Praise for Sophie Littlefield and *Garden of Stones*

"Littlefield...makes her tale resonant and universal...gripping."
—*Publishers Weekly*

"Suspense, mystery, and love drive the intricate plot in this moving drama of women in a Japanese American family over the course of three generations....The shocking revelation is unforgettable."
—*Booklist*

"Mesmerizing...it possesses elements of mystery that give way to shocking revelations and heartbreaking yet inevitable conclusions. A story of unspeakable injustice and bitter sacrifice, it will leave you shaken."
—*RT Book Reviews*

"*Garden of Stones* is a remarkable work of fiction...that is quite engaging and unique. The book and writing are immediately engrossing and engage the reader's sympathies deeply. Reading this dramatic, affecting account is an illuminating and insightful journey."
—*Bookreporter.com*

Also available from Sophie Littlefield and Harlequin MIRA

GARDEN OF STONES

House of Glass

Sophie Littlefield

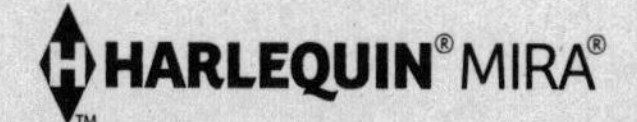

ISBN-13: 978-0-7783-1478-3

HOUSE OF GLASS

For questions and comments about the quality of this book, please contact us at CustomerService@Harlequin.com.

Printed in U.S.A.

First printing: March 2014
10 9 8 7 6 5 4 3 2 1

For S.A.L. and K.W.

House of Glass

Chapter One

On Jen Glass's Saturday to-do list, she scheduled an hour to visit the apartment her father died in, and another for the morgue. Only half an hour for the funeral home, since you could make just about anything go faster when you were willing to write a big check.

And Jen was willing. With every passing mile of frozen fields, every tinny song on the classic rock station, every time her sister snapped her gum, she was growing ever more willing.

The to-do list was written in her neat handwriting in the fabric-covered notebook in her purse. On the page before were the notes she'd taken at the parents' association meeting. On the page before that, a list of tree services that had been recommended by friends. Both of those lists were written before she knew her father was dead. But according to the police, he had been dead for several days when the landlady found him. So it was entirely possible that while Jen wrote down *ArborWorks (Margeurite) ask for Gerald,* he had already taken his last breath. When she was sitting in the library at Teddy's preschool, writing *Teacher appreciation, Thursday, two dozen cupcakes (carrot? cream cheese frost?)* his corpse could well have been beginning to smell.

Tanya always made fun of Jen's list making, so she had kept this one hidden away. But what Tanya didn't understand was that when you wrote a list, it forced you to organize your thoughts, so when the time came to act, you didn't waste time on false starts and dead ends. A list could make an unpleasant task go more quickly. And this day, attending to the details of the passing of a man Jen hadn't seen or talked to in almost three decades, couldn't go quickly enough.

They reached Murdoch in the early afternoon, after a stop at a roadside Subway because Tanya had a coupon. She paid for lunch. Jen was paying for everything else, and that knowledge sat between them like a screen that muffled what they wanted to say. But it was an inescapable fact: being a Calumet housewife of a global management consultant—even a laid-off one—paid far better than being a single mom with a high school education and a call center job.

Jen exited the highway when the phone app told her to. There wasn't much to look at. A couple hundred miles north of Minneapolis, the land was flat and gray. Murdoch had no visible means of support, no smokestacks or office parks or hospital complexes. A cluster of motels and fast-food restaurants gave way to a depressing little town that spilled out on either side of a straight-shot four-lane road littered with strip malls and auto shops. Jen estimated that a quarter of the businesses they passed were boarded up.

"Jeez, this place isn't much," Tanya said, yawning. "Guess Sid didn't exactly move up in the world."

The phone took them into a neighborhood of shabby bungalows. Sid's apartment building was a run-down two-story sandwiched between a vacant lot and a squat little cinder block bar whose neon Budweiser sign struck a jarring note in the colorless afternoon. No one had bothered to shovel the sidewalk leading up to the apartment building's entrance after the last storm, and the snow had melted unevenly, dirty banks of it giving way to icy patches. One of the units still had Christmas lights up around the window; the strand had come loose from the nails and dangled against the building.

Tanya dug the keys out of her purse. The management company had overnighted them to her. Monday, they were hauling away whatever was left in the apartment.

"Ready?" she said, opening the door.

Jen steeled herself to face the residents they might pass in the hall. She imagined men in threadbare wool coats, old ladies with cats for company and the TV on all day long. But inside the building it was empty and still, the carved wood moldings and newel posts in surprisingly good shape. Someone in the twin cities would pay a bundle for them, Jen couldn't help thinking. Up here in the sticks, people didn't know what they had.

"One-oh-one." Tanya read the numerals on the doors. "One-oh-two. Where the hell is apartment one?"

"Can I see?" Jen took the keys from Tanya. The little round tag had a number one printed clearly on it.

Tanya glared at her as she took the keys back. She was older, by almost two years, and even though they were in their forties now, she still sometimes seemed to need to be in charge.

"Satisfied? Maybe next time trust me to read a number? I bet it's downstairs."

A narrow staircase at the back of the hall led to the basement. It smelled of both mold and bleach. There was a washer and dryer up on blocks, splintery plywood cupboards with padlocks. The light from a naked bulb overhead and a few narrow windows near the ceiling wasn't enough to cut the gloom. At the far end of the basement was a door set in unpainted Sheetrock that blocked off the rest of the basement.

"No way this is a legal apartment," Tanya said. She tried the key, and the door opened.

Inside, the odor of bleach was stronger, but there was another faint smell underneath, ripe and awful and somehow sweet. *So that's the smell of death,* Jen thought.

The apartment was a single room. A bank of cabinets and a sink anchored one wall; a tiny bathroom and closet were built into the other. A high, cobwebbed window looked out on a dead shrub. There was a bookcase, a table under the window covered with a patterned cloth, a soiled couch facing a television set on a pressboard console. A bed stripped down to the mattress, which looked none too clean.

"I bet he died in the bed," Tanya said. "Otherwise the sheets and stuff would still be on there."

"Um." Jen felt faintly nauseous. "They didn't say when they called?"

"They hardly said *anything* when they called. I think it was just some secretary or something. She was, like, when was the last time you saw your father? I wanted to tell her to shove the death certificate up her ass."

"Tanya," Jen said reprovingly. "She didn't mean anything."

"How do you know? You weren't there."

Jen let it go. They were both on edge today. Tanya just said whatever she was thinking, a trait that had always gotten her into trouble. Jen had learned a long time ago to think before speaking, to filter out the emotions first.

Tanya picked up a glass that had been sitting on top of the television and inspected the contents. "There's nothing in here that's worth anything. Look at this. The Salvation Army probably wouldn't even take it."

"Well, then I guess it's good that we don't have to deal with it."

"I asked the management company if there was a security deposit," Tanya said, putting her hand on the metal headboard and giving it an experimental shove. "They gave me the runaround."

Why are we even here? Jen was thinking, but she knew the answer. For her, anyway. She had to see the room, the place where Sid had lived, to believe he was truly gone. She had to feel his absence, the emptiness that he left behind.

And there was the curiosity, too. That faint uneasiness—was it hope? Dread?—that there would be some clue to who he'd been, or more specifically, who they'd been to him. Some evidence that their lives had once been tangled together.

Tanya moved briskly through the room, opening cabinets, picking up papers and CDs from the shelves and examining the covers, flicking through the half dozen shirts hanging in the closet. Jen stood near the window, watching. A yellowing newspaper was stacked on one end of the couch. A chipped bowl holding loose change sat next to the TV.

"Found his cash," Tanya said, holding up a plastic baking soda container. She shook out the bills and counted. "One-eighty."

"There's nothing else here you want to take back with us," Jen said. "Is there?"

"I guess not." Tanya looked around, frowning. "I guess I just wanted to know if he had pictures of us. Of Mom. Anything, from then."

"Are you disappointed?"

Tanya shook her head. "Not really. I guess I'm almost relieved. But I just had to see it for myself. Like, if he'd secretly saved things from then, it would be like part of him was still alive. And not in a good way."

"Yeah, I know what you mean."

"Oh, wait." Tanya reached up on the closet shelf and took down a faded cardboard shoe box. She brought it over to the table and dumped out the contents. Papers, mostly. She flipped through them. "Central Valley Tool and Die…it's just HR stuff. Benefits, employee handbook. These look really old. Wonder how long he even worked there?"

An envelope fell out, two words written in black ink on the outside. "The Girls." Jen didn't know until that second that she knew her father's handwriting, that the memory of it had lodged fast and hidden all these years.

Tanya shook out three pictures. Two were their school pictures from the year before Sid moved away: shy grins, their hair curving out in Farrah Fawcett waves, sleeveless cotton shirts revealing thin suntanned arms. The third picture was of the whole family, much earlier: their mother in the middle, Jen no more than six or seven and wearing a sundress printed with anchors. Sid with a mustache, looking out of the frame, scowling with impatience, as though there was somewhere else he needed to be.

The afternoon held no more surprises. Forms to sign at the morgue, where it turned out that they were not required to view the body. A brief tug-of-war at the mortuary until Jen gave in to the pitch and bought their cheapest urn for the ashes she had no intention of ever claiming.

It was dark by the time they checked into the Double Tree. Their room had a view of the parking lot. The heater cycled on with a vengeance, something rattling deep within.

“Is it okay with you if we do room service?” Jen asked. “I really don’t want to go back outside in the cold.”

“I’ve got something better,” Tanya said, setting her overnight bag down on the nearest bed. She unzipped the bag and pulled out a bottle of wine, and then another. “I even remembered the corkscrew. And check it out. Snacks.”

Jen feigned enthusiasm. She knew Tanya was just trying to contribute, and she didn’t really need anything more than the canned nuts and snack mix. While Tanya was setting it all up on the nightstand between the two beds, laying out a hand towel for a tablecloth and pouring wine into the plastic cups, Jen called Ted, but there was no answer. She took off her makeup and changed into her pajamas.

“Wow, look at you,” Tanya said, when Jen came out of the bathroom. She was lounging against the pillows in her bed, watching television. She picked up the remote and shut it off. “Got big plans later?”

Jen looked down at her pajamas, a silky navy blue set that

Ted had given her for Christmas. "These aren't anything special," she said, blushing.

"Seriously? I don't dress like that unless I'm getting some action." She grinned, her teeth pink from the wine. She was wearing a faded T-shirt over sweats. Her cup was almost empty.

Jen got into her bed, pulling the covers up over her legs and taking a sip of her wine. She was always embarrassed when Tanya talked about the men she was seeing. They never lasted long, and they were never anywhere near as good as Tanya made them sound when she first met them.

"I feel like we ought to drink a toast to the old bastard," Tanya said, and it took a minute for Jen to realize that she was talking about their father. "Only, I can't think of a single thing to toast him for."

Jen raised her cup, reaching across the space between the two beds. She was going to say *May he rest in peace,* but something stopped her; she had never seen Sid at rest during her entire childhood. He was always on the move, fidgeting, pacing, coming and going.

Until Tanya called, Jen had barely thought about her father in years. Sid Bennett was often away from home when his daughters were young, disappearing for days at a time. Later he took pipeline work in Alaska and his absences stretched to months. When he was around, he wanted little to do with two solemn, skittish little girls, and spent his time antagonizing their mother instead until she finally told him not to bother to come back.

And then the summer that Jen was thirteen and Tanya a rebellious, sullen fifteen, their mother got sick. Sid started coming around again, looking for an opening, wooing her with smooth talk and cheap flowers when he needed a tank of gas or money to tide him over. She was unable to resist, the cancer rendering her silent and listless. He might have persisted right up to her death, but a bar fight landed him in the hospital for a long stay at the end of that dismal summer.

When he was released, he headed north, ending up here in Murdoch. They only found out where he was when the court tracked him down after their mother died, but by then Jen and Tanya were settled into their aunt's basement, a solution everyone agreed was better than trying to extract any support out of Sid.

"He never got in touch with us, not once," Jen said, after they both drank.

"That never seemed to bother you before."

"It doesn't. I mean, I don't know what I would have done if he had. It's just that now he's dead, I'm realizing that it's like he never aged, for me. I never saw him get old."

"I guess it was too much to hope that he would have gotten remarried. Left someone else to deal with all his shit." Tanya's voice was bitter.

"At least it's all done. After today we don't ever have to think of him again."

"So we just walk away." Tanya sighed. "I guess at least we got a night away from the kids. Speaking of which—what's Ted doing with his big night to himself?"

"Working on the bathroom, supposedly."

"He's *still* not done?"

Jen grimaced. Ted had been laid off for almost six months, and the renovation project was supposed to keep him busy while he looked for a new job, but lately he hadn't done much job searching *or* renovating. In the past few weeks there had been several times when he went out "for supplies," and came home empty-handed. "He swore he was going to get a lot done this weekend."

"Good luck with *that.*" Tanya laughed. Jake's father left when he was a baby, and she took a dim view of men in general, other than the brief infatuations at the start of her relationships. "With his wife and kids gone for the weekend? I bet he went out and painted the town."

"I guess..." Jen said, more morosely than she meant to.

Tanya looked at her keenly. "Hey, I was kidding. Everything's okay with you guys, isn't it?"

"No, no, it's fine. Just, you know, I wish he'd find something. It's hard having him underfoot all the time."

Tanya looked at her doubtfully, picking up the bottle. "Here, give me your glass."

As Tanya topped off her wine, Jen couldn't help thinking of the little slip of goldenrod notepaper Ted had tossed in the tray on his dresser along with his change. The feminine handwriting that wasn't hers, the initials SEB in a curvy script at the top. On it, Sarah Elizabeth Baker had written *Thx tons, Thursday 2pm Firehouse xoxoxo.*

Sarah had been his assistant before he was laid off. She wasn't gorgeous, but she had a knowing, sensual way about her that was hard to miss; she could make a Brooks Brothers blouse look like an invitation. At the Christmas party, when she'd had too much to drink, she'd kissed Ted on the mouth when she said goodbye.

None of which necessarily meant anything—except that

Ted left Flores Martin months ago. And yes, for a while there was a weekly bundle of his mail, delivered with one of these little gold notes paper clipped on top.

But there hadn't been mail from work in a long time.

Jen wondered if she could tell Tanya about Sarah. But Tanya would be too quick to turn on Ted, too quick to castigate him for crimes he might not have even committed.

So Jen drank her wine and changed the subject, and when the bottle was empty Tanya opened the second one, and they made a good dent in it before Jen finally turned the light out. They mumbled their good-nights just like all those years ago when they shared a bedroom and a bunk bed. Tanya was asleep in minutes, her breathing even and deep. Jen lay awake for a while despite the blurry wine buzz, thinking about Sarah and her glossy hair, the x's and o's at the bottom of her note.

When Jen finally slept, her nightmare had nothing to do with Sarah, or even Sid. She dreamed the red bird, its beak opening wider and wider, its screams ever louder, uncoiling and unfurling until there was nothing else.

Chapter Two

Livvy woke up shivering. Her shirt was wet against her back. Something cold had seeped into her sleeping bag, the room smelled like vomit and her head felt thick.

Faint light came from the hall at the top of the stairs, enough for her to make out the others, asleep in the basement rec room. Paige and Rachel and Collin. The girls were huddled in the sleeping bags Rachel got from the garage, and Collin was making do on the couch with a blanket from Rachel's room. No one else was awake. Someone snored softly.

Livvy sat up groggily, peeling the damp sleeping bag from her skin. It smelled like stale beer—and there was the overturned plastic cup. Rachel must have set it down between them before she fell asleep. Livvy patted the floor; the spill hadn't reached Rachel, only her. And soaked through the carpet. How were they going to clean it up before Rachel's parents got back?

Not to mention where Collin had vomited, over by the TV. They'd gotten most of it up then, holding their breath and laughing. It had seemed funny last night. Livvy knew that he wasn't the only one: Paige had thrown up behind the fraternity before they'd walked home from the party.

"Are you up?" It was Paige, whispering from her other side. They'd lined up on the floor, the three of them, just like they used to do in middle school when they fell asleep watching movies during sleepovers. "Let's go upstairs."

"Rachel spilled beer on my sleeping bag."

"Eww. Leave it. Come on."

They tiptoed upstairs to Rachel's bedroom, sneaking through the house as if Mr. and Mrs. Crane were sleeping upstairs. But they weren't even home; they had taken Rachel's sister to some out-of-town tournament, leaving Rachel home by herself. She was supposed to be on the school ski trip—they all were. Instead they'd walked the half mile to the edge of campus, to Collin's brother's fraternity, where the party was still in full swing hours later when they left.

Paige flopped on Rachel's bed. "Did you get it on you?"

"Just on my shirt." Livvy pulled the shirt over her head. She got clean clothes out of the overnight bag she'd stowed in Rachel's room last night. Her pajamas, yellow flannel with snowflakes, were still folded neatly at the bottom of the bag. She felt guilty as she pulled on her clothes; she could smell the fabric softener her mom used.

Paige yawned. "Did you end up talking to Sean?"

Livvy didn't look at Paige. Even hearing his name, even that hurt. "A little," she said, like she didn't care. "They weren't there long."

"You looked so good last night. It must have killed him. Oh, my God, especially when that guy…remember?"

Paige laughed, still riding the giddy thrill of their lie. She'd told everyone they were freshman from Ann Arbor, visiting for the weekend. No one questioned it, not for a second. People flowed in and out of the fraternity, tracking snow in on their shoes, leaving the door open, standing around the keg on the back porch like it was summer. No one seemed cold. Rachel was gorgeous and Paige was fearless and Collin made them laugh, and Livvy kept to the center of them all, where no one seemed to expect her to talk. Just to dance, as the night wore on and she drank more and Paige convinced her to get up on the coffee table, and she'd shut her eyes and felt the music go through her and then when she opened them, there was Sean, standing in the doorway watching her with an expression she couldn't read.

"Stay here. I'm going to go get us a couple Red Bulls," Paige said, bounding off the bed.

"Okay." Livvy crawled under the covers. Maybe she and Paige could sleep here a little longer. She wasn't supposed to be home until after lunch. With any luck, when she got home she would go straight to her room and her parents would leave her alone for once. At dinner if they asked her about the skiing she'd just lie—no big deal.

Except the thing with her mom's dad. Livvy squeezed her eyes shut and burrowed down deeper in Rachel's bed. It was so weird, not to even know she had a grandfather, that he had been alive all this time. Then all of a sudden he was dead, and Mom was going up there with Aunt Tanya to get him cremated or something.

At least her mom would be distracted and maybe she wouldn't ask her a million questions about the ski trip. But still. It was her mom's *dad*. Her mom and Aunt Tanya had been really poor growing up and their mother died when they were in high school and they had to go live with relatives, and her mom never talked about it except to constantly say how grateful they should all be for their blessings. So her dad must have been a real dick, not even taking care of them when their mom died, but still, not to ever even mention him?

Paige came back with the drinks. She slid in next to Livvy, and they popped the tops and drank. "So, what did you say to Sean?"

Livvy shrugged. "I told him I heard Allie has herpes. Then he told me I didn't know what I was missing, and I told him to go fuck himself."

"You didn't!" Paige cracked up. "You can do so much better, anyway. Did you give that guy your number last night?"

"Are you kidding? My parents would *kill* me."

"So? They don't know about last night, right? You got away with it once, you can do it again. We just have to be careful."

But as Paige chatted on about the night before, Livvy could only think of the way Sean had looked at her over his shoulder as he left. She knew her parents hated him, and even her friends thought he was a loser since he got suspended again, but none of them knew what it was like when he looked at you as though you were the answer to every question he ever had.

Last fall, for a few months, Sean had made her his world. And even if Livvy pretended she hated him now, even if he was with that skank Allie, whose cousins supposedly were in a gang, even if he never thought about her anymore, she knew that being with him had changed her and she would never be the same.

She hadn't told Paige the truth about what really happened.

Sean and Allie came up to the keg together, holding hands, not seeing Livvy standing there until they already got their drinks. Sean looked like someone slapped him, and Allie said something, and Livvy tried to get past them but Allie blocked her way.

"I heard you have herpes," she muttered so only Livvy could hear.

And Livvy couldn't think of anything to say back, because she was drunk and about to cry, and so she shoved Allie hard and the full cup of beer went all down her front, splashing up into her face and soaking her hair. As Sean dragged Allie off, she was yelling that Livvy would be sorry.

Livvy was already sorry. But not about Allie.

Chapter Three

When they got back to Tanya's apartment, Jen parked and turned off the car. "Let me help you take your stuff up."

Tanya had fallen asleep on the drive, and there was a crease on her face from where it was pressed against the hood of her coat. "What stuff?" she said irritably. "All's I've got is just the one bag. Plus I need to pick up Jake from next door."

She already had her hand on the door handle, and Jen didn't know how to tell her that she wasn't ready to leave her, that she'd replayed that desperate little apartment over in her head the whole way back and her stomach felt like it had a giant hole in it. That there were things somebody needed to say and she didn't know what they were or how to say them.

"Have lunch next week?" she asked.

Tanya was out of the car, and she ducked back down to peer in. "We never have lunch. There's nothing around the office except that Arby's."

She looked both perplexed and irritated. It was true that they never met for lunch—Jen wasn't sure she could even find the building where Tanya worked.

"Or just call me," she settled for.

Tanya got her bag and shut the door. Jen watched her walk to the stairs of her building, but drove away before Tanya reached the landing.

Jen managed to compose herself before she picked up Teddy from the Sterns'. Cricket Stern was one of her best friends, not to mention the mother of Teddy's best friend, Mark, but even so Jen hadn't been able to bring herself to tell her the real reason she'd gone out of town. Spa weekend with her sister, she'd claimed, a late birthday gift to Tanya. It wasn't like Cricket's and Tanya's paths would ever cross, so it was a safe lie, but Jen felt guilty, anyway. But if she hadn't been able to talk about Sid before the trip, she was even less willing now, so when Cricket asked she just said that the spa treatments were relaxing, the restaurant very good.

Teddy fell asleep in his car seat on the way home. She carried him up to his room and put him to bed; a nap wouldn't hurt, considering the boys had been up late the night before. Ted was taking a shower in the hall bathroom, and Livvy's door was closed, which only deepened Jen's dark mood as she went to unpack.

The door to their own bathroom, the one Ted was renovating, was closed. On the floor of their bedroom was a mound of clothes, a sweatshirt and jeans and socks that were still warm when Jen picked them up to toss them in the hamper. She had lifted the wicker lid and was about to drop the clothes in when she noticed something odd: in the bottom of the hamper was only a single pair of boxer shorts.

Jen stared at the boxer shorts, thinking. She had emptied the hamper Friday when she did the laundry. In her arms were the clothes Ted had worn today while he worked on the bathroom. The flannel pants and T-shirt he slept in were on the floor by the bed, where he left them every morning for Jen to fold and put under his pillow.

She dropped the clothes in and let the lid fall shut, and went looking for his gym bag. She found it on the floor of the closet, unzipped it and confirmed there was nothing in it but his MP3 player and a couple of water bottles. Nowhere was there another set of dirty clothes.

Ted hadn't done laundry since Livvy was a baby, and he never wore the same clothes twice. Which meant he had hidden or disposed of yesterday's clothes for some reason.

Or left them somewhere else. He could have left the house yesterday with a change of clothes in his gym bag, gone somewhere else where he showered and changed, leaving the clothes for someone else to wash. Sarah, for instance. Sarah, who probably had one of those stackable units in her condo, who was in training to take on the role that Jen played, learning how Ted liked his T-shirts folded and his socks rolled and—

"No," Jen whispered. There had to be a good explanation. It was crazy to equate a note and some missing laundry with a full-blown affair.

Ted walked into the bedroom, a towel wrapped around his waist, a thin sliver of shaving cream under his chin. He looked exhausted. Jen toed the gym bag out of sight in the corner of the closet.

"Hey," he said, giving her a tired smile. "Welcome back."

She watched him get socks and underwear from the dresser, clean clothes from the closet. He dressed unhurriedly, tossing the damp towel across the hamper. If he was covering up a guilty conscience, he was putting on a hell of an act.

"How was the drive?" he asked. "Any snow on your way back?"

"A few flurries. Nothing that stuck." She forced a smile. "So, I can't wait to see what you've been up to all weekend."

His expression slipped, and his eyes darted to the closed bathroom door. "Okay, look," he said nervously. "Don't lose it when you see the tub. I mean, where the tub was. It was a big job getting it out of there."

"What do you mean? What happened?"

"Nothing *happened.* Look, Jen, that thing weighed a ton. It would have been a job no matter who took it out." He opened the bathroom door, and light poured in from the window.

"I hit the wall trying to get it out of here," Ted continued, talking fast, his face going slightly red. "And listen, there's a little damage to the subfloor, too, but I was lucky, I lost my grip, and I'm telling you, if I'd dropped that thing there'd be a crater there and not just a dent."

Jen pushed the door open the rest of the way, willing herself not to react. No matter how bad it was, it could be fixed, and—

"Oh, wow," she said, putting her hand over her mouth. Where the old tub had been, she saw a gaping hole edged with ragged plasterboard, wallpaper hanging in strips. The wall tile was gone, leaving exposed lath and scarred plaster. The subfloor was filthy and gashed, and the whole thing looked like a bomb had gone off in it.

And nothing else appeared to have been done. Ted had promised to finish stripping the wallpaper and replace the light fixtures—not to mention replacing the bathtub—by the time she was back from Murdoch. Instead, he'd gotten the tub out and then…what?

"Like I said, I know it looks bad," Ted said.

"It's just…I don't understand what you've been *doing* all weekend. With us gone and the house to yourself—" She stopped, because if she kept going he might actually *tell* her, and she wasn't sure she wanted to know. "Never mind. Just never mind."

"Don't you think I'm trying?" Ted said. "Is this really about the job search? Is that what this is?"

"*What?* No, I know you're trying. I know it's a tough market out there, and—"

"No. You don't know what it's like to send out thirty résumés and get only four callbacks. You can't know what it's like when a guy you trained—a guy who got out of business school in two thousand *five,* for Chrissakes, gets hired instead of you."

"Ted, please. The kids'll hear."

"Hear *what?* We're just talking, and it's long overdue. I guess you've been wanting to say this to me for a while, and—"

"I didn't even say anything! *You* brought it up. I have never once criticized you for not looking harder, not trying hard enough." Tears welled up in her eyes, and she swiped them away.

"Hey, hey," Ted said, instantly abashed. "Jen. Jesus. I'm sorry. Don't cry. God, I'm sorry, I didn't mean to go off on you like that."

He reached for her, and after a moment she stepped into his arms. She pressed her face pressed against the soft cotton of his sweater, feeling his heart beat against her cheek. What *was* she doing? How could she really believe Ted would cheat, would risk everything they had built together?

"Jen, look…it's my fault, too. I don't—I know I've let you down. I've let the family down. It's just, knowing that I'm not providing for you guys, it eats away at me."

"Oh, Ted…" Jen closed her eyes and inhaled, his soapy shower scent tinged with the faint metallic sweet smell he had when he drank too much the night before.

A tiny leftover spike of suspicion flared inside her, but she fought it back down. He probably took a break to watch a game, have a beer…and just let the afternoon overtake him, that was all. She could hardly hold it against him, considering she'd had more than enough herself last night.

"We're going to get through this," she said as much for her own benefit as his. "They say the economy's picking up, and even if it doesn't, we're fine—we have money put away for exactly this situation. We could go another *year* before we have to worry."

"Oh, Jesus," Ted said heavily. "I don't think I could take that."

"No, that's not what I meant, honey. You'll find something long before that. I just mean that there's nothing to worry about."

They held each other for a moment longer before Ted pulled gently away. There was something in his eyes, some troubled emotion. God, she hoped he found something soon.

"I'm going to do better," he muttered. "I'm going to make things right."

Chapter Four

In the hours before dawn on Wednesday, Jen dreamed the red bird again. It was bright as blood, coiled in a circle, its beak open and angry. In the dream, the bird slowly unfurled its wings, expanding until it filled her mind, its screams growing hungrier and its beak widening until it seemed that it meant to consume her from the inside out.

She'd first had this nightmare years ago, when she was fresh out of college and just starting to date Ted. The bird didn't do anything but scream, its beak open wide, spinning and getting larger and larger until she woke up. It had been years since she had the dream, but now it had come twice in one week.

When it first happened, Jen had researched the meaning of birds in dreams and decided the bird was nothing more than a symbol of her struggle—to put herself through school, to get her first job, to pay back her loans, to survive the stress of trying to fit into the society she had worked so hard to join. She struggled to erase her past, to project the ease and confidence that her colleagues and friends seemed to come by naturally, to be the mother she hadn't had, the wife her own mother hadn't had a chance to be.

But none of that had been a problem for years. So why was the dream returning now?

Jen was tired and irritable as she got Teddy fed and ready for preschool. Livvy refused to eat breakfast and dashed out the door so she didn't miss the bus. Ted took his car to the dealership to have the oil changed and a dent fixed. He'd been complaining about the dent for weeks—someone had dinged him at the Target Center parking lot during a Timberwolves game.

After preschool, Cricket Stern brought the boys over for their standing playdate. "Listen, Jen, something happened today," she said as Mark and Teddy shot past her into the house. "I thought you'd want to know."

Instantly Jen was on alert. She had worked so hard to get the speech pathologist and Teddy's teacher on the same page. A year ago, when he was three, Teddy stopped talking to strangers; when he stopped speaking to his babysitters and then to his friends and teachers, Jen and Ted became concerned enough to have him evaluated, and Teddy had been diagnosed with selective mutism.

For the past year, he hadn't spoken to anyone outside his immediate family, but the speech pathologist said that Teddy was responding well to the self-modeling and desensitization exercises. She thought Teddy was very close to verbalizing one-on-one with a trusted adult.

"It's nothing," Cricket said hastily. "Just, the kids are starting to pick on him. Well, not all the kids. Mack and Jordan. Of course, right?"

"Oh. *Shit.*"

"I know." Cricket grimaced. "Sometimes I just want to

smack Tessa. It's like she *wants* to raise a couple of delinquents, the way she lets them run wild."

The twins had been a problem since the beginning of the year. Recently they pushed a kid out of the castle in the play yard and knocked out two of his teeth.

"What did they do?" Jen asked, steeling herself.

"They had him in the corner by the dress-up box, and they were trying to make him talk. Mack was making fun of him and calling him retarded. Or maybe it was Jordan—I can't tell them apart."

Jen's anger was tempered with dismay. "What did Teddy do?"

"He managed to get past them. They're big, but he's fast, you know?"

"Well, it could have been worse. Did he look upset?"

"Not too bad. More like aggravated. I said something to Mrs. Bray, and she talked to the boys. I thought you could decide whether you want to have her talk to Tessa."

"No, I feel like that'll make it worse. You know, like he's a tattletale. Damn it. He's so close. He's been talking to the speech therapist over Skype. She says any day now..." She felt her eyes tearing up.

"Oh, honey, it's okay. I didn't mean to upset you," Cricket said, pulling a packet of tissues from her purse.

"No, it's not even that," Jen said, taking a tissue and dabbing at her eyes. "It's...just, things are kind of a mess right now."

"Is it Ted's job search?" Cricket asked sympathetically.

Jen hesitated. She hadn't told Cricket about Sid's death, or about Sarah's note. She didn't like to make her problems public, even to her best friends. "Yes, I guess," she said, settling for a partial truth.

Cricket nodded sympathetically. "When Brad was laid off a few years ago he was unbearable. I finally made him rent office space to get out of the house. We pretended he was 'consulting.'" She smiled as she made air quotes. "Luckily it was only for a few months or we'd be divorced."

"Oh, it's not that bad." Jen had heard rumors that Brad was seeing a woman he'd met on one of his accounts while he was supposed to be at that rented office. "Just a blip, that's all."

As Jen watched Cricket drive away, she had the strange sensation that she could be watching herself. Sometimes it felt like she and her friends were all the same, well-preserved Calumet housewives in expensive sunglasses and recent-model SUVs.

Jen closed the door and wondered how many other secrets they kept from each other.

Thursday afternoon, Jen decided to bundle Teddy into the car and pick Livvy up from school so she wouldn't have to take the bus. Livvy had been hostile and distant all week, and the gesture was meant to be conciliatory, to let her daughter know she was trying.

As she inched forward in the car-pool line, she caught sight of Livvy with her cluster of friends. Standing a few feet away was a gangly boy with shaggy black hair and a threadbare backpack repaired with duct tape. Sean—Livvy's first boyfriend, the one who had broken her heart over the Christmas holidays. He was talking to a girl in pink UGG boots and a pink knit cap, his hands jammed in his pockets, and Jen had a momentary urge to get out of the car and shake him, to demand to know who he thought he was to hurt her daughter's feelings, an unspectacular boy with a dusting of acne on his forehead and gauge earrings he was surely going to regret in a few years.

Livvy got into the car without sparing Sean a glance. She said hi to Teddy and lapsed into sullen silence.

"How was your day?" Jen tried. "Anything interesting happen?"

"My day was like every other day of my life," Livvy muttered. "So no, I would say that nothing interesting happened."

"Well, mine was fascinating. After I worked at your school, I did your laundry and made you a dentist appointment and picked up your sweaters from the cleaners."

"Good for you."

Jen tightened her grip on the steering wheel and pressed her lips together. They rode the rest of the way in silence. When she turned onto Crabapple Court, she realized she'd been holding her breath. She exhaled with relief as the garage door glided up, and she saw Ted's BMW parked in his side of the garage. So he'd come home from wherever he'd been all day.

Jen had barely turned off the car when Livvy opened her door and bolted into the house. Teddy started whimpering to get out of his car seat, shoving at the restraints, and Jen hurried out of the car to help him. But even as she worked at the tangled strap, his protestations turned to frustrated tears.

Even though Jen could swear she was doing everything right—even though she was trying just as hard as she knew how—the more she strove to connect with her family, the further she seemed to drive them away.

★ ★ ★

Jen set her purse on the hall table and headed for the kitchen. She could hear Livvy's footsteps racing up the stairs, and she winced, waiting for the slam of her daughter's bedroom door.

Jen filled a plastic cup with snack crackers and got Teddy settled in front of the TV, his tears forgotten. She felt guilty using *Dinosaur Train* as a babysitter, but she just needed a few minutes to change into yoga pants and put her hair in a ponytail before she started dinner.

Jen went upstairs to her bedroom, steeling herself for whatever Ted had done to the room now. There he was, on his knees by the wall under the windows. It wasn't really all that bad. He had put a drop cloth on the bed and the nightstand, and the lengths of baseboard that he'd pried away from the wall were stacked neatly. But there were several gouges and scrapes in the plaster. And there was a long, thin scratch in the finish on the walnut-stained floor.

Jen pushed her hair behind her ears as she looked around the room. *It's fine, it's fine.*

Ted set down his pry bar and got to his feet. "Hey, hon," he said, a note of guilt in his voice. "I had to go to the lumber store to order a few trim pieces. Thought I'd get these baseboards taken care of."

"Uh-huh. Listen, I was wondering, maybe you could watch Teddy while I get changed and start dinner."

"Jen…" Ted ran his hand through his hair. "All I'm doing is trying to get this thing finished. I know you're tired of the mess. I got that message, loud and clear, and I'm just trying to get it put back together."

Frustration mixed with fatigue in his voice, and Jen tried

not to rise to the bait. "I appreciate that you're trying to get some work done up here. I just wonder if you could have done it while Teddy was at preschool instead of going…wherever you went."

"I just told you, I was at the lumberyard. And a couple of errands." Ted's face darkened with anger. "Look, I don't think it's the end of the world if our kid watches half an hour of PBS. I guess that makes me a crappy parent on top of everything else, but I wish you'd stop and think once in a while that maybe your way isn't the only way to raise a kid."

"Could you keep your voice down?"

"Why? A little disagreement's normal, Jen. It's not going to break us. It's good for the kids to hear it once in a while, instead of growing up thinking everything has to be perfect all the time."

Jen flinched. "If you really want to go there, I'm not going to have our daughter listening," she said, hurrying to shut the bedroom door.

"Look," Ted said carefully, waiting until she came back. "I'm sorry if that came out wrong. But there's no need to get hysterical about every little thing."

Hysterical, Jen repeated in her mind. Was that how her husband saw her? She was trying to think of how to respond without sounding defensive when there was a knock at the bedroom door.

She and Ted both froze. Ted wiped his hand across his forehead, muttering softly.

"I'll get it," Jen said.

As she crossed the room, she thought about how the smallest reminder of one's children could make a person feel guilty even when there was no rational reason. The air, charged with tension seconds earlier, was now weighted with wistful failure.

Jen put her hand on the brass knob. Later, she would remember this detail, the warmth of the old brass to her touch, the way she had to tug to clear the slight jam.

Standing in the hall was her beautiful daughter, her face exquisitely frozen, her lips parted and her long-lashed eyes wide with terror.

On her left, a man Jen had never seen before held Teddy in his arms, her little boy flailing ineffectively against his grip.

On her right, a man who looked unnervingly like Orlando Bloom pressed a gun to Livvy's head.

Chapter Five

"This is where you stay real quiet," the younger man snapped, jabbing Livvy's skin with the barrel of his gun, making her head jerk. He was wearing gloves, his hands pale and dead-looking through the thin latex.

"Mom," she whimpered, and Jen didn't think, she threw herself at her daughter, her fingertips brushing Livvy's arm before she was struck from the side and went crashing to the floor. The other one had kicked her in the knees, still holding her son in his arms, and as Jen pushed herself up on her hands, she saw the rough work boots he was wearing and wondered if he had broken something in her leg.

Ted was yelling: *no, stop,* but he stayed rooted to the spot. Which was what she should have done, because she had endangered her daughter. The young one had Livvy's hair in his fist, dragging her backward, out of the range of Jen's flailing feet.

"That was stupid," he snarled, and gave Livvy's hair a hard yank, forcing her head back and exposing the long pale expanse of her throat. Her whimpering escalated to shrieking until he put his hand around her throat and squeezed. "Shut the fuck up *now,*" he yelled, and she did.

Jen scrambled backward on her hands and knees. Ted grabbed her arm and pulled her up, holding her around the waist against him. "What do you want?" he demanded.

The older one held Teddy tightly, absorbing the impact of Teddy's silent kicking and flailing. He looked like he was in his fifties, but he was powerfully built, his forearms roped with muscle. He, too, was wearing latex gloves. "Tell this kid to calm the fuck down."

"It's all right, honey," Jen gasped, thinking *please please don't hurt him.* "Mommy's here. It's all right."

But Teddy only struggled harder, trying to twist around in the older man's arms so he could see her. Jen knew how strong a four-year-old could be—Teddy could grab your hand so hard you felt the bones squeeze together; he could hug you so tight it was hard to breathe.

"Goddamn it," Ted said, pushing her roughly behind him, putting his body between her and the intruders. "What the hell is going on here?"

"Take him," the man said, holding Teddy out like a sack of cement. The minute Ted grabbed Teddy, the man reached for a gun he'd jammed in the waistband of his pants. It seemed to take less than a second, the movement of his arm and the way he held it still and sure, pointed right at Jen's face. She gave an involuntary gasp and felt her body slacken with fear, her bladder almost releasing. She imagined the bullet striking her full in the face, shattering the bones, liquefying her brains.

Teddy wrapped his arms tightly around his father's neck and immediately calmed. Livvy was gurgling, her neck craned awkwardly backward, the young man not seeming to care that he was hurting her. A half grin on his face—as though this all amused him, as though he was deriving pleasure from their fear.

"Let me have her, let my daughter go," she pleaded. "Please. We won't do anything. We won't go anywhere."

The young man held Livvy in place for another moment and then shoved her toward Jen. Livvy's neck snapped forward; she stumbled and went down on one knee. Her hair flew across her face, obscuring her terror for a fraction of a second. Jen rushed to help her, wrapping Livvy in her arms, tensed for the bullet, waiting for the gunshot, but it didn't come.

"Mom, Mom," Livvy wailed, holding her so tightly the air was crushed from her lungs. But Jen held on, dragging Livvy backward until they were standing next to Ted. Teddy's shoe was wedged against her shoulder and they were all touching, jammed together in a family scrum, facing the strangers outside the bedroom door.

"What do you want?" Ted demanded for the second time. The question echoed through the room, which Ted had stripped of its carpets and drapes in preparation for painting.

"Downstairs. Now." The older man motioned with the gun. There was a faint sheen of perspiration along his hairline, and broken capillaries marred his sallow, broad cheeks. A few flakes of dandruff rested on the shoulders of his shirt.

For a moment they didn't move. Jen felt the warmth of Ted's body through their clothes, his shoulder pressed against hers.

"Now!" the man bellowed, and she took a step forward, still holding Livvy tightly.

"The girl first," the younger man said. He reached toward her with the gun, caressing Livvy's arm with the barrel while she trembled. His eyes roved up and down her body, lingering on her small breasts. "Don't be scared."

He seemed relaxed, grinning faintly. He wore his hair buzzed short, and he had skipped a shave or two, but his beard grew in fine and strawberry blond—the beard of a boy rather than a man. There were tattooed spikes on his neck; the rest of the design was hidden under his collar and Jen couldn't tell what it was supposed to be. As they passed, his gaze stayed fixed on Livvy, watching her walk.

Livvy reached the stairs first and went down with her hand on the rail, barely pausing on the landing. Jen followed close behind. At the bottom of the staircase was the front door, heavy and solid. Jen could slip past Livvy and yank the door open. She could push her daughter out into the night, to safety. It would only take a second. One of the men might shoot her, but unless he got lucky the wound probably wouldn't kill her. As long as she made it out the door, someone was bound to see her and Livvy on the front porch. It was dinnertime on Crabapple Court, and fathers were arriving home from work and kids from sports and clubs and music lessons. Moms were returning from grocery runs and yoga classes. Jen would scream and help would come.

Except she couldn't leave her little boy behind, not even for a second, unprotected and vulnerable. She couldn't leave Ted. So she walked past the front door and into the family room, the others close behind her.

"Sit." The older man's voice was terse and impatient.

Jen pulled Livvy down with her in the corner of the sectional. On the television, Dora the Explorer hid behind a cartoon tree.

"You don't have to do this," Ted said. "Come on."

"Oh, yeah?" The man turned on Ted. The two men glared at each other, something passing between them. Jen looked from one to the other, trying to figure it out. "Turn that shit off."

"Have you seen him before?" she whispered as Ted reached for the remote on the coffee table and turned off the set.

"No, never," he muttered, sitting down on the other side of Livvy with Teddy on his lap.

The two men stood in front of them, one on either side of the television armoire. The younger one slouched against it, his gun practically dangling from his hand. The older man stood ramrod straight.

"We're here to do a job," he said angrily as though the Glasses had inconvenienced him in some way. "You make it easy, cooperate, you'll be okay. You get in our way, we hurt you."

Next to him the other man coughed, only Jen was pretty sure the cough covered up a laugh.

"What do you want?" she asked. "Because you can have it, I don't care—"

"You don't talk," the man snapped. "*I* talk. I'm Dan. This is Ryan. You only talk when we tell you. You got something to say?"

Was she supposed to talk now? Jen tried to ignore the pounding of her heart, "I'm sorry. I'm just scared. Please don't hurt my family. How can we help you get what you want so you can go?"

"Hah," Ryan said. "She wants to *help* us. You like that, Dan?"

Jen realized something deeply terrifying: they had made no effort to disguise themselves. No knitted caps or Nixon masks, which meant they didn't care if the Glasses knew what they looked like.

They're going to kill us, Jen thought, terror slicing through her.

Dan ignored the younger man. "All you need to know right now is don't talk until I tell you to. Keep your hands to yourself. Do what you're told and don't make me ask twice."

"Just tell us what you want," Ted demanded. "Whatever it is, we can help you get it."

"That right…Ted?" Dan drawled.

"How do you know his name?" Jen asked. Ryan swung the gun in her direction, instantly tense.

"Aren't you paying attention? Shut up!"

"Please," Jen whispered. "I'm sorry. Can I ask, just one question—"

"Go. Fast." Dan watched her impatiently.

"Let the kids go," Jen said quickly, pleadingly. "Please, just let the kids go. They can walk over to my sister's. It's less than a mile."

Ryan laughed, lips pulling back from slightly crooked teeth. "Right! Great idea. Livvy here's gonna take her bratty little brother over to her aunt's house and forget to mention that her parents are being held hostage."

Jen felt her daughter stiffen in her arms. They knew Livvy's name. Ted's name. Ryan spun his gun so the barrel was pointing down, reached out and caressed Livvy's cheek with the grip. Livvy flinched and pulled away with a whimper, and Ryan laughed.

"Get up," Dan said. "Time to go downstairs."

Chapter Six

"Oh, *God,*" Livvy said, a split second after they heard the lock at the top of the stairs. She was standing apart from her parents, her arms hugging her body. Tears threatened to spill from her eyes. "It smells so *bad* down here!"

Ted reached for Livvy, and she fell against him. He wrapped his arms around her and hugged her close, and she sobbed against his chest. Jen picked Teddy up and rocked him gently, whispering that he shouldn't worry about Livvy, that his sister would be just fine.

After a few moments Livvy's sobs subsided and she pulled away from Ted. She went to stand near the shelf where all her trophies were lined up—Mini Marlins swim, eight years of soccer, a few for softball, one from the American Legion speech contest back in middle school. Jen could see her shoulders trembling.

"Honey, it's going to be okay," Jen said, handing Teddy to her husband and approaching Livvy cautiously. She had to keep her calm, had to make her believe she and Ted had things under control. "Once they get what they want, they'll go."

"But what do they even want?"

Jen put her hand on Livvy's shoulder and gently turned her so she could look into her eyes. "Anything they can sell, I would guess. There's the silver, my jewelry, the computers—any number of things. They'll take it and they'll go."

She could see Livvy trying, *wanting,* to believe her. She tried to make herself believe it, so her face would convince Livvy.

"I need to talk to Daddy," she said as calmly as she could. "Can you play with Teddy and keep him busy for a few minutes?"

Livvy nodded. She looked a little better, some of the panic gone from her eyes.

"His old toys are in here," Jen said, getting a cardboard box down off the shelf. "I haven't had a chance to get them over to St. Vincent De Paul's yet. Go ahead and get them out. Whatever he wants."

Livvy talked softly to her brother, kneeling down on the cold concrete floor next to him and peeling the tape off the box. Jen and Ted went to the far side of the basement where the old living room furniture was stored, the pieces that Ted kept meaning to put on Craigslist. Ted lifted the old lamp shades off the couch and brushed off the cushions. When they sat down, he took her hands in his.

"I don't understand why they picked us," Jen said in a low voice. "It's not like we have the biggest house in the neighborhood. And we were *home.* Why wouldn't they pick a place where nobody was home? I mean, all they had to do was keep knocking on doors until they found one that nobody answered. Then they could just go around the back and break in."

"I don't know, maybe they were worried about alarms. Everybody's got those signs in their yard, those ADT warnings."

"Not everyone," Jen said. "Lots of people don't." *They* didn't, for instance. They'd talked about a home alarm system, but they'd felt that Livvy was too young to be depended on to arm and disarm the system.

"I think we have to assume it's just random," Ted said. "Just bad luck."

"But you'd think they'd at least watch the house for a few days. I mean, that's what you always read in the papers—they watch the house to figure out when the owners come and go, right? But these guys came at exactly the *wrong* time. This is the time of day there's most likely to be someone home. It doesn't make any sense."

I'm scared, she wanted to say. She wanted Ted to put his arms around her and tell her everything was fine. She wanted him to do for her what he had done for Livvy, to hide his own fear and promise her they would be safe. But she wasn't Livvy. She and Ted were the adults, and they had to face the truth.

"I don't know, Jen," Ted said. His voice was oddly detached, and he was looking past her shoulder at the shelves behind her. "I'm guessing they'll have one of us go up there and show them where everything is. Where your jewelry is, the safe, stuff like that."

"Oh, God." Jen felt a wave of nausea, and she doubled over her knees, letting go of Ted's hands. "There's nothing in the safe but papers. What if they're expecting more? Like cash or something—what if they're angry that there isn't more to take?"

"Well, there's the electronics, the silver—there's lots of stuff," Ted said, putting his hand on her back and rubbing absently. His offhand touch was the opposite of comfort; it made her flinch and shrink away.

If the men upstairs were disappointed with what they could take from the house, they might take it out on her family. She pictured them opening the safe, and—once they had seen that there was nothing but insurance policies, passports, copies of the will—becoming enraged. In her imagination, Dan swung his gun around, his eyes accusing, and pointed it at her face.

She whimpered.

"Oh, hon," Ted said. He gathered her into his arms and held her tightly. "You can't let yourself think the worst. Do you hear me? We're just going to take this one step at a time. We have to stay calm and trust that—*believe* that things will be all right. These aren't some hopped-up drug addicts up there—they're professionals. Professional thieves. Believe me, they want things to go smoothly just as badly as we do."

"How do you know that?" Jen drew back and looked deeply into his eyes, trying to find the source of his certainty. "How can you be sure?"

"I'm not *sure*—how could I be?" His gaze skittered away, avoiding hers. "But what choice do we have but to believe it?"

"I just feel like there's some connection, that if we thought about it we could figure it out. You're sure you've never seen these guys anywhere?" Jen's mind raced through her routines, the small world she inhabited: the kids' schools and the grocery store and the yoga studio and the restaurants and coffee shops downtown. She was sure she'd never seen these men anywhere she went on a regular basis.

She thought of something. "Remember when your wallet was stolen from the locker room?"

"That was almost a year ago. Even if someone had kept it all this time, why would they wait so long to come here?"

"But they knew your *name.*" She remembered the faint smirk on Dan's face, as he looked down on her in her own family room.

"Jen, they could have found out our names on a two-second Google search of the address. Hell, they could have gotten our names on their way up the sidewalk by just looking on their phones. That doesn't mean anything."

Jen was silent a minute, thinking through her family's routines. Teddy was always with her unless he was at school or the Sterns' house. Livvy went to school and soccer and out with her friends, less often since she'd been grounded last fall—

"What about Sean?" she said. "He had trouble with the police. Remember?"

"Sean's sixteen years old, Jen," Ted said incredulously. "He's a *child.*"

"But he was arrested."

"You mean that vandalism thing? That was just a stupid prank. He wasn't even the instigator."

It had happened after a football game, shortly after Livvy had started dating him. One of Sean's friends had a key to the equipment shed, and they'd broken in and dragged the lacrosse goals into the parking lot and shot smashed beer cans into them. When the police came, Sean and one of the others were drunk enough that they fought ineffectively back and got assault charges tagged on, which were later dropped. The school got involved and suspended the boys for a week.

"I'm just saying he might know the young one. Ryan." Jen tried to sort it out. "He could be friends with him. He could have told him to come here. Sean was in our house half a dozen times. He could have a grudge against Livvy from the breakup...or maybe all he did was tell them about the house, our stuff...."

"*He* broke up with *her,* Jen. Why would Sean have a grudge against her? It doesn't make any sense."

Jen's mind raced with possibilities. "Or what about Renaldo?"

Ted stared at her, his eyebrows knit together. "Seriously? Our yard guy?"

"He has access. I mean, I know anyone could come through the gate, but he's been in our yard so many times." She felt ashamed of the betrayal even before she stopped speaking. Renaldo was a nice guy, respectful and dependable, and he never forgot to blow the bits of grass off the patio after the first time she had to remind him.

"Jen. How would Renaldo know those guys? And even if he did, why would he send them here—why wouldn't he just come when he knew we were out of town? You always call to let him know when we'll be away."

Jen tried to corral the swirling thoughts in her head. She looked at her children, sitting on the carpet remnant Ted had laid out in the middle of the concrete floor. Livvy was talking softly, moving a plastic car along an imaginary track, a row of Playmobil people looking on. Teddy's bubbling laughter was punctuated by growling engine noises and honking horns. Livvy was so good with him; she'd managed to banish the fear from his mind, somehow tamping down her own terror for his sake.

Because that's what you do, Jen thought. *When you love some-*

one, you make yourself stronger for their sake. As strong as you can, as strong as you must—stronger than you ever believed you could be. Your love makes the other person all that matters, and how can you let your fear rule you when you have something so much more important to protect? Livvy had been shaking with fear when they came down the stairs, but now she was sitting cross-legged with a smile on her face, a smile she had conjured from nothing for her little brother.

And now she had to do the same for Livvy. For both of her children, and for Ted, too, because she was the center of their family. She was the axis on which the rest of them turned, and if she'd occasionally resented it, if sometimes it seemed thankless and even pointless, she had also spent the past fifteen years of her life building a core of strength that could support all of them even now. She would take over for Livvy and let her daughter be a child, and she would do her job.

"I'm sorry," she said, running her hands through her hair. "You're right. About Renaldo, and Sean—I was just trying to figure it out, but like you say, it's probably just random. Just bad luck. Listen, can you see if you can talk to Livvy? Who knows what's going through her head right now—just tell her what you told me, that everything's going to be all right. And I'll take over with Teddy."

Jen knelt on the floor with her children. "Wow, I haven't seen these old toys in a long time," she said.

"Shepherd," Teddy said, holding up an androgynous plastic figure with a yellow bowl haircut and a crook in its hand.

"That's right, shepherd! Where are the sheep, do you think? I wonder if they're in the box?"

While she upended the box of toys on the carpet, Ted took

Livvy by the arm and led her to the couch. He sat with his arm around her and Livvy pressed her face to his shirt, shaking with silent sobs. She was trying to stay quiet for Teddy's sake—and Ted enfolded her in his strong arms, comforting her like he always did after the worst disappointments. When her soccer team lost in the semifinals. When Sean had broken up with her. Ted was the one Livvy wanted when her world was falling apart.

Teddy's eyes went wide at the pile of toys on the carpet. A few round pieces from the K'Nex set rolled across the floor. The poor kid was never allowed to make a mess like this; Jen was forever cleaning up around him, sorting his toys into their various bins and baskets. Well. If—when—they got out of this, she would try to loosen up a little.

She plowed her hand through the center of the pile, the figurines and building toys and vehicles clattering against each other. She dug out a Star Wars figurine. She didn't know its name—it was from the new movie, some sort of soldier with a head scarf obscuring his face.

Teddy took it from her solemnly. "Bad mans," he whispered. He stared at the inscrutable painted eyes, the plastic rifle nearly as tall as the figurine itself.

Jen took a deep breath. "You mean the men upstairs? They were a little scary, weren't they?"

Teddy nodded, his lips quivering. He gripped the toy tightly. "He didn't put me down. I wanted him to put me down but he didn't."

"Oh, I see. I can understand why that was upsetting."

"They had *guns*."

What the hell was she supposed to say now? In all the

women's magazines Jen had read over the years, the ones that promised solutions to everything from dry skin to marital disharmony to kids' behavioral issues, there had never been a single piece of advice for what to do when your child is threatened at gunpoint. Jen flashed through the possibilities and decided to lie. If it was the wrong decision, she'd do her penance later.

"Oh, those were just pretend. Those guns? Toys, like these, only bigger."

Jen took the toy back from Teddy and bent the rifle's stock. She waggled it back and forth.

"Don't break it, Mommy!"

"Oh, sorry. Here you go." She handed the little soldier back to Teddy. "They were playing a game, kind of like when you and Rand and Mark play in the backyard. Remember? With the Super Soakers? Those were pretend guns."

"I shot Rand," Teddy said. "Rand shot me *and* Mark."

"That's right!" Jen said, warming to her lie. "And remember when Mark was crying because he didn't understand that it was just a game? And I had to take the Super Soakers away and you guys all had quiet time? Well, upstairs it was kind of like that. Daddy and I didn't understand it was just a game at first and so we were kind of upset. And now we're having some quiet time down here so everyone can calm down."

Teddy regarded her skeptically. Jen's smile felt frozen in place. "They have to leave now," he said. "I'm hungry."

"Oh, yes, it is almost dinnertime, isn't it?" Jen said, faking surprise. "But I'm just having a nice time down here with you guys. Let's play for a while longer, okay?"

"Tell Livvy," Teddy said.

"Tell her what?"

"That it's a game because she was scared." Before Jen could react, he reached into the pile of toys and pulled out a chubby little sheep. "I found him!"

Jen helped him find the other sheep, the lambs, the pieces of fence and the plastic bushes. Livvy joined them on the rug, helping Teddy assemble the imaginary pen. Jen looked at the windows and saw that it had grown pitch-dark outside. What did that make it, seven? The lights worked down here, thank God, even if it was just a few naked bulbs in the ceiling.

Ted was sorting through the shelves, pulling bottles of water from the emergency supplies. Jen went to help him.

"You got Teddy calmed down," Ted said quietly.

"How's Livvy?"

"Okay, I think. I think I convinced her that they weren't here to hurt anyone."

"I just wish I knew if they were coming back. I mean, maybe they just took what they wanted and left already."

"No, they would have had to bring a car to load it all, and gone through the garage, unless they were really stupid. We would have heard the garage door. Besides, I hear them moving around up there."

"Oh." Jen tried to keep the disappointment from her voice. Why were they still in her home? "Maybe they're just waiting until everyone's in for the night, so they don't call attention to themselves."

"Maybe. Though pulling up a car late at night has its own risks, if someone sees them. They'd be more likely to notice a strange car at three in the morning."

"Who's up at three in the morning?" Jen demanded, and

then wished she hadn't, because the look Ted gave her conveyed what they both knew: that she was up at that hour as often as not. Lately, sleeping through the night had been nearly impossible for her; her doctor said it might be from perimenopause.

"I think we need to prepare for the possibility that we might be stuck here overnight," Ted said.

"Oh, my God—there's no way. They can't just leave us down here—"

Ted reached for her, gently pushing the hair from her eyes, tilting up her face to look at him. "I know, sweetheart, I know." His voice was heavy with emotion. "But maybe the kids can get some rest, if we just try to make it seem as normal as possible."

"There's nothing normal about this!" Jen felt the panic nipping at her. She wasn't sure she could keep acting like nothing was wrong—pretending even for a few minutes with Teddy had exhausted her.

"We can do this," Ted said as though sensing what she was feeling. "Together. We'll stay busy and keep our minds off it, okay? And you're right—they could leave at any time. And meanwhile we can move stuff around to make it comfortable down here for the kids. We can set it up kind of like it used to be upstairs."

Jen looked around her at the crowded shelves, the furniture stacked up near the wall. When they'd bought the new living room furniture a couple years ago, Ted decided to sell the old stuff on Craigslist and dragged it all down to the basement, where it sat gathering dust. It had been one of their first arguments after he was laid off: Jen asked if he couldn't finally get rid of all that junk now that he had time on his hands.

"Okay," she whispered, because she couldn't think of anything better to do, especially since Livvy and Teddy were occupied with the play set, and she didn't want to interrupt and risk upsetting them.

First they took down the old dining room chairs, fussy dark walnut things with uncomfortable thin red damask cushions, and lined them up along the basement wall. The love seat was heavy and narrowly missed crushing Jen's toe as it slid to the floor. They lifted the old coffee table down and set it next to the kids on the carpet.

Ted searched the shelves for the nonperishable food he thought he'd stored during his emergency preparedness phase, and Jen dug out the old quilts her grandmother had made. She found them packed in a box on a high shelf, and laid them out on the sofa. Livvy looked up from the floor.

"We're going to *sleep* down here?" she asked, and then before Jen could answer, "What's Daddy doing?"

Jen followed her gaze. Ted was at the top of the stairs with a flashlight and a screwdriver. Little light carried up the stairs, and his face was shadowed as he poked around at the knob.

Fear constricted Jen's throat. If Ted managed to get the door open, he could get himself shot—or even worse, he might enrage the men upstairs, and invite their wrath on all of them. Before she could react, the door crashed open, sending Ted scrambling. The flashlight and screwdriver clattered down the wooden steps, and Ted cursed, falling a few steps until he was able to right himself by grabbing the handrail.

The door banged against the wall and swung back. A man

stood in the door frame, but Jen couldn't tell if it was Dan or Ryan. Something glinted dully, but Jen didn't realize it was a gun until it had gone off, the report echoing dully. The man disappeared back into the hall, slamming the door shut behind him.

Jen raced up the steps. She heard Livvy screaming and the sound of the key turning on the other side of the door. Ted was holding his shin, muttering. Blood trickled down his forearm.

"What happened? Are you hurt?" Jen heard the panic in her own voice and knew the kids could hear it, too. She forced herself to stay calm.

"I'm fine."

"But the gun—he shot—"

"Didn't hit me. This is just from running into the handrail. I think he was just aiming for the wall." Ted grimaced, wiping at the blood with the tail of his shirt. In the poor light Jen couldn't see how bad it was. "Trying to make a point, I guess."

"Daddy, come down here!" Livvy wailed frantically, and behind her, Teddy started to cry.

"I'm fine, I'm fine," Ted said, getting up painfully and holding on to the handrail. Jen did her best to help him down the steps, as he favored his bruised hip. In the light she could see that the gash on his forearm wasn't bad.

Livvy seized her father's good arm. "Daddy, you can't go up there! They could have killed you!"

"No, that was just…laying out the rules," Ted said, managing a tight smile. "They never meant to hurt me. They're not killers."

"How do you know that?" Livvy demanded as Jen went to Teddy, lifting him into her arms.

"They're just not." Jen knew Ted was trying to reassure Livvy, to convince her they were safe. But even if the men fired this time as a warning, how could he be sure that next time they wouldn't shoot to kill? "I don't know what they want, but if they were going to hurt us they would have done it already. They're probably just trying to figure out what's worth taking."

Teddy whimpered against Jen's neck, and she rocked him, trying to calm him, feeling guilty about the lie she'd told him.

"That was scary, wasn't it?" she asked quietly. "I don't think I like this game anymore, do you?"

Teddy shook his head against her neck. She felt the dampness of his tears against her skin. Looking around the room for something to distract him with, she had an idea.

"Let's do the wash, okay?" she said. "Do you want to help?"

Teddy stopped snuffling and allowed her to put him down. "Laundry baseball," he said, running for the basket of soiled towels.

Laundry baseball was a game Jen had invented to keep Teddy occupied. She tossed items from the dirty laundry pile to him, and he batted them with a hollow plastic bat, sorting them into dark and light piles. She always had to sort them again afterward, but the sound of his laughter more than made up for the extra effort.

Teddy found his bat under the folding table and swung it. Jen tossed the washcloths to him, and he batted them to the ground. She poured the detergent into the plastic cup and picked him up so he could empty it into the receptacle. They put the towels in together, and Jen held him so he could press the start button, and he watched as the water began to spray against the convex round window.

She backed away cautiously, making sure he was truly distracted. He'd often stay rapt through most of the cycle when she let him, watching the slap of the drenched towels, the sloshing of the suds and waves of water.

Ted and Livvy were picking the toys up off the floor and putting them back into the box, both looking dazed. Jen crouched next to Livvy and touched her shoulder, making her jump. "You're doing fine, sweetheart," she murmured. "You're so good with Teddy. I'm so glad you're here for him."

Livvy picked up the toys one at a time and tossed them into the box, her lips moving slightly, as if she were talking to herself.

"Let's let Livvy finish this up," Jen said pointedly. Ted straightened up and they went back to the corner of the basement.

"What were you *thinking?*" Jen hissed, the moment she judged herself out of range of Livvy hearing. "That was a crazy chance to take, Ted. You could have—"

Ted held up his hands to stop her. "I know, I know, I'm sorry. It was…" He swallowed, looked away. "I thought maybe I could… I thought if something happened, I could at least hold them off long enough, and you and the kids—" He slammed his fist into the sleeping bags stored on the shelf, making the shelves shake.

"Ted, don't!" But Livvy hadn't looked up. She had slumped against the coffee table, and she was trying to untangle a length of string that was attached to a toy spacecraft. "Please. I need you to keep it together. All right. I understand, you wanted to *do* something—"

"To stop them. To protect my family."

"And instead, now Livvy's twice as scared."

"I didn't know they were going to shoot—"

"You didn't *know?* Two guys come in our house with guns and you didn't know it was a possibility? And then telling her that they're not going to hurt us, practically guaranteeing it, how can she trust you? She's not stupid, Ted, she has to know how bad this is, and lying to her isn't going to help."

"I wasn't lying, Jen, I just really didn't think—don't think— they have any intention of hurting us. If they got caught, that would make the charges against them so much worse. They know that. They aren't some out-of-control tweakers looking for their next fix. They've got to have a plan."

"Maybe, or maybe it's like you said—they saw the house and looked it up on the phone and came in here just to take whatever they could find. I don't think we can assume they've got a plan at all." There was something off about Ryan, a crazy burning intensity in his eyes. "They don't seem…stable."

Ted frowned and rubbed a hand over his face. He hadn't shaved this morning, and the day's growth shadowed his face, making him look older. "Look, what do you want me to say here? I'm trying to stay positive. For you, for the kids. It isn't going to do anyone any good if we start going to worst-case scenarios."

Jen knew he was right. Someone had to keep the kids' spirits up; someone had to make sure Livvy didn't get hysterical. "I'm sorry," she said. "You're right. It was just, the moment and the gun and then when you fell…"

Ted took her into his arms. "You're shaking," he murmured, his face against her hair. "Sweetheart. It's going to be okay. Come on now."

Jen closed her eyes and tried to concentrate on the feel of his hands against her back, holding her, supporting her. She hadn't known she was trembling until he held her, but now she felt the zigzag racing of her heart, the throbbing of her pulse in her temples, the weakness in her limbs.

But she couldn't give in, couldn't let herself fall apart in his arms. For one thing, she knew that Livvy saw everything, even when she pretended not to. And for another, it wasn't fair to Ted. It wasn't fair to expect him to be the strong one, the only one to hold them all up.

"I'm okay," she said, gently pushing him away. She took a breath and pushed her hair away from her face. "I'm good. Really. Look, let's try again. There's got to be some—some sort of clue we've missed. About what they want. I mean, why not just take what they want and go, now that we're stuck down here? What are they *doing* up there?"

"Look at it the other way—now that we're stuck down here, why hurry? Why not take their time and make sure they get what they came for?"

"But leaving us in the basement for so long, that's a risk, isn't it?"

"Not really. There's only the one door and now we know they're keeping an eye on it. And if they're looking for big-ticket stuff, they might just be trying to break us down, make us less likely to resist when they come looking for it."

"But they can just *take* whatever they want. We can't stop them."

"They don't know where we keep things…so once they take the obvious stuff, the electronics and art, they'll come down here and want to know what we have hidden away."

"But what are we going to tell them?"

"Whatever they want to know. It's all insured. We tell them where the silver is, your jewelry, everything. Hell, we'll tell them where the suitcases are and they can pack it all up. We *cooperate,* that is the important thing. Make it easy for them to get the job done."

"Okay," Jen said, nodding reluctantly. "I just, I guess I'm worried it won't be enough."

"Honey," Ted said, taking her hand. "I know it's hard, but you need to just stay calm and assume these guys are pros. Hell, for all we know they've done this before. There might have been a whole string of robberies around here. I mean, think about it, it's not bad for one night's work, right?"

"What, you think they've been breaking into houses all over Calumet? We would have heard about it."

"It wouldn't have to be just Calumet," Ted said. "They could go all over the Twin Cities."

"But, Ted, it would be in all the papers. The news would be all over it!"

A sound behind her caught Jen short.

"Stop it," Livvy whispered. She was standing a few feet away, her arms hugging herself; she'd approached so quietly that they hadn't heard her. "Please. Stop talking about it."

Jen pulled her into her arms, shushing her, smoothing her hair. "I'm sorry, sweetie. Daddy and I didn't mean to upset you."

"Just do what they want," Livvy pleaded. "Don't let Daddy try to fight with them."

As Jen comforted her, she thought she heard voices up above and felt the vibrations of footsteps through the basement floor. It had to be her mind playing tricks on her. In the moments since she first saw the strangers standing in her bedroom door, it was as though the edges of her mind were disintegrating, like a tablet dissolving in water. The core was still there—her rational mind, her focus on her family—but how long could she sustain it?

And in a way, it hadn't started upstairs, today, with the arrival of this threat. Sid's death. Sarah's note. Ted's evasiveness. And even before that—his job loss, Livvy's hostility...what had happened to her perfect family, the beautiful home she had created so carefully for all of them? What had she done to invite all these destructive forces in?

She was doing her best, trying to be strong, but she was beginning to imagine the walls cracking, the house bearing down on them, old sins from the past clamoring to come back.

Chapter Seven

Livvy fell asleep first. Jen figured it was her body's way of shutting down in the face of her terror. Jen covered her with one of the quilts and turned her attention to Teddy, who had finally gotten bored with the laundry when the wash cycle ended.

It had to be past his bedtime. Jen tried to get him to lie down on the couch, but he kept sitting up and fussing with his covers. Jen stroked his soft, downy hair and sang to him, and eventually his hand fell against his chest and his breathing grew steady and slow. She covered him with a second quilt, butterflies appliqued onto its square blocks, the colors faded to the palest greens and oranges and pinks. She had a vague memory of the quilt from her childhood, a time when her mother had used it for her own bed, after Sid left.

Ted was sitting in one of the old dining room chairs holding a spool of copper wire. Jen remembered seeing the wire in one of the jumbled bins of hardware and tools on the shelves above the workbench. The wire had become loose and slipped off the spool in tangled coils, and Ted was methodically working out the knots, rewinding it carefully around the spool.

Jen watched him for a few moments, feeling her gut con-tract and her breath go shallow until finally she couldn't stand it anymore. "What in heaven's name are you *doing?*"

Ted didn't answer her for a moment. He wrapped a few more coils around the spool, then set it carefully—gently, as though it were something precious—on the coffee table. He didn't look at her, pulling at a loose thread in the seam of his pants and clearing his throat. "Jen, there's something I need to tell you—"

The door opened at the top of the stairs. "Oh, God," Jen whispered. She accidentally dragged the quilt halfway off Teddy as she scrambled off the couch. He mumbled in his sleep.

"Don't move." Dan descended the stairs, slowly, holding a garbage bag in one hand and his gun in the other. When he reached the base of the stairs, he looked around the room, then let the bag drop to the floor with a muffled thud. "Here's food. And I threw a few of the kid's toys in, too."

"Wait," Jen said. She searched Dan's face. His beard grew in unevenly, with a few bare patches that looked like he'd taken an indifferent swipe with a razor before giving up, more pepper than salt. Her father had that look, when he first came back from Alaska. He never made much of an effort at grooming. "Couldn't you just let the kids go? They won't say anything, they're—"

He held up a hand to stop her. "Not going to happen, okay, so let it fucking drop. Trust me, it'll go easier."

He backed slowly up the stairs, one hand on the rail, finding his footing a little clumsily, moving with the bearing of a middle-aged man who got too little exercise. Then he was gone, the door closing behind him.

Jen stood motionless for a moment before bending to pick up the trash bag. It was one of the black lawn bags, the good ones. She upended it carefully on the rug, and four water bottles rolled out. Jen set them on the coffee table and shook out the rest of the food. Juice boxes, half a dozen of the little ones Jen sent to preschool with Teddy. A box of Triscuits. Another, half-full of cheddar goldfish. A mesh bag of those little round wax-covered cheese wheels, still cold from the fridge. Bruised fruit—a couple of bananas and three pears.

Jen picked up a pear, remembering choosing it from the bin at Whole Foods—was it just yesterday? She'd chosen the Bosc because the other ones were so hard and green, like they'd never ripen, and she'd come home and arranged them in the white ceramic bowl on the counter.

"You hungry?" Ted picked up the Triscuits, tore open the box.

"Are you *kidding?*"

Ted paused and stared at her. "Look, Jen, I'm not the enemy here."

"I get that. But how can you eat?" Her own stomach had growled in protest, and she hadn't eaten since taking Teddy to Jamba Juice after preschool, an outing that seemed like it had taken place days ago, not just hours earlier. But the thought of food was impossible.

Ted looked down at the cracker in his hand. "I'm…I just thought we should eat something."

He looked so lost, and Jen wished he'd lie to her again, like he had before. Anything to stop her mind from chasing itself in desperate circles. She should never have come down on him so hard when he was only trying to keep their spirits up.

But she'd questioned him then, and now she'd done it again, eroding his strength right in front of her eyes. It was all wrong. Her job was to bolster him, to help him be the strong one, to help him take care of them all.

But the poison was in her mind, in her imagination. She kept getting flashes of the dark schemes the men upstairs might have in mind. Especially the young one. He seemed unbalanced, like someone who could hurt others without feeling remorse. Like he might enjoy it.

The way he looked at Livvy, his gaze sharpening and his mouth going tight, and she didn't even know what he was seeing. When he looked at her daughter, did he imagine tearing her clothes off her? Doing things to her, making her do things—

Jen let out a whimper of terror, unable to stop the terrifying parade of images. Ted dropped the cracker on the coffee table and reached for her. "Honey. Jen. What is it?"

"It's Ryan. I just don't trust him. With Livvy. I mean, didn't you see him watching her? When he pulled her head back—when he touched her with his gun? Even if what you said about Dan is true, even if he just wants to take our things and leave, how's he going to stop Ryan if he wants to..." She couldn't bear to say it, to name her fear.

"Dan's not going to let things get out of control. He's in charge here. There's no way he'd risk that. Anything goes wrong, it takes them both down."

Jen seized on the hope he was offering her, willing it to be true. "I know it *seems* like he's in charge. But what if Ryan tries something, anyway?"

"Dan won't let that happen." Ted shook his head. "Look, I

know guys like Ryan. There's one in every locker room. On every team at work. They're the guys who are always looking for an opening, trying to see what they can get away with. They always end up digging their own hole and getting fired."

"This isn't an office—"

"No, but Dan's not going to let Ryan get the upper hand. Guys like that are tricky, but they're weak."

Jen considered, dubious. It seemed like Ted's theory was woven from the thinnest threads, but it was better than anything she had, and it had the advantage—the enormous advantage—of giving her hope.

"I thought of something else," Ted said. "A reason why they're waiting."

"What?"

"The cars. If they want to take the cars, they can't risk driving out of here and being seen by someone who knows us. They could change the plates while they're still in the garage, drive out in the middle of the night when there's no one on the street. They could—come to think of it—" he snapped his fingers "—they could have a truck nearby. Make a few trips in our cars, get everything out and none of the neighbors would ever notice because everyone's asleep."

"But then they'd need a third person, right? To drive the truck? Besides, how much could they possibly take? More than they could fit in two cars?"

"Well, maybe that's why they came so early. So they could take their time looking around."

"Or maybe they already *knew* what we have," Jen said. "If there's someone else involved, like we were talking about before. Like where the safe is, my jewelry, the art, your dad's coins—all of it."

"I still think that's such a long shot. I mean, someone who knew us well enough to know where all of that is—I just don't know who that would be."

Or Livvy, Jen thought. *Someone who knew Livvy.* But she had promised herself to try to stay calm, to keep a grip on her fears.

They were silent for a moment, both of them listening, both deep in their own thoughts. But upstairs, all was quiet.

"Look—take the love seat," Ted said after a while. "You might be able to get some sleep on it. I'll take the floor."

"Well..." She thought about letting him have the love seat, since one of them might as well be comfortable, and she was pretty sure she would be wide-awake all night, no matter what. But she had to try, for the kids' sake if not her own. "If you're sure you'll be all right."

"Yeah, the floor's nice and firm, probably be good for my back."

He tried to smile, and for a moment Jen watched him, really looking at him the way she hadn't in a long time. Something was different—some flicker in the depths of his eyes, some extra lines around his mouth. Of course it was probably just fear and exhaustion, the sheer weight of worry, but as Ted busied himself with spreading out some quilts on the floor, she couldn't help feeling there was something else.

She arranged her blanket on the love seat and curled up on her side, using a sofa cushion for a pillow. When Ted snapped off the light, the basement was completely dark, the kind of dark where you almost feel like you're in another dimension, adrift, without even the glow of the moon through a window or a night-light down the hall to orient you.

After a few seconds Ted turned the light back on. “I don’t want the kids to be scared if they wake up,” he whispered. “Will this be okay for you?”

“It’s fine,” Jen whispered back, and rolled over so her face was pressed against the back of the love seat, finding her own total darkness.

As she closed her eyes and waited for sleep, she tried to force her thoughts away from this horrible day, back to when things were normal. Yesterday, she’d gotten out of bed, brushed her teeth, got the paper, made the coffee. Packed a snack for Teddy and ironed a shirt for Livvy. Planned the details of her day, the errands, the car pools, the dinner menu, never dreaming that thirty-six hours later her life would be yanked out from under her. She’d had an extra cup of coffee with Ted before he went…where had he gone yesterday? Some errand…then she remembered, Ted had spent the afternoon at the BMW dealer having the oil changed and the dent fixed.

Except when she came home tonight with Livvy, she could swear the dent had still been there.

She dreamed a dinner party, impossibly detailed, and even as she walked the rooms of her house she suspected that she wasn’t really there. It happened that way, sometimes, in dreams. She touched the stemware, the silky petals of roses in the pewter bowls. She walked among her guests, but she barely greeted them. She brushed past the hired bartender, through the butler’s pantry, a quick tour of her kitchen, where several of the women from her Zumba class were standing near the bay window, wearing those skimpy outfits they all bought at the new fitness store that had opened in the old Blockbuster space. Jen was annoyed that they hadn't dressed for her party, but still she didn't stop.

She was looking for something.

She made her way up the stairs, leaving the crowd behind. The kids' doors were open; they were with friends for the evening. The hall bath was tidy. It smelled like disinfectant, which Jen found soothing.

She hesitated at the door of her bedroom. It had been milled to match the rest of the doors in the house, solid six-panel construction. It was standing slightly ajar, and Jen tapped it with a fingertip and it opened a few more inches. Did she really want to do this? She could turn around; she could go back downstairs; she could have a glass of wine, a second, a third, however many it took to dull this wanting to know, this need, the one she couldn't bring herself to separate from, the way she knew was best, the way other women did. Choosing not to know—it was one of the most important tools in a wife's arsenal.

Some defiant spark wouldn't let her turn away. She pushed the door open, hard enough for it to bang against the wall, and there they were. In her bed. Sarah Elizabeth Baker sitting astride her husband with her head thrown back, all that luxurious hair tangled around her shoulders as if she'd ridden through a windstorm to come to him. Ted's hands were on her hips, pressing her against him, grinding up into her, and they were so consumed by the moment that even as they twisted around to see her, they didn't stop their rhythm and the sight of them thrusting together was like an ax in Jen's heart.

Chapter Eight

"Jen. Jen."

Ted was shaking her, his hand on her shoulder. Jen shuddered, trying to banish the nightmare, and then she remembered where she was.

The basement was lit by the single overhead bulb, casting its small, gloomy pool of light down on the four of them. The kids were fast asleep, Livvy burrowed so far under her quilt that only her hair was visible, Teddy tangled up in his covers. Ted was on his knees at the foot of the love seat, staring up at her. Jen blinked and put her hand over her mouth.

"You were having a nightmare," he said. "You were thrashing around. Are you all right?"

The last bits of the dream dissolved and were replaced with guilt. Absurd though it was, Jen felt like she'd been caught in a moment of betrayal, walking in on the scene between her husband and his lover.

"I'm fine," she said shortly.

"I couldn't sleep. I thought I might try to eat again. I don't think I've had a real meal since breakfast yesterday. You want something? We probably ought to."

Jen didn't answer, but she watched Ted open the crackers, peel the wax off a cheese round, then another. He split the cheese into four squishy quadrants and stacked each on a cracker, brushing the crumbs into a little pile in the center of the plate. When he picked up a cracker and handed it to her, Jen was surprised that her stomach rumbled in response, and she was able to take a bite.

They ate quietly, Ted opening a water bottle and sharing that with her, too. There were no sounds from upstairs, no footfalls, no water running in the taps. Jen wondered where the intruders were sleeping. Her bedroom? The guest room? Somewhere in this house they lay under blankets she had tucked under the mattresses herself, their heads on pillows that she had fluffed.

Would they ever be all right in this house again? If they made it, if they lived? Probably not. They would have to sell it. Move to another neighborhood, another town.

What about her marriage? The strain of this—this event, this crime, this tragedy, whatever they would come to think of it later—it was sure to be too much to bear, especially if Ted really had been having an affair. Jen wondered if she had been in some sort of denial. His afternoons away from the house, the calls and notes from Sarah—what kind of assistant gives that much attention to a former boss?—and now, lying about where he'd been. The trip to the auto dealership that he never made; the missing change of clothes. Why hadn't she added it all up before?

Jen watched Ted eat his crackers, his jaw working as he chewed. She'd always loved his jaw. He had the perfectly masculine bone structure of a 1940s movie star. She felt the pull she'd always felt toward him, the longing that she'd assumed would always be there for both of them. She couldn't bear to believe he didn't still feel the same for her, that he could have slowly grown away from her, little by little, until he was too distant for her to reach him.

"If we get out of this..." she started, her voice wavering.

"Hey, hey, what's this 'if'? There is no if," Ted said. "Come on, honey, this is the hardest part, getting through the night, but it's going to be okay. I swear it."

Jen swallowed, wanting so badly to believe him. She stared at his shirt, focusing on the plaid, and asked the question. "Okay, not if. When. When we get out of this, are you going to leave me?"

"Am I *what?*" Ted sounded genuinely shocked, and Jen stole a look at his face. His eyes were stricken, reflecting confusion and dismay. "Why would you even ask that?"

"The car," Jen said, trying to keep her voice even, to keep the tears from forming. She couldn't cry now, she *wouldn't* cry, and it was ridiculous to have this conversation now, but she needed to know. Suddenly the idea of never knowing—if things went wrong, if she ended up dead, shot by one of the strangers upstairs—was intolerable. "You said you took the car in yesterday, but the dent was still there. And you've been seeing Sarah. Don't tell me you haven't, Ted. I'm not stupid. And all those afternoons you disappear—you really want me to believe you've been sitting in Starbucks checking your LinkedIn account? When you haven't had an interview in over a month?"

"Jen...look. Whatever you think I've been doing, I haven't been having an affair. I swear to you." He put a hand on the back of the couch for support. "Sarah's just—there's nothing there, honest."

"Then what have you been doing all this time?" Jen gave up her battle not to cry, angrily pushing the tears away with the back of her hand. "What am I supposed to think?"

Ted reached for her, and she pushed his hands away. *"Don't,"* she snapped, and Teddy stirred, murmuring in his sleep. That couldn't happen; she couldn't let the kids hear them fighting. "Tell me," she whispered angrily.

"I've..." Ted's shoulders drooped, and he suddenly looked exhausted. There were deep smudges under his eyes, the skin loose and pouchy, the skin of an old man.

The huddled form on the couch shifted, and Teddy emerged from the nest of quilts, rubbing his eyes. "Mommy?" he said sleepily. He looked around him, blinking, and his face crumpled. The basement, shadowed and rearranged, looked nothing like it did before, and Teddy must have thought he'd woken up in a strange place.

"Oh, sweetie," Jen said, picking him up off the couch. "Hush, it's all right."

"I want Daddy," Teddy snuffled, reaching out for Ted, and Jen handed him over, gently untangling the quilt that had been twisted around him. Ted cradled his son in his arms, hitching him up so Teddy's cheek rested on his shoulder.

"Hey, little buddy," Ted whispered. "It's okay."

"I lost my truck," Teddy said, pointing somewhere off into the dark. Jen looked where he was pointing, but didn't see anything other than a stack of boxes. "Livvy dropped it over there."

"Well, we can look for it in the morning," Ted said. "Listen, how about you and me sleep down here on the floor. Like camping, what do you say?"

"Camping?" Teddy asked, yawning.

"Yup. Just us guys, the ladies have to sleep on couches because they're not tough enough."

"Can we go to Moose Lake?"

Ted pushed the coffee table away from the couch with his foot, making a space wide enough to stretch out. He set Teddy down and lay next to him, curving his body around his son. "Sure, we can go back to Moose Lake next summer. This is just practice, okay? We'll practice down here so that when we're in the tent, we'll be really good at it. But you have to go back to sleep, and show me you're ready for camping, okay?"

It broke Jen's heart to see how tender Ted was with their son, how gently he caressed the downy blond hair that never lay flat. Ted looked up and met her eyes, and he mouthed, "I'm sorry," but Teddy's eyelashes were already fluttering down. Their little boy would be asleep again in moments.

Jen draped the quilt over them, tucking it around. She made a pillow of one of the folded quilts and slipped it under Ted's head. Ted reached up and grabbed her wrist, not hard, but holding her there.

"Jen. You believe me, don't you? I would never… I don't want any other woman. It's you. It's only you."

Jen wanted to lie down in his arms, press her face to his chest and hear his heartbeat. Maybe then she could believe. Maybe she could detect in its rhythm the truth about his love for her.

But that wasn't possible, not now. Teddy needed him, and

Jen gently pulled her hand away and sat back onto the couch, reaching for the last of the quilts.

"Good night," she said softly, and turned off the lamp, casting them all into total darkness.

Chapter Nine

"Mom. Mom!"

Jen woke to Livvy's urgent whisper, her daughter shaking her by the shoulder. Groggily, she sat up. She'd finally fallen into a dreamless sleep, and it took her a second to remember. She was alone on the couch, and Ted was asleep on the floor with Teddy.

Livvy's face was stark with fear. "I can hear them up there!"

Weak light streamed through the window wells. It probably wasn't even seven yet. Jen didn't have a watch—who wore them anymore?—and Dan had taken their phones, all three of them. Livvy would have received dozens of texts by now, from her many friends. Jen wondered if Dan had thought of that. Then again, she doubted any of Livvy's friends would notice anything amiss for a while. Sometimes Livvy got into a mood and refused to text anyone back. She was known among her friends for being a bit artistic, a bit prickly. Sensitive, Jen would have said, though some days her daughter seemed anything but.

She pushed the quilt out of the way to make room for her daughter. Livvy sat next to her, stepping over her dad and brother, who didn't even stir. She was holding something tightly in her hands, one of Teddy's colorful toys. "I can hear them," she repeated. "What do you think they're doing?"

"I don't know." Jen tried to think, to force herself to process what was happening. Of course she had hoped they would be gone, that they would have loaded up their cars with everything they could fit and driven away in the early hours of dawn.

That hadn't happened, which begged all kinds of questions, all of them ominous. But she didn't want to communicate her fear to Livvy, to make things any worse. She caressed her daughter's cheek, pushing a wayward lock of hair out of her eyes. "I imagine they're doing what anyone does in the morning. Using the bathroom, maybe getting something to eat. But don't think about that, sweetie. It doesn't matter. You're here with us. With me and Daddy."

"Mom. They're *criminals.*"

"Oh, baby, I don't think they're all that dangerous," Jen said, praying it was true. "Guys like this, they're probably just in a jam. You know, with the economy the way it is, everyone struggling, all it takes is a missed paycheck or two and normal people start facing difficult decisions, and they do desperate things."

"Yeah, but they don't go around holding people hostage in their basements. You have to be sociopathic to do that."

Jen hugged Livvy tighter. "Don't jump to conclusions."

Livvy opened her hands, revealing the stubby little purple-and-orange plastic receiver of a walkie-talkie set that Ted had recently given Jake for his birthday. It had been a double-edged gift—the real reason Ted wanted Jake to have it was so that he would play with it with Teddy. It had led to an argument with Jen; she hated it when Ted tried to second-guess the speech pathologist, when he complained that Teddy's progress wasn't fast enough. But she had to admit that the toy had been a huge hit: Jake called every night from his bedroom in Tanya's apartment across the ravine in Hastings, and Teddy answered. If Ted didn't mind that he was the one who ended up talking to Jake when Teddy got tired of playing with the buttons, then Jen supposed it was a good thing, especially because Jake could certainly use a father figure.

"I found this," Livvy said. "When Dan brought Teddy's toys down from the living room, this was in the pile. Jake probably called after dinner, but we missed it because it wasn't turned on. But look, it's still charged." She pushed the button and the little light glowed orange. "Maybe we can call Aunt Tanya."

"That's—that's a great idea, Liv," Jen said. "But they don't work down here, remember? You have to be upstairs or the signal doesn't come through."

Livvy looked crestfallen. She switched the receiver off. "Maybe one of us could sneak upstairs."

"But it only works if the other one's on, too. And Aunt Tanya only lets Jake use it after dinner so he doesn't run down the battery. I just don't think it's going to work. I'm sorry, honey."

The door at the top of the stairs opened, and they heard heavy footsteps. "I'm coming down." Dan's voice. "Stay where you are."

Livvy quickly jammed the receiver under the couch and grabbed Jen's wrist tightly, and they watched Dan descend the steps. Ted groaned softly and shifted on the floor, his joints popping. Teddy turned in his sleep, a soft sigh escaping his lips.

Dan came down the stairs, looking better than he had the day before: well rested, clean shaven and wearing one of Ted's shirts. The shirt was snug on Dan, and he'd rolled the cuffs up over his forearms unevenly, the latex gloves looking fussy on his big hands.

Ted rolled onto his side and blinked, then lurched to his feet, cursing. Dan's hand went to the gun jammed in the waistband of his pants. The pants were Ted's, as well; Dan's gut hung over the waistband.

"Watch it," Dan barked. "Get up. Hands up."

Ted complied instantly. "I wasn't—"

"Save it. It's showtime."

Ted rubbed his hand over his eyes. "Is that—is that my shirt?"

"Ted," Jen warned. She pulled Livvy against her, instinctively shielding her daughter's face from the stranger.

"You and me," Dan said, ignoring Ted and pointing at Jen. "We're going on a little trip. Time to get ready."

Jen pulled Livvy tighter against her, trying to read Dan's expression. His eyes were calculating, not cruel, but not kind. "Where do you…"

Ted cut her off. "You're not taking my wife anywhere!"

"Calm down. Nothing's going to happen to her." Dan barely glanced at Ted. "Jen, we're leaving at ten after nine. I'm taking you upstairs now so you can take a shower and get dressed. Ted, we'll only be gone an hour or so. Stay here, feed your kids—it'll be over soon."

"I need to know where you're taking her."

"You don't *need* to know anything." Dan took a step toward Ted, his hand never leaving the gun. "You don't call the shots anymore, remember?"

"Listen," Ted said, standing his ground. "How about this. How about I'll go with you, whatever it is you need us to do, okay? Leave my wife here. I can promise you I won't give you any trouble."

Dan laughed harshly. "That right, Tonto? You gonna come along quietly?"

Ted paled, and closed his mouth. Jen glanced sharply at him, but he wouldn't look at her. *Tonto*...the nickname he'd earned in business school, when he had a reputation for reckless bravado, volunteering in class even when he wasn't prepared and playing pickup rugby in the quad. The nickname had stuck with him, but only among the handful of guys from school who still got together to ski every March, to relive the youth that seemed more distant as they settled more and more comfortably into middle age.

"Why did he call you that?" she asked. Livvy was staring, too, confused.

Ted merely shook his head. Dan looked from him to Jen, smirking. "You can discuss it later. *Now,* Jen."

Livvy whimpered and slid her hand into Jen's. "She stays with me," Jen said, trying not to show her fear.

"She can come upstairs, but only for a few minutes. Then she comes back down here. You'll both be fine. Let's go."

Jen refused to look at her husband as she followed Dan up the stairs. *Tonto, Tonto,* the stupid name echoed in her head. Something incomprehensible was going on. Ted knew something, he'd done something and she could barely contain the fury brewing inside of her.

When they reached the top of the stairs, Dan locked the door behind him. Jen and Livvy blinked in the bright sun streaming through the front door. They'd been in the basement for less than twelve hours, but Jen felt like she'd been released from a prison. She turned her face to the light and let it blind her.

Dan hurried her along. "Come on, upstairs."

As they passed the kitchen, Jen spotted Ryan standing at the counter. The fridge door was open and he was drinking straight from the orange juice carton. When he saw them, he set down the juice and licked his lips slowly, staring at Livvy.

"Ladies," he drawled, the sound rippling up Jen's spine.

"Come on, sweetie," she muttered, tugging Livvy's hand.

Upstairs, the hall bath was already steamy. One of the green towels was wadded on the floor.

"I'll give you five minutes," Dan said. "Then you go back downstairs, Livvy."

Livvy looked beseechingly at her mother. "Come in with me," she begged.

"Just give me a sec, and I will," she said, touching Livvy's cheek. "Go on in, now, sweetie. I'll be right here."

Livvy's eyes were red and puffy, but she nodded and closed the door quietly behind her.

Jen knew she didn't have much time. "How did you know about his nickname?" she demanded, speaking quietly so Livvy wouldn't hear. "About Tonto?"

Dan raised his eyebrows. That smirk—Jen wished she could smack it right off his face. "Lucky guess?"

"How did you *know?*" Jen said, closing the gap between them, her face inches from his, fury making spittle fly from her mouth.

Dan reached up deliberately and wiped a fleck of spit from his cheek. "I think you have more important things to worry about right now. Go in there with your daughter. She needs you."

"If I go with you—" Jen stopped herself, took a breath and tried again. "Can you promise me that Ryan will leave my daughter alone?"

"What—yeah," Dan said, but Jen didn't miss the flicker of uncertainty that crossed his face. She thought of the way Ryan had looked at Livvy, his gaze sliding over her body, and her nerves twisted.

She had no reason to believe Dan when he said that their errand would be brief or that she would return safely. It was possible he meant to take her somewhere, rape her, kill her, leave her body in a shack or a culvert—but that didn't seem right. He was too…calculating, and when he looked at her, she didn't sense anything predatory or sexual. But Ryan was something else entirely.

"Look, I know I'm not in a position to ask you for anything. But I won't give you any trouble. Just please promise me that nothing will happen to her while we're gone."

"Jen," Dan said, and maybe it was her desperation, but she thought he softened, just a little. "I want this to be over as much as you do. Nothing bad's going to happen, okay?"

Jen nodded, but as she put her hand on the bathroom doorknob, she had a terrible feeling that it was a promise he couldn't keep.

Inside the bathroom, Livvy was staring at herself in the mirror, her eyes glazed over. “Here, sweetheart,” Jen murmured, taking a washcloth from the white wicker basket and running cool water over it. She squeezed out the excess and then patted her daughter’s face gently, dotting away the sleep from her eyes, the red blotches on her cheeks. She picked up the boar’s-hair brush, a splurge last Christmas from a fancy bath store, and began to brush Livvy’s hair, taking care not to tug. The ends were tangled, and as she patiently worked out the knots she hummed softly, tunelessly at first, and then seguing into the Brahm’s “Lullaby,” something she’d sung to Livvy every single day when she was a baby.

When Livvy’s hair was neat and straight, Jen set down the brush and put her hands on her daughter’s face, turning her gently toward her. “Livvy, listen to me. I’m going to go with Dan now.”

“Are you coming back?”

Not *when* are you coming back, but…*are* you. Jen forced the muscles of her face to relax, pulled a smile out of some desperate last reserve of maternal will. “Of course I am, sweetie. Dan’s just, he just needs me to… I am going to find out how to get them the things they want, the money and all that.”

Livvy knew she was making it up. Jen could tell by the way her lip trembled, her breath huffed out in tiny puffs. She *had* to do better. “Dan is not going to hurt me,” she said carefully. “You just have to have faith in that, honey. *I* do. I really do.”

“Mommy,” Livvy whispered, her eyes filling with tears. “Please. I need you. Come back as fast as you can.” She put her own hands over Jen’s and squeezed them, and then hugged her hard.

"Oh, sweetie, you're my brave, brave girl," Jen murmured, just like she had when Livvy was seven and ran into the drinking fountain and had to have stitches in her scalp. "I'm so proud of you. Everything is going to be fine."

Livvy finally pulled back and wiped her eyes on her sleeve. "I'm sorry, Mom. I'm fine. Really."

"I know you are. Just stay close to Teddy and Dad. There are three of you. Just one of him. And he's going to be upstairs. Okay? I'll be back just as soon as I can."

"Hey, come on," Dan said, knocking. "Let's go, Livvy."

Livvy swallowed and nodded, and Jen gently shooed her out the door. "Go on now, sweetheart." She watched her walk down the hall, padding in her socks, her blond hair streaming over her shoulders. Livvy walked quickly, not turning around, with Dan close behind her. Jen's longing to chase after her took her breath and made her weak: if she died today, this would be the last time she saw her daughter.

When Dan returned in less than a minute, Jen was holding on to the sink for support. He didn't seem to notice.

"Put these on." He handed her a stack of clothes: a pair of black pants, a soft lavender twin set, things Jen stored in her dresser because she rarely wore them. "Make yourself up. Make it look good, like you have a meeting or whatever. Conservative, tasteful, not slutty." He paused before closing the door and shutting her in the bathroom. "You fuck up, I'll make you do it over, but we're on a schedule so don't fuck up."

Jen locked the door and turned the shower on full blast and skimmed off her clothes. She stepped under the scalding water and welcomed its burn, the stinging spray against her arms and chest. She didn't dare take long in the shower, so she didn't get her hair wet, just scrubbed her body.

She shut her eyes and let the hot spray wash over her, trying to see herself from an outsider's point of view. From Dan's point of view. He wanted her "conservative"—was that a euphemism for rich? Did he think she'd been born with a silver spoon in her mouth? Was that—God help her—a turn-on for him?

Again her mind refused to accept the possibility; whatever Dan wanted from her, she was convinced it wasn't sexual. But still, he had an idea in mind of who she was. How was he to know that she'd come from nothing? She'd worked so hard to expunge all traces of the past, the faint rural Great Lakes accent, the bad haircuts and the unschooled manners. But she'd been poor, and she'd been desperate. She remembered what it felt like.

Jen toweled off quickly, trying to push those thoughts away. She folded her towel and hung it from the rack. She dressed, her heart racing. It felt like her pulse hadn't slowed down since she first opened the bedroom door last night and saw their lives, changed forever, reflected in her daughter's terrified eyes.

She brushed her teeth and rinsed twice, trying to get the sour taste out of her mouth. For a moment she stood motionless, staring at her reflection, her feet cold on the tile floor. Her face looked dead: pale, expressionless, the faint lines bracketing her mouth and at the corner of her eyes more pronounced than usual. But she could do this; she could paint herself to look like what he wanted. She smoothed on foundation, dusted with powder, lined her eyes with the charcoal pencil. A swipe of eye shadow, two coats of mascara, lipstick in a shade of berry that the Chanel girl said complemented her coloring.

Jen considered the result. She hadn't been able to conceal the hollowness of her eyes, but she'd done a passable job with the cosmetics. It would have to do. She picked up Livvy's brush and did her best with her hair, dampening it where it stood up, smoothing it as flat as she could.

When she was finished, she took a deep breath, let it out slowly and opened the door.

Dan was gone.

She walked quietly down the hall, her bare feet making no sound. She heard voices when she got to the stairs.

"...*my* operation." Dan's voice, angry but controlled, came from the kitchen.

"Yeah, Uncle Richie, it's all you, ain't it. You're the big guy." Ryan didn't bother to hide his sarcasm.

When Jen entered the kitchen, Dan—Richie?—glared at her, turning his back on Ryan. "Tell me where the car keys are, Jen, and we'll go."

"Not until I say goodbye to my family." Jen's heart thudded so hard she could feel it in her throat.

"They're fine. I took Livvy back downstairs," Dan said.

"She's fine, all right," Ryan said, ignoring Dan. "She's so damn fine..." And then his tongue caressed his lower lip and he pantomimed a shudder.

"That's my *daughter,*" Jen snapped. She took two steps toward him, clenching her fists. "That's my *daughter* you're talking about, you—you *cocksucker*—"

Dan grabbed her, his hands on her shoulders, maneuvering himself between her and Ryan, yelling at her to calm down.

The word she'd said, the worst one Jen could think of, hung in the air, and Ryan's smirk broadened.

"Ignore him," Dan muttered, backing her out of the kitchen, his grip strong enough to hurt.

"I need to see them. My children. Before we go. I can't—I can't do this if I don't know that they're all right."

She twisted her hands around his wrists so they were locked together. She dug her fingers into his skin above the gloves, trying to hurt him with her nails. But Dan's arms were hard and corded, and he didn't even wince. Not like her husband's at all, not even with all those years of squash, all his home improvement projects.

"Ryan," Dan said in a low and dangerous voice, without taking his eyes off Jen's face. "Go upstairs *now.*"

Ryan shrugged, pushing himself with exaggerated effort away from the wall, and exited the kitchen. Jen heard his footsteps, taking his time, through the living room and up the stairs. Not until she heard his tread on the hall above did Jen relax her grip on Dan. "Please," she repeated.

Dan walked her to the basement door, pulling her by the upper arm, and turned the dead bolt. It was a good lock, and Jen recalled how she'd had the lock replaced when Teddy started walking. The man at Calumet Hardware told her it was the finest available. A small price to pay for the sense of security she had whenever she turned the key that Teddy couldn't reach.

Dan opened the door but didn't release her. "Five seconds," he said. "Just to look."

It took a moment for her eyes to adjust to the dim light. But there they were—Teddy was watching the washing machine again, a mesh bug net dangling from one hand. Ted sat on the sofa, holding Livvy in his arms. They stared up at her, the two of them, as if they didn't recognize her. It looked like Livvy had been crying.

"See, they're fine. Everything's fine," Dan said, pulling Jen back into the hall and closing the door, sliding the lock into place.

He looked at her appraisingly. "You look nice, by the way."

Chapter Ten

They were barely out of the cul-de-sac when Dan told her.

"We're going to the bank. It's payday and you're paying."

The bank. So it *was* just money, nothing more. Jen closed her eyes with relief, said a silent prayer. *Thank you. Thank you.*

She didn't dare show how relieved she felt, in case Dan somehow decided it wasn't enough, that they weren't taking enough from her. She had to resist, at least a little. "There's only a few hundred dollars in my checking account," she said. Her voice sounded strained even to her; she had never been a good liar.

"I don't give a shit about your checking account." He took his eyes off the road, his eyes boring into hers. "You know it damn well. I want the money market."

"How do you—"

"Never the fuck mind how. Now we need to be smart about this," Dan said. "It's not like you can take all that money out of the ATM."

The balance in the money market was seventy thousand, eighty-two dollars and some change the last time she looked. But how could Dan know that their balance was that high?

The vast majority of people didn't have that much liquid cash, especially in today's economy. Even in affluent Calumet, a lot of families had drawn down their savings and were living paycheck to paycheck. What made Dan think the Glasses were any different?

The way Dan looked at her at the next stop sign made Jen shiver: it was like he somehow saw inside her. Like he knew that having a lot of cash on hand was one of the ways she reminded herself of how far she'd come from the hardscrabble way she grew up. Seventy thousand covered six months of fixed living expenses and medical deductibles, but that was only part of it. In the back of her mind was another list, a secret one called Things That Can Go Horribly Wrong At The Worst Possible Time, and it included every shameful episode from her childhood as the daughter of an unlucky and eternally broke single mother: running out of milk before payday, not being able to go on class trips or play sports, never answering the phone because it might be a bill collector.

But no one knew about that. And no one but Ted and the bank—which, nowadays, was so disconnected from any human interface as not to count—knew about the money market. So how did *Dan* know? Could he possibly have made such a lucky guess? Or did he think every affluent family had cash squirreled away?

Jen's nerves tightened, squeezing her lungs, making it hard to breathe. She forced herself to look at Dan. He was driving right at the speed limit, his right hand draped casually on the wheel. In profile he looked relaxed, just a regular guy headed into town for a few errands.

"All right," she said, trying to keep her voice calm. "I'll

get your money. I'll talk to one of the personal bankers and get a cashier's check."

"That's more like it."

She bit her lip, thinking it through. "You made me come instead of Ted because it won't look as strange this way. You and him together, two men, that would raise eyebrows, but they'll just think we're..."

"Married," Dan said. "You can say it. I guess I'm not your type. You think I couldn't get a woman like you."

"I never— I don't—"

"You wouldn't give me the time of day," he went on, ignoring her. "We met in a bar, you'd tell me to fuck off. Which is kind of funny, if you think about it."

His hands were tense on the wheel now. She'd made him angry; his jaw was tight and his shoulders stiff, a stark contrast to how relaxed he'd been moments earlier. But what was responsible for the change? Just because he thought she considered herself...too *good* for him?

She wondered again if he had thought of her...that way, if he was even now thinking of pulling the car off the road, after he got what he wanted at the bank, and doing things to her. If she was somehow giving off signals that she found him repugnant, and that made him want to hurt her, defile her. Humiliate her.

She stared at his large hands. They were fleshy and sunspotted, reddish hairs springing from the knuckles in clumps. She imagined them fumbling at her blouse, yanking down her pants. Covering her mouth when she tried to scream.

"I wouldn't tell you to..." she started, but her voice trembled and she couldn't finish the sentence, couldn't say the words. *Fuck off.* "I don't think I'm better than you."

Dan laughed, a harsh and abrasive sound. "That's a good one. That's right, you're not—and we both know it, don't we? We both know you came from nothing. Your daddy didn't have two nickels to rub together. Took off on you and your sister and never looked back."

He leered at her, giving her a complicit wink as the car started moving through the intersection. He turned his attention back to the road, where he'd drifted from the center of the lane, earning a dirty look from the other morning commuters.

Jen fought the numbing horror of his words. How could he know? But the answer was right there, glaringly obvious, and she must have been working hard to stay in denial, because everything pointed to it, once she gave it a moment's thought.

"You knew my dad," she said, her voice barely more than a whisper.

"Oh, I've known plenty of guys like him. And I've known their dirty little trailer trash kids, too. Not too often one grows up like you. *Princess.* You act so high and mighty. But in my book if you come from trash, that makes you trash, too."

His voice had hardened with disgust. He didn't glance at her as Jen tried to absorb what he'd said. He switched lanes without signaling, cutting in front of a slow-moving sedan full of old women.

"What did Sid tell you?"

He snorted. "That's enough of that," he muttered. "Shut up now. I'll tell you when to talk."

In her mind, the pieces reshuffled, like the gears of a music box spinning. Dan knew Sid. Maybe they worked together at one low-end job or another. Ryan, too. Maybe they drank at the same bar. The few friends Sid used to have were always drinking buddies, men he met at dives and taverns all over town.

How would it have happened? Sid's life, practically empty from the looks of his pathetic apartment, wouldn't have given him much conversational fodder. Sitting at the bar late at night, talk among the regulars would turn to bragging and blaming: the scheming ex-wives, bosses who were out to screw them, cops who had it in for them.

Ungrateful children.

Never even write to me, she could imagine Sid saying. *Live a few hours away and I ain't never even met my grandkids. Not even a fuckin' Christmas card.*

He'd get a lot of sympathy for that, Jen imagined, his drinking buddies egging him on. Over a few nights, or years maybe, he'd refine his bitter tale. *One of 'em rich enough to buy the damn town, couldn't even help out with a few bucks.* He might easily have talked himself into believing Jen didn't deserve all her good fortune—how hard would it be to convince strangers?

And then he'd died—

He'd died, and what if Dan and Ryan had actually been *good* friends? Sid could have convinced them he had been screwed over by his life. As the bitter seed planted during those drunken conversations took shape into a plan, they could have felt justified in coming after Jen and her family. In some twisted way, maybe they even felt like they were honoring his memory.

She wanted to protest. She wanted Dan to know exactly what kind of father Sid had been, but what good would it do? And who cared, anyway? Sid was *dead.* Let Dan have the money. She could get more; she could cash in some investments and replenish the rainy-day fund. Once she got through this ordeal she would put it behind her just like she had put Sid behind her. She would choose not to let it matter; she would move on.

She just had to get through it. One step at a time. *Focus.* It was hard, but each moment on its own was manageable. Walking into the bank. Getting the money. Returning home, being locked up in the basement again. Dan and Ryan leaving with their money. They would wait for help to come. Livvy and Teddy didn't show up for school today; that wouldn't go unnoticed. Jen would be absent from her yoga class and her assigned hour helping in the high school library. And she was supposed to meet Elaine Cavanaugh tonight at a wine bar for a drink. Elaine would wonder why she didn't show up.

Maybe Elaine would be worried enough to stop by the house when Jen didn't answer her calls. Or if not Elaine, maybe one of Livvy's friends, when she didn't come to school tomorrow and didn't answer her texts. *Someone* would come for them. There would be cops and investigations and calls from the media, insurance adjusters and counselors to make sure the kids were processing their emotions, and they would get through all of it.

But what about Ryan? Here in the car with Dan, even with what he'd said about Sid, Jen could convince herself that he wouldn't hurt her family. He only wanted their money. But Ryan was another matter. She couldn't put his face out of her mind, that sneer that never left him, those pale eyes that lingered on Livvy's body. Jen felt her pulse quickening, her blood pressure rising, and she tried again to think only of the moment. Walk into the bank, get the money....

Breathe in. Let it out slowly. One...two...three...

There was construction along Glenn Road, and traffic was down to one lane. Flaggers in orange vests stopped traffic for the cars coming the other way. Dan drove slowly through the construction, keeping pace with traffic.

Away from town. In the opposite direction of the bank.

"Where are you taking me?" Jen demanded, her voice shrill and frightened.

"You think I'm taking you to your own branch? That make sense to you? Risk running into one of your friends, or your neighbors?" Dan signaled and eased into the turn lane. And Jen figured it out a second before he said it: "We're going to Hastings. I don't guess you know many people there."

They crossed the ravine, and Glen Hollow Road turned into 17th Street and curved straight into the blighted part of town that was hidden from Calumet by the thick band of trees that grew along the bluff. Erosion was slowly claiming the trees, but erosion was also to thank for keeping the bluff from being built on, so that Calumet could continue to ignore its neighbor to the east.

Dan drove past Tanya's street—if Jen craned her neck she could probably see her sister's building—and into Hastings' struggling downtown. There was a pawnshop, a halal market, an Ethiopian restaurant. In the next block, a tire shop and a discount grocery. And, of course, the bank.

A car pulled out of a parking space right in front, and Dan gave the driver a thumbs-up before pulling in. Jen felt oddly detached, looking at the bank's familiar logo on the sign above the doors. The bank branch was blocky and unattractive and small, a humble brick building that might have been an insurance office or a drugstore before, nothing like the beautiful restored granite building that housed the Calumet branch. This, it occurred to Jen, was where Tanya banked.

Before getting out of the car Dan turned in his seat to face Jen. "I never hurt anyone, never served any time. I got a plan and I mean to stick to it. But that don't mean I won't do what I need to. Don't fuck with me in there. You draw attention to us, do something stupid like call for help—you'll regret it. If Ryan sees anybody but me come through the door of your house today, it's your family that's going to pay."

"I—I understand."

He nodded and reached into the backseat where he'd tossed Jen's purse. He handed it to her, but didn't let go until he finished talking. "Don't look for your phone because it's not there. You got your ID, your ATM card. That's all you need to get the money. Now let's go inside and get this done."

Dan peeled off his gloves and stuffed them into his pocket as they went into the bank. There were two customers talking to bankers in cramped cubicles, and a few more standing in line waiting for tellers. Most of the customers were elderly. None of them looked like they were dressed for work.

A man who couldn't be more than twenty-five stepped toward them, smiling.

"May I help you?"

Jen felt the slight pressure of Dan's hand on the small of her back. She forced a smile. "I need to make a withdrawal. A significant one, actually...I'd like to close out a money market account."

"I see. All right. I'm happy to help. Why don't we sit... over here, please."

He led them to the only empty cubicle, and Jen and Dan took seats in the two chairs across the desk from him.

"If I could have your debit card, I'll be able to access all your accounts...."

Jen took it out of her wallet and slid it across the desk. She watched the man carefully as his fingers tapped at the keyboard. The little nameplate on his desk read Terrence Jurgenssen, which seemed like a lot of name for his bland features.

"And which of your accounts are you interested in withdrawing funds from, Mrs. Glass?"

"The money market account ending in 4611."

"And you want to take the funds in...?"

"A cashier's check, please."

"All right." He reached for a slip of paper and began to write. "Now with a cash withdrawal of over five thousand dollars, I will need to ask my supervisor to join us."

Jen watched him write. He worked slowly, his movements laborious and careful. Terrence Jurgenssen's handwriting was precise, and Jen had no trouble reading the figure he wrote, even upside down.

Ten thousand eighty-two dollars and sixteen cents.

"Wait," she said. "Wait. What is my balance, please?"

"Ten thousand eighty-two dollars and sixteen cents."

When Jen didn't respond, immobilized by shock, Terrence spun his monitor around so she and Dan could see the screen. There—there was the list of accounts: Livvy's, with eight hundred some dollars at the top, and then the household account and their personal accounts—and then the personal line of credit that had been at zero since the day she opened it all those years ago, a prudent precaution she'd never had to use and never meant to.

And there it was. Just as he'd told her, just as he'd written on the little slip of paper: *$10,082.16.*

Dan leaned close, his hot breath on her face. Terrence looked away, clasping his hands on his lap. "What the fuck," Dan whispered, too low for Terrence to hear. "That's not enough. I want all of it. I know there's more."

How did he *know?* With every new revelation, each bit of evidence that Dan had somehow wormed his way even more deeply into their lives, she found it more excruciating to be near him. She wanted to jump out of the chair and run. Freedom was tantalizingly close—he couldn't hurt her here, she could be out the door and gone in seconds.

And then he would return to her home. Her family. Where he could take his fury out on them.

Jen pressed her knees together, trying to contain her horror. She nodded, her mouth dry. "If you could...if I could see the recent transaction detail," she said, hearing the tremor in her own voice.

Terrence clicked obligingly, and after a very brief pause the screen populated with the recent transactions. The monthly interest on the thirty-first. There, down at the bottom, the January adjustment she made every year, transferring the accrued interest into checking to keep the balance right at seventy thousand.

And at the top, dated three days ago, a withdrawal of sixty thousand dollars.

Chapter Eleven

"That one," Jen said hoarsely. "At the top. The withdrawal..."

"Yes." Terrence moved the cursor over the numbers. "That would have been, let's see, Monday. Right here in the Hastings West Plaza branch, and it looks like it was also taken in the form of a cashier's check."

"But I don't..." Ted, dear God, what had Ted done, what had he been thinking? She checked her accounts every Sunday night—he knew that, he'd teased her about it for years. He said he could set the clocks by her. He had to have known she would look this Sunday, only two days away.

Ted had withdrawn the money four days ago. From this very branch, for God's sake—what had he been doing here? It was nowhere near the BMW dealership, that was for sure.

A flash of goldenrod, a memory of perfume. Sarah Elizabeth Baker with her long white neck, the smooth rounded tops of her breasts in that dress she wore to the holiday party. *Thx tons, Thursday 2pm Firehouse xoxoxo.* Ted could have withdrawn the money, planned to meet her...

But no, that was crazy. Ted had held her last night, had sworn to her that he wasn't having an affair. And even if he had lied, even if he was planning to leave Jen to be with Sarah, he wouldn't do it like this. Ted was many things, among them impetuous and passionate, but he was first and foremost a family man. He would never destroy everything they'd built together, not this way.

Terrence cleared his throat. He was looking at her oddly. "Is there…something I can help with?" he asked lamely. Under the desk, Dan put his hand on her leg and squeezed, hard enough to hurt, his fingers digging into the soft flesh behind the knee. She was mucking this up, raising suspicion, doing exactly what he had warned her about. *It's your family that's going to pay.*

"I'm sorry," she said, forcing a smile to her lips. "If I could just have a second."

She took another look at the accounts and did some quick math in her head. Excluding Livvy's account, the rest added up to about four thousand. Another fifteen from the line of credit, though she was uncertain about whether she could do that all in one day. As for the rest, the easiest thing would be a wire transfer from their investments, but it would take a day for the funds to clear.

The thought filled her with dread. Could she convince Dan to give her the extra time? How would they bear another night in the basement? But there wasn't any other choice.

"Thank you," she said to Terrence, forcing herself to stay calm. "All right, here's what I'd like to do. I'll take what's in the account now in a cashier's check. Then I'm going to have some funds wired from an investment account today, and I'll come back to withdraw that. When is the earliest I could make the second withdrawal?"

"If the funds clear by 1:00 p.m. tomorrow, you can withdraw them after that. We're open until 5:30 p.m."

Terrence busied himself with the paperwork. While Jen waited, she stared at his nameplate, reading the letters of his name over and over. She tried to ignore Dan, to pretend she was alone here, doing some routine transaction on an ordinary day.

It seemed to take forever, but finally Terrence excused himself for a moment and returned with the check, which he slipped into an envelope.

"May I help you with anything else today?" he asked, handing the envelope to Jen.

"No, thank you, that will be all," Jen said, standing and offering him her hand.

"All right. Thank you, Mrs. Glass. Mr. Glass. Have a great day."

As Dan shook Terrence's hand, Jen was already walking unsteadily toward the door, suddenly desperate for fresh air. On the sidewalk next to her car she paused, and Dan almost ran into her.

"What the fuck—" he started, but she held up her hand to silence him.

His face was inches from hers. Half a dozen black hairs protruded from his nostrils. He had a mole on his eyelid and flecks of gold sparked in his otherwise unremarkable brown eyes.

"How did you know how much money was in the account?" she demanded.

He was already shaking his head before she got the words out. "None of your fucking business. Give me the check."

She handed it to him, and he folded the envelope and put

it in his pocket without looking at it. "Okay. That's a down payment. Now all you need to concern yourself with is getting the rest of it to me."

"All right. I'll get it. I just need to make a few calls. I have to transfer the funds."

Dan's face was mottled red with anger. "Do it now."

"I would, if I could, I swear to you. But it takes a day to wire the funds. There's no way to get it today, by law."

Dan turned away from her, his fists clenched, and for a moment Jen thought he was going to hit the parking meter. Instead he seized her upper arm and dragged her to the passenger door. "Get in."

Jen did, barely managing to get her legs in before he slammed her door. By the time he came around and got in the driver's side, he was breathing hard. He sat rigidly for a moment and then slammed the steering wheel with his hand. The car shook from the impact.

"God*damn* it. The price just went up. Double. I want a hundred fifty."

"I'm not sure if I can—"

"Call them. Now." He had the gun in his hand; he must have gotten it out of his jacket when he got in the car.

Jen didn't believe he would shoot her in the car, in the middle of the day, right here in depressing downtown Hastings, but she wasn't about to test him. When he handed her his phone she was shaking so badly she nearly dropped it. It was warm from his pocket, the screen blurred with a greasy smudge.

She found the phone number on the internet and dialed,

staring at the console between them, not wanting to see the gun he was holding in his lap.

An assistant answered. That was a stroke of luck; Jen wasn't sure she could have pulled off the transaction if her broker had answered, with his friendly inquiries about Ted and the kids, questions that Jen doubted she could have managed in her current state.

But the young woman who took the call sounded bored as she went through the authentication and the details of the transaction. Jen could hear her fingers on the keyboard as she keyed in the amounts.

"The funds will wire by eleven o'clock tomorrow morning. Is there anything else I can help you with?"

"No, thank you."

"Thank you for your business today, Mrs. Glass, and I hope I have provided you with excellent service. Have a great day." She hung up before Jen could respond.

"So?" Dan asked impatiently.

Jen stared at the phone, the number disappearing from the caller ID. "It's taken care of. They're wiring it in the morning. We can pick it up tomorrow afternoon."

Dan nodded curtly and started the car, saying nothing. He let it idle for a moment before backing out of the parking space. He made the turn at the next stoplight, but instead of going around the block and heading back the way they'd come, he drove straight through the heart of town.

They passed vacant department stores and shuttered shop windows. At a green light, they had to wait while a group of young men in enormous puffy coats and sneakers took their time ambling across the street. A plastic bag rode a wind current and rested for a moment against the windshield before drifting away.

Jen wondered if Dan was lost, if she should tell him he was going the wrong way. If he was her father's crony, if he lived up in Murdoch, he wouldn't know his way around. He might have memorized the route to the bank, but not the reverse directions.

She was about to say something when it suddenly occurred to her where Dan was going. Surely not…there wasn't any way he could know. Was there? She waited, holding her breath, thinking that at any moment he'd take another turn and start heading back west.

But no. They passed the Kmart, the outer limit of Jen's childhood, the farthest she was allowed to ride her bike alone. Down Lowry Street, past the narrow wedge of a public park, where even in the middle of the day, in the biting cold, she could see a few homeless men sleeping on the benches. Past the turnoff to the elementary school, where her mother—in a brief happy phase when she'd had the occasional weekday off—had once been a playground monitor.

"This isn't the way," Jen finally blurted, when they were almost to her old street. She felt like she couldn't breathe. But Dan slowed, until the car was barely doing twenty in the right-most lane. A car honked and passed them on the left.

"It's not even there anymore," he said irritably as though it was her idea to come here. "It's nothing but a parking lot now. A shitty one."

He turned on Russell. That's what the road used to be called, anyway, before they bulldozed the half dozen run-down little houses arranged in a crooked loop off what used to be the route to the paper mill. The mill had been shuttered a long time ago, and now there was a shabby strip mall anchored by a dollar store and a Pet Express. Not even a quarter of the parking lot was full.

Jen had been here exactly once in the past decade, propelled by curiosity and the wistful mood that used to accompany the anniversary of her mother's death. Tanya had told her the old house was gone, but she still wasn't prepared for the way the parking lot obliterated even the contours of the old neighborhood. She'd driven slowly along the Dumpsters and loading bays in the back of the mall, looking for proof that what was once Russell Street lay beneath the asphalt. Finally she'd managed to find the approximate spot by looking out into the field beyond and lining up landmarks with her memory—the barn that still stood next to a clump of black walnut trees, the stagnant drainage pond. Development, it seemed, had not reached very far into the outer edge of Hastings.

No one could argue that the demolishing of those houses was any great loss. So Jen hadn't been prepared for the emotional turmoil that visit invited. She'd ended up having to pull over near what was once the far end of Russell Road, where a long-ago neighbor kept a pair of mangy dogs on wire leads tied to trees, and vomit onto the pavement. She'd wiped her mouth off and driven home, and never mentioned the trip to anyone.

Dan drove past the parking lot, where the road dead-ended at the gravel turnaround in front of a cattle guard. Jen doubted that anyone grazed cattle here anymore. It was only a matter of time until the field ended up being studded with cheap little tract homes. She hoped Dan would just turn around and head back, but he pulled the car up so close that the front fender was almost touching the gate and the tires rested on the bars of the cattle guard, and let the engine idle.

"Why are we stopping?" Jen asked.

"I just thought you might need a reminder." Dan sounded even angrier than he had outside the bank. "This is what you come from. Everything you did, trying to hide it, it don't change anything. You're still from the wrong side of town and you always will be."

"Did my dad tell you we used to live here?" Jen's teeth were chattering, even though the interior of the car was still warm. "Did he tell you he abandoned us? Took off and never sent any child support? That when my mom got sick, all he ever cared about was whether he could get his hands on her money?"

"I don't know what the hell you're talking about," Dan said. "I don't give a shit about your dad. Just you. I just want you to see that I know you're nothing. And you screw up and don't get my money, you'll end up worse off than if you still lived here. I'll make sure of it."

"I won't screw up. I promise."

"You think I'm some dumbass who can't count," Dan continued, as though she hadn't even spoken. "You think I don't have what it takes to pull something like this off, that I'll settle for a few bucks when I know you've got a lot more stashed away. You're wrong. Dead wrong," he repeated as he finally put the car in Reverse and started backing into a turn.

Neither he nor Jen spoke as he drove back the way he'd come, past the Kmart and gas stations, back down Lowry and over the bridge on 17th.

The farther they got from what had once been Jen's home,

the more the panic receded. She still didn't know how he knew: Sid, maybe, but maybe there was a much simpler explanation. One of those online search services—they could have found out all kinds of things about her background. For fifty bucks he could have had all her prior addresses.

By the time they crossed the ravine, heading back into Calumet, Jen had managed to convince herself that Dan was just trying to push her buttons, using whatever thin threads he'd been able to discover in a basic exploration of her history. She didn't have to react. She didn't have to let paranoia and fear take over. She should be grateful that at least they hadn't raised suspicion at the bank. She should reassure Dan that everything was taken care of.

Maybe she'd been forced to endure one too many spikes in her adrenaline, one too many rushes of pure terror, because deep inside her, the fear was beginning to harden into something else. Being forced to leave her family behind in the home she loved, at the mercy of an armed psycho, had altered something inside Jen. She had no idea how Dan had known about the account. No idea if her father had planted the seed that led to this disaster. No idea what Ted had done with the money. And suddenly, those things didn't matter.

At the edge of her mind were the things she could not think about—her children in the basement, her husband with his secrets, the life she had worked so hard for, that she had convinced herself could change things. Things, she now saw, that could never be changed. She would never be able to shed her past.

But now all the cards were on the table, and she had nothing else to lose. And the realization brought a simmering, dangerous rage.

Chapter Twelve

Ryan was in their kitchen making Stouffer's French Bread Pizzas. Livvy recognized the smell even all the way down in the basement because it was her favorite after-school snack, and because whenever the little bits of cheese got on the pan they burned and made the whole house smell.

She was never going to eat one of those pizzas again, if she ever got out of here.

All morning she had been trying to decide if she should tell her parents about the text, but then her mom left with Dan and her dad was losing it, she could tell. He kept picking Teddy up and putting him down, and then he'd come over and tell her everything was going to be just fine, with this horrible fake smile on his face that told her he was really scared. So it didn't seem right to say anything, especially since there wasn't anything he could do about it.

The only person who could have done anything about it was her, but now it was too late. Allie was one crazy, unpredictable bitch—everyone said so, and besides, once her cousins got involved that was a whole other thing. They were supposedly in a gang. Livvy didn't know anything about it except for the rumors, which she didn't believe half of, but she also figured some of it was probably true.

Monday when she got to school there had been a shirt hanging out of her locker. Poked through the vent slit, only part of it hung free, and since Livvy had an A period and got to school early, she didn't think anyone saw it but her. It was a gym shirt, a dirty one, gray, with CALUMET PHYS ED on the front. Under that someone had written *Whore* in red lipstick. Bright red, like blood.

The shirt wasn't any mystery—anyone could steal them out of the PE lost and found. Livvy stuffed it in the trash, her face burning with shame. When she saw Allie across the cafeteria at lunch, Allie smirked at her and gave her the finger, her hand half-hidden under the tray.

Livvy figured that was the end of it. She didn't tell anyone, not even Paige. Allie was constantly getting into trouble at school, and if Livvy went to the counselor she was pretty sure they'd take it seriously, call Allie in, maybe suspend her again. But then Sean would find out. And he would…she wasn't sure what he would do, because she didn't know what he thought about her now, if he ever thought of her at all. But maybe he'd be angry, maybe he'd hate her, and while that shouldn't matter, because she was so much better off without him and he had never been good enough for her in the first place, she still hadn't been able to stop thinking about him, remembering all the times they'd been together. Wishing. Missing him.

Allie knew it, too. Somehow she knew how bad it hurt, because when she passed Livvy in the hall on Wednesday, she pretended to drop something in front of her so Livvy had to stop walking and then Allie stood up and said, real quiet, "He told me everything. He told me you didn't even know what to do. When you were together. He fucked you as a *favor.*" She smiled, revealing her sharp little teeth with the gap between. Livvy was close enough to see her eyelashes clotted with mascara, to smell her perfume.

Livvy had gone through the day numb, hardly even hearing anything the teachers said. Paige asked her if she was sick. She looked for Sean after Spanish and saw him heading into the robotics lab, high-fiving Mr. Jenkins, and he was so much like he used to be with her, funny and kind of silly and smart; he always did well in the classes he liked, it was just the ones where he was bored that he had trouble. And it was more than Livvy could stand. She just had to know if it was true. What Sean really thought. If he ever thought of her at all.

She waited for him near his locker, pretending to text, her face flaming. "Livvy," he'd said, sounding surprised, sounding maybe a little glad she was there, and she'd tried to say what she'd rehearsed, but it didn't come out. She would have gotten around to it, she was working up to it and Sean was sort of half smiling, letting his backpack slide down to the floor, putting his hand on the locker next to her so she was between him and the locker.

Then Allie showed up. She didn't say anything, just slid her hand into Sean's back pocket and moved her body in front of him, edging Livvy out of the way. She kissed him on the lips and put her arms around him so his face was in her neck, and Livvy backed away. The look Allie gave her was pure hate, and when Livvy got off the bus, she had a text from a number she didn't know.

You will pay for that I told you to stay away from him youll be sorry

Well, she was sorry now, really sorry, because all Allie would have had to do was tell her cousins to send someone, to take care of it. There were rumors her cousins had killed someone who was going to testify against them, that one of them had killed another prisoner at Hennepin County jail, so sending someone to rob Livvy's house would have been nothing to them. Ryan was probably in the gang with them, and Dan…well, Livvy didn't know how that worked, how he fit in, but now he was off with her mom doing God knew what.

Which she couldn't think about. Because that was her fault, too.

The basement door opened and Ryan came down the stairs. Teddy was sitting next to her on the couch playing with the paper from an origami set that she had never used, folding the pretty colored squares into random shapes. Livvy had tried to teach him how to fold a fortune-teller, but he was too little still, he couldn't do it, so Livvy just let him do whatever he wanted with the paper. Her dad had been sitting next to them looking at nothing. Every once in a while he would reach over and pat Livvy's knee, very gently, like he was afraid he might hurt her. Like he was making sure she was still there.

But when Ryan started coming down the stairs, her dad threw his arm in front of her and Teddy the same way he did when they were driving and he had to put on the brakes suddenly, his big arm pushing them back against the couch cushions.

As if that would help anything. As if he could stop anything.

Ryan stood in front of them with one hand resting on the gun he kept in his pants. He had something on his face, a fleck of white that it took Livvy a minute to figure out was shaving cream. Ryan had shaved in her house—he had used her dad's stuff. She felt like she was going to throw up.

"I made lunch. Livvy, you come up and eat and then you can bring the rest down here for them."

"Absolutely not." Her dad stood up. He was taller than Ryan, though not by much. Ryan stepped back and raised the gun and pointed it right at his chest.

"Back off," Ryan said.

Her dad raised his hands halfway, but he didn't sit back down. "You won't take her upstairs alone." He wasn't scared, not for himself.

"What are you going to do about it?" Ryan demanded.

"You try to take my daughter up there with you, and I'm coming after you. You can shoot me if you want, but you'd better be damn sure you stop me with one shot."

"That's all it would take, man."

"Maybe." Her dad stayed calm. "Maybe not. You shoot me, you got a whole other set of problems on your hands. Just go back upstairs, and leave us alone down here. We have food. We're fine."

Ryan's mouth twitched at the corner. She could tell he was trying to decide what to do.

For a minute they glared at each other, and then Ryan laughed. Teddy had put down the paper squares and crawled into Livvy's lap, and she wrapped her arms around him.

"Whatever. You can all come up. Make the kid go first, then her, then you. Go straight to the kitchen table."

Livvy couldn't believe he was going to let them upstairs while Dan was gone, but she didn't have to be told twice. She picked up Teddy and started up the stairs, pretending not to be scared. Her dad was right behind her. At the top she put her hand on the doorknob and imagined slamming it into the wall so hard it wouldn't lock again, taking a hammer to it, the old ax her dad kept in the shed. Something, anything. But instead she just opened the door and went into the hall. She carried Teddy to his chair. Her dad sat in the one he always did.

"Hurry up," Ryan said, even though she was going as fast as she could. But Teddy was fighting her, wiggling to avoid getting in the chair. Livvy thought she knew what the problem was.

"He has to go to the bathroom."

"Oh, Christ, tell him to hold it. He can go after lunch."

"Kids *can't* hold it," Livvy said, not even trying to keep herself from sounding like she thought he was an idiot. "Besides, he always washes his hands before we eat."

"Well, then take him." He waved his gun at the powder room across from the kitchen. "But the food's going to get cold."

Only then did she notice that he had laid out lunch on the counter: two plates with pizza on them, two glasses of milk. Two napkins folded in half. He'd gotten it all ready for the two of them, had planned it out. Livvy shivered with revulsion.

"We're fine, Daddy," she said, making her voice sound upbeat, knowing he could see the two plates, too. She carried Teddy into the bathroom and locked the door behind her and turned on the fan.

Teddy got the step stool and scrambled up on the toilet. It always took him a while, and he often sang or tried to whistle while he sat and waited. Livvy got on her knees in front of him. "Listen to me, Teddy," she said, suddenly sure of what had to happen next. She couldn't take back what had happened already, but at least she could help Teddy get away. "This is really important, okay?"

Teddy looked at her skeptically, his face twisted in concentration. She knew he wouldn't talk now, not even with the door closed and locked. Not while there was a stranger in the house.

"When we go out of the bathroom, I'm going to go in the kitchen and make a lot of noise. And you are going to run to the front door and unlock the lock, as fast as you can, and then run to the Sterns' house, okay? Run as *fast* as you can, because Mark is waiting for you to come over for your playdate. You don't want to be late, do you?"

Teddy thought about it for a moment, then shook his head.

"Listen to me really carefully, Teddy. No matter what happens…" She stopped, trying to think of what to say that wouldn't scare him. "I'm going to pretend to get mad at Daddy and Ryan. But it's just a game, okay? I'm tricking them. But I'm going to yell and it might be loud, but you just have to go as fast as you can and don't turn around. Don't come back, no matter what. You *have* to run to Mark's."

Teddy said nothing. He closed his eyes and his urine finally trickled into the bowl. Livvy waited, her heart pounding with each passing second. When he was finished, she repeated the plan as he got down from the toilet.

"You remember how to turn the lock?" she asked as she ran water and helped him wash his hands. "Grab the lock and make it go this way." She took his right hand in hers and made the twisting motion. "Just like this. Remember? Then grab the door and open it and *run*."

Now, suddenly, she *was* really scared. But she couldn't let him see. "Teddy, you can do this. Promise me, you're going to go as fast as you can. Run to the door, do the lock, open it and *go*. No matter what you hear. No matter if you feel scared. No one is going to be mad, I promise. Mom's going to be really proud of you when I tell her."

She was messing this up. She had told him it was a game, but she could see that she was scaring him now. She rinsed his hands and he dried them on the hand towel and she knelt before him. She made herself smile and she kissed his cheek, the skin that was softer than anything she had ever touched, softer than her mom's, softer than her own. "You ready?"

After a moment, Teddy nodded.

"I love you," she whispered, and he nodded again.

She took a deep breath and opened the door. She gave Teddy a shove down the hall, and he ran, his shoes slapping on the wood, and he didn't look back, just like she told him. But she had to turn away from him; she had to run into the kitchen and pick up the coffeepot—it was sitting right there on the kitchen island. And even though Ryan was already moving toward her, running, yelling something, she managed to crash it against his shoulder. She saw her dad rising from the table, but it was all so slow, too slow. Her arm hurt from the impact of the pot against Ryan's shoulder, but she hadn't even managed to stop him.

The pot clattered to the floor, and her dad tripped on it as Ryan fired the first shot, and Livvy waited for her body to register where she had been hit. She grabbed for the pan on the stove, the pizzas sliding to the counter, the metal still hot in her hand. She hit Ryan with the pan, but it was too light to hurt him and it just bounced off him. Her dad was on his knees, tackling Ryan around the legs, and she threw herself at Ryan, too, trying to grab for his gun hand, but he bucked her off and she slammed into the cabinets, hitting the back of her head on the knob. Someone grunted, and she couldn't tell if it was Ryan or her dad, but her dad was reaching for Ryan's throat, and she knew if he could just get his hand around it he would crush the life from it, her strong and fearless father, but the gun went off a second time and her dad fell against the cabinet, spraying red against the white paint.

Chapter Thirteen

Neither of them spoke as Dan pulled into Crabapple Court.

Dan and Ryan would have their money by tomorrow afternoon, and this nightmare would be over. Jen thought she could detect the effects of stress on Dan—the sallowness of his skin, the depth of the lines on his face. The past twenty-four hours had cost him.

Her home appeared eerily unchanged on the outside. There was no hint of the terror that was taking place inside, nothing out of place to indicate that the Glass family was under siege. Peeking from the snow was one of Teddy's toys, a bright blue plastic boomerang he must have been playing with before the last snowstorm. Other than that flash of color, their house was like every other house on the block: tasteful if a little ostentatious, a suburban stronghold.

After he parked, Dan pulled his gloves back on. Jen wondered what he planned to do about the prints on the steering wheel. She guessed that Ted had been right—they were going to take the cars when they left.

She followed Dan into the house, wiping her feet on the mat from habit. But two steps inside the mudroom, she went still.

Something was wrong. The interior of the house had been altered in her absence. Some faintly unpleasant smell tainted the air, and the silence was edged with tension.

Surely it was just her imagination, the physical embodiment of her fear. Jen steadied herself, putting a hand to the wall, brushing against Ted's parka that hung there. She steeled herself to walk into the kitchen when she heard what sounded like a moan coming from upstairs.

"What was that?"

Jen hesitated for only a second before sprinting toward the living room. She felt Dan grab at her and miss. But she knew this house like the back of her own hand. She grabbed the door frame for balance and slid around the corner on the polished floors, catapulted into the living room and skidded. There was Ryan, stretched out on the sofa with his feet up on the ottoman.

"What happened?" she demanded, her voice rising.

Dan caught up with Jen and seized her shirt in his fist, yanking her backward. "Settle down," he snapped, wrapping his elbow around her neck and cutting off her air. Only when she went limp and stopped fighting him did he ease up the pressure on her throat.

"What was that noise upstairs?" she gasped.

"Nothing. Things…well, things kind of happened while you were gone." Ryan lifted his hand and let it drop, an oh-well-what-can-you-do gesture.

"What do you mean? Is everyone all right?"

"Well…that." Ryan sighed. "Some shit went down, see? It was totally not my fault. Suddenly people want to mess with the plan, they get what they have coming."

Jen wrenched herself free of Dan's grasp, crashing against the coffee table and rebounding off the sofa. By the time she got her balance, Ryan had his gun out and resting casually on his lap. Jen held up her hands and stayed where she was.

"Where is my husband?"

Dan pushed between her and Ryan, forcing her to sit down on the sofa. He sat down with her, wedging her into the corner, trapping her there. The look on his face was clouded with uncertainty. Because he didn't know the answer to Jen's question. He didn't know what had happened while he and Jen had been gone. He'd lost control, he'd left Ryan in charge, and now even he looked like he was afraid of the answer.

"Ted's just having a little rest upstairs." Ryan sounded weary and irritated. "He got in the way of a bullet."

Chapter Fourteen

Once Teddy had pulled the heavy door open and run out into the freezing gray afternoon, he remembered that he didn't have a coat, and wondered why Livvy would send him outside without it. She had never spoken to him the way she did in the bathroom, and he was trying to make sense of what was happening. Livvy said that he had to run fast, and he did, not even going slow on the steps the way mom always insisted, because there could be ice.

Halfway across the yard he heard Livvy scream, and he almost turned around. But she had said not to. She said no matter what happened, he had to go to the Sterns' and to run as fast as he could and so that's what he did.

Teddy ran on the edges of the lawns along the street, where the snow had melted and frozen again, leaving the dead grass stiff and crunchy under his feet. He had learned the hard way that running on the sidewalk in the winter, even when the snow had mostly melted, often ended up with a hard fall on the concrete. He pumped his fists and kept his eyes on the stop sign, pushing himself to go faster and faster, just like he did when they had races at Blue Devils summer camp.

When he got to the stop sign, Teddy looked back to see if Livvy was coming after him, but the street was empty. Nobody at all was outside, no moms or kids or the mailman or delivery guys. The front door of their house was closed, and Teddy wondered if Livvy or his dad had closed it—or if it had been the stranger called Ryan. Teddy didn't like thinking of the strangers, whose presence in his house was yet another confusing and frightening thing. He was pretty sure his parents were afraid of the two men, something that struck him as astonishing—that they, especially his father, could be afraid of other grown-ups.

Teddy started running again, though not as fast, partly because he was breathing hard and partly because he was beginning to think that leaving had been a bad choice. Maybe Livvy made a mistake. His mom always took him to Mark Stern's house, but she was gone on her errand.

Once, when his mom wasn't feeling well, Mrs. Stern had come to pick him up, and she had even brought him a muffin. Teddy brightened at the memory. Maybe Mrs. Stern was on her way, and would see him and pull over in her red minivan and he could ride back with her and Mark. Mark had K'Nex, too, and they had built a tower last time that was very tall, and maybe this time they could make one that was even taller.

A car drove by, but it wasn't Mrs. Stern, and Teddy kept going.

The cold was making him shiver. The tips of his fingers were getting achy and his nose was crusty. Wiping his nose on his sleeve only made it sore. Teddy looked in the windows of the houses he passed, wondering if other people had visitors like theirs, strangers who stayed overnight and used their things and used mad voices. Teddy had liked sleeping in the basement, but he wasn't sure he wanted to sleep there again tonight. What he most wanted was for the strangers to leave, and to sleep in his own bed.

At the next corner, Teddy stood for a long time trying to remember which direction Mark's house was. Nothing looked the same with snow. You couldn't see anyone's grass or flowers, and there were cars that still had snow on top of them even though it had been a long time since the snowstorm. After a while, Teddy decided to go left, partly because the sidewalk looked less icy in that direction and he especially didn't want to fall down now because he had started to cry a little. If he fell, someone might think he was crying because of the fall, which wasn't the case at all. Teddy was brave about things like falls. His mom said he was brave all the time, in fact.

He was only crying because Livvy had spoken to him in that way that frightened him, and because he was cold and because he wasn't sure where the Sterns' house was. And, maybe a little, because he was afraid the stranger named Ryan would be the one who would come find him and take him back.

When they came yesterday, Teddy had been looking for a Lego piece that went under the couch, part of his Imperial V-Wing Starfighter. When Livvy went to answer the knock at the front door, Teddy had had spotted the little red piece just beyond his reach and was straining to get his fingers around it, so he didn't see the strangers until they had already come into the living room.

"Teddy," Livvy had said, "get up from there." He didn't like abandoning the Lego piece, and he was planning to ask Livvy to push the couch over for him, when he saw the strangers' legs on either side of Livvy's. He stood up and looked the visitors over. One was old like his dad, and the other one was younger, with a smile that wasn't friendly.

"Hey, kid," the older one said. He had his hand behind Livvy's back, and she didn't seem very happy about it. In fact, she looked scared, so Teddy was scared, too, and his voice disappeared all the way inside him.

Livvy started to pick him up, but the older one said *"no."* She put her hands on Teddy's shoulders, squeezing too hard. Teddy waited for her to explain who the men were, but she didn't.

"I'll get him," the old one said and then he picked Teddy up himself. His fingers felt hard and unfamiliar under Teddy's arms, digging into his ribs, and Teddy wiggled to get down. The man just held on tighter and squeezed Teddy against his chest. It didn't hurt until Teddy accidentally hit the man in the chin as he was trying to wriggle free. The man grabbed his arm and twisted it and said, "Cut that shit out."

Teddy knew that grown-ups weren't supposed to say "shit," that they had to remind each other sometimes, but no one told the stranger not to talk that way in front of him. So that was also strange and worrisome.

Teddy stopped struggling. The curse word was worse than the twisted arm. Teddy didn't know what the man would do next, but he felt certain that it wouldn't be good, and he began to cry a little. As the man carried him up the stairs, Teddy watched the walls go by, the pictures he rarely looked at because they were hung high above his eye level. Pictures of his parents, then his parents with Livvy when she was little, and finally his favorite, the large one of all four of them, dressed in white shirts and pressed close together, smiling. Teddy remembered that day, how they practiced pressing together and smiling over and over while the photographer took their picture, how he could smell his mother's perfume and his father's shirt, the dry cleaner smell.

The stranger carried him down the hall to his parents' room, with the other stranger and Livvy behind them. The older one knocked on the door, and his parents were surprised to see the men's guns. Teddy's father took him away from the older one, and Teddy was so relieved that he burrowed as close to his dad as he could and stopped paying attention to what they were saying. Everyone seemed angry. Teddy hoped his father would tell the strangers to leave, but they all went down in the basement instead.

It was nice once the strangers went upstairs and left them alone, and his dad put the furniture together like it was a living room instead of a basement. Teddy wasn't sure why they had the sleepover in the basement, but his father explained that it was like camping, that they were practicing for a trip to Moose Lake. In the morning Teddy felt better. His mother let him help with the laundry until she had to go on her errand, but his father didn't feel well, and had to rest up on the couch. Livvy played with him though, and usually she was too busy to play for very long, so that was fun. Everything had been fine until lunchtime, when his mom still hadn't come back so the stranger named Ryan had to make lunch. Teddy had to go to the bathroom, and that was when Livvy told him that he had to run out the door and keep going.

Teddy felt like he had been walking for a very long time, but he didn't see the Sterns' house, and he was starting to worry that he was lost. But then he took another turn and realized where he was: across the street was his second-favorite park. It would have been more fun if Mark had been there, too, because there was a wooden bridge that was fun to jump on if you had two people. Maybe Mrs. Stern would bring Mark to the park. Maybe they were on their way.

Teddy decided to wait in the little playhouse at the top of the climbing structure, where he had a clear view of the parking lot. Also, the wind couldn't get inside the house so it was warmer in there. He tucked his knees under his chin and blew on his fingers and the cold-ache went away a little. In the field, a woman with a ponytail threw a ball for her dog, and Teddy watched the dog run and jump into the air to catch the ball in its jaws. *Good boy,* Teddy said each time, though he said it on the inside, with words that only he could hear.

Chapter Fifteen

He wasn't dead.

When Jen wouldn't stop screaming, Ryan took her upstairs to her bedroom to prove it, Dan trailing behind them. Ted was stretched out on the bed, his feet tied to the footboard with white plastic rope that Jen didn't recognize. One hand was tied to the headboard, and the other lay awkwardly on the bedcovers, a bloody pulp at the elbow. Bits of bone showed through the torn flesh, and his hand was swollen, twitching and purple. Under his ruined arm, the bed was saturated with blood; more blood crusted his shirt. The stain on the bed was bright at the center, glistening wetly, and Jen imagined the blood seeping through the down blanket and sheets and mattress pad.

"Jen," Ted said when he saw her, wincing from the effort.

"Oh, my God, Ted—" Jen tried to yank herself free from Ryan's grip, but he held tight.

"That's far enough," Ryan said. "You can see him from here."

"Why did you have to shoot him?" She fought Ryan, twisting and trying to get some leverage with her elbows, but he was stronger than he appeared, and he managed to pull her against his chest with her arms behind her back. When he spoke, his breath was hot against her neck. He smelled of sweat and ham and Ted's cologne.

"Now *look,*" he snapped, yanking her arms painfully. "You *fight* me, shit's going to happen. That's what happened to your damn husband. Just calm down or things are going to get a lot worse."

"Okay." She let her arms go limp to show she wouldn't give him any more trouble. "Can I please just see how bad it is?"

"You can see from here. It's just his arm. He'll live."

"I'm all right, Jen," Ted said, but his voice was weak and thready.

"Where are the kids? Are they downstairs?"

"Look, don't freak." Ryan tightened his grip again. "It's Livvy's fault—she let that damn kid run away. That's how this whole thing happened."

"What do you *mean,* he ran away? Teddy? Do you mean Teddy?"

"She was trying to help," Ted wheezed. "Livvy helped him get out."

"Is he okay? Oh, my God, is Teddy *okay?*"

"Well, he was when he left here. Look, is he retarded or something?" Ryan said. "Because Livvy said he doesn't talk. That damn well better be true."

"He's not retarded…he just has a condition. He never talks to anyone outside the family. He won't say anything." Jen couldn't believe all of this was happening, that things had gotten so much worse while she and Dan had been gone. She couldn't keep the panic out of her voice. "Where did he go? Is Livvy okay?"

"Livvy's all right. She's in the basement," Ted said. He paused, his face contorted with pain, before continuing. "She...told Teddy to go to the Sterns'."

"Christ, Ryan!" Dan exploded. "I can't *believe* you." He turned on Jen. "Who the fuck are the Sterns?"

"They're a family from school. Teddy's best friend. He goes there every Friday for a playdate." Jen tried to calculate if the truth served her better than a lie. "You should be glad. They would have been suspicious if he *didn't* show up."

"Jesus!" Dan said. "I told you to leave them in the basement. How hard is that? I'm gone one hour—"

"You were gone more than an hour," Ryan said testily. "Everyone was hungry. What was I supposed to do, let them starve?"

"So you just let them come upstairs and have the run of the place? Did you even stop for one minute and think about the *plan?*"

"No, I didn't let them have the *run of the place,*" Ryan snapped, mocking Dan with a reedy falsetto. "Livvy had to take her brother to the bathroom and I was getting drinks. She threw a coffeepot at me. I'm supposed to know she's going to throw a *coffeepot* at me?"

"Listen to me," Dan said, grabbing Ryan's arm so hard he nearly fell down. For a moment Jen thought Ryan was going to fight back, his eyes sparking dangerously, but he just shook off the older man's hand. "Go wait for me downstairs. Don't do one goddamn thing. Just sit there."

For a moment they glared at each other, and then Ryan

stomped out of the room, muttering. Ted moaned and Jen started to go to him, but Dan grabbed her arm roughly and yanked her back.

Things were falling apart at a dangerous rate, the potential for things going irrevocably wrong expanding much too fast. Ted looked like he was going to pass out at any moment. Livvy had somehow given Teddy the chance to get away. If he ran to the Sterns', he'd be safe, but Cricket would wonder why he was by himself, since Jen had never let him walk over alone before. And certainly not without a coat. She was probably calling, even now. If Jen didn't answer, what would she do? Would she come over?

Jen forced herself to think it through. If it was her, she'd call Cricket and tell her to call her back as soon as she got the message. And then she'd get the boys settled, and she'd wait. How long? An hour? Two? The Friday playdate frequently turned into dinner and sometimes even a sleepover, if the boys were getting along well.

Jen felt a tiny, desperate ray of hope. Teddy would be safe at the Sterns', as long as she could keep Cricket from coming over. "Let me call her," she said. "Let me tell her to keep him for a sleepover."

"I'm supposed to trust you to talk to her?" Dan rubbed his temples as though he had a ferocious headache. "God*damn* it."

"I'll make it quick, I'll tell her something came up, that Livvy got invited to the city and I have to drive—she won't think anything of it."

"Right, and if he isn't there? If he *didn't* show up? You don't think your friend's going to find it a little strange that neither of you know where he is? I'm damn sure not going to have the whole neighborhood looking for him."

For a moment nobody spoke. Jen tried to weigh the possibilities. Either Teddy was at the Sterns', in which case he was safe. Or else he was outside somewhere, in the cold. But someone would see him. There were only so many places he could go, and there were people everywhere. Someone would find him and take care of him. Wouldn't they?

"Look." Dan took a deep breath and let it out, scowling. "Your kid doesn't talk, right? He's got some kind of disability?"

"He has selective mutism. He doesn't talk to strangers, ever."

"What about his friend? His friend's mom? He wouldn't talk to them, even if he was upset? Even if they were asking him why the hell he wasn't wearing a coat?"

"He only talks to us. Me, Ted, Livvy, that's all. I swear it."

"It's true," Ted said, gritting his teeth against the pain. "Doesn't—talk."

Dan raked his hand through his hair, loosing flakes of dandruff that settled on his shoulders, on Ted's shirt. "You'd better be telling me the goddamn truth. Because if that kid does talk, he's going to make trouble for all of us. And you aren't calling anyone. If your friend comes over here, you're going to answer the door and lie your ass off, and I'll be standing right next to the door where she can't see me. You screw up, I'll shoot her first, and then you. You think I won't do it, you just test me. Her I can kill. You I keep alive until I get my money."

Jen nodded. There were so many ways his plan could go wrong, but she didn't have anything better. She had to trust that Cricket would take care of Teddy. Maybe Mark answered the door; then Cricket would assume Jen waited in the car to make sure Teddy got in the house before driving off. Mark loved to answer the door, so it seemed entirely possible.

She just had to have faith that Teddy was safe at the Sterns'. That left Livvy and Ted, who was looking worse by the minute.

"We've got to get Ted help," Jen implored Dan. "He can't spend the night like that."

"He's not going anywhere until I get what I came here for. Besides, he has some explaining to do. He'd damn well better not pass out before he tells us what happened to the money. Ask him. Go on, ask him, Jen."

It took her a second to understand what he meant. The events of the morning seemed impossibly long ago. "He means the account, Ted. Dan took me to the bank to cash out the money market, but most of it was gone. There was a withdrawal, sixty thousand dollars."

For a moment Ted didn't react. Then his face crumpled. "Oh, God, what have I done?"

So it was true. Jen realized that she had been holding out hope that there was some explanation, some error on the part of the bank, that her husband hadn't actually secretly done something so monumental.

What have *you done?* She wanted to scream it, to launch herself at him. Because it didn't really matter how it came about, or why, only that Ted had been the one who'd risked their lives, their *children's* lives.

Except that Ted would never intentionally do anything to hurt any of them. And now he was lying in his own blood, his arm mangled, and it was clear that he was desperately remorseful. What good would it do to make it worse? They still had to get through this. It wasn't over; the bad news kept coming. If they were going to turn this around they would have to work together.

"Can you get it back?" Dan asked coldly.

A second shuddering sob racked his body. "No, no…it's gone. It's *gone.*"

Jen couldn't bear to watch her husband's agony. She pulled free of Dan, and he didn't try to stop her. "Shoot me if you want," she said. "What's one more bullet?"

She went to the bed and sat down on the edge of the soiled mattress, her body tensed in anticipation of a bullet, of Dan's fist smashing into her, but he didn't move. Jen touched Ted's head, stroking his hair, forcing herself to set aside her anger. "It's all right," she said. "We're taking it out of the investment account. We'll get their money that way. Don't worry, we'll get through this."

"I can't stand that I've done this to you." Ted tried to sit up, sinking back when pain seized him, making him whimper.

"Very touching," Dan snapped. "But the price just went up. You're going to show me your investments, Jen, and you're going to transfer every damn penny. You hear me? All of it."

"They won't let me touch the 401(k)s," she protested. "That would take days. You have to fill out all kinds of forms."

"That's not what I'm talking about. I know you got other accounts. Big fat ones full of rainy-day savings. How much more do you have? And don't bother lying, unless you want to see what happens when you push me too far."

Jen didn't have to calculate—she knew the sum practically down to the dollar from looking over the end of year statements. "Just over three hundred," she whispered. "Three eleven."

"Three hundred *thousand?*" Dan whistled. "Holy shit. Holy mother of God shit..." He shook his head slowly. "Well, that puts a new spin on things. Don't know about you—actually, I do know about you, but *my* day just got a little brighter."

"It's my fault," Ted gasped. A smell wafted from him, the smell she'd noticed downstairs. She'd read that blood smelled metallic, but the odor coming off her husband was something else, dirt and fear and chemicals and misery. "This is all my fault."

"It doesn't matter," she whispered, her mind already spinning, trying to work through the details of the account transfer.

"She's right, buddy. It doesn't matter, long as we get paid. But listen, just for kicks, I know *I'm* dying to know—what did you do with the cash?"

Ted closed his eyes, and his head lolled back against the pillows.

And Jen wondered if she really wanted to know. He looked so vulnerable, so damaged. She had no idea how badly injured his arm was. No matter what happened, he had paid heavily for whatever he had done. She stroked his face and tried to communicate forgiveness through her touch.

But Dan grabbed Ted's foot, still clad in one of the old running shoes he wore for working on the house, and shook it. "Hey. I asked you a question."

When Ted only moaned, Dan took hold of the hand of his wounded arm and gave it a shove. Not hard—but it was enough: Ted screamed and blood seeped from the wound. Jen grabbed Dan's arm, trying to tear him away from her husband. He shoved her hard enough to send her crashing into the corner of the dresser, the edge connecting painfully with her hip.

"Now," Dan said, all traces of amusement gone from his voice. "Tell us what you did with the money."

Ted's eyes were shiny with unshed tears, and he looked at Jen as he spoke, his voice breaking. "I've done something really bad. I wanted…I've been trying to make it right, and I've only made it worse. I…"

"It's all right," Jen said, easing back down next to him on the bed, trying not to cause him any more pain. She stroked the hair away from his eyes. "Whatever it is, it's all right."

But even as she spoke the words of forgiveness, Jen's dread grew. What if the truth was too big? Too much? What if she *couldn't* forgive him?

"I started gambling again." He stumbled over the words, as if he could read her thoughts and wanted to get the truth out before she changed her mind. "After I got laid off. Just the track, at first. Just a few times, with some guys from business school."

Jen tried to wrap her mind around what he was telling her. Gambling. Sure, he and his friends from the old days used to go to the track sometimes, but it didn't mean anything. It was supposed to be ironic, like the cigars and bourbon and the dinners at the Palm…wasn't it? And he hadn't mentioned his old friends in a long time. He barely saw them since they'd moved to the suburbs.

"We went out…. I told you about it, after I got laid off. Remember? And then a couple of the other guys got laid off, too, and we started betting on the games. It was supposed to be a joke. You know, little bets, fifty bucks, we said if any of us won we'd buy rounds for all the poor slobs who were out of a job. I didn't tell you about it because...well, because it seemed sort of pathetic." He swallowed and looked away.

Jen thought of all the nights Ted said he was going to the city for networking events, coming home late after he said he had a drink with some potential employer or fellow job searcher. She'd been naive enough to believe him, because she wanted so badly for him to be looking for work.

And all along, he'd already given up.

"Then what?"

Ted swallowed. "I lost a few thousand—from what Uncle Gar left us, not our savings. And I kept almost winning it back and then some. I'd get so close... Then I placed a big bet on a Lakers game. It should have been a sure thing. I mean, I put everything on it. I could have made up the gap and more. And then I was going to quit. It was going to be the last time, I swear it to you."

Dan snorted. "If I had a nickel..."

"When the Raptors won, I...I couldn't believe it," Ted continued. "I'd taken a loan to buy in, and I told the guy I just need a couple days to get the cash. But he wouldn't give it to me. He..." His face contorted in agony and Jen put her hand on his cheek, gently turning his head toward her.

"Look at me, sweetheart," she whispered. "Just look at me. Right here."

"He emailed me Sunday night," Ted said, making no effort to stop the tears that spilled down his cheeks. "He'd found me on Facebook. He had pictures of the *kids,* Jen. Livvy in her soccer uniform, and Teddy at the pool at the club. He didn't come out and say he was going to hurt them, but the threat was there. I was desperate. I got him the money on Monday. And, Jen…not that it matters now, not that you'll ever believe me—Christ, I don't deserve your forgiveness, but I won't ever, I wouldn't ever—"

Jen brushed away his tears with her fingertips. "It's done, it's over. It's all right."

"And that, folks, is how to really fuck up your life in three easy steps," Dan said, almost jovially. "Well, I guess that about does it. No further questions for the witness. Come on, Jen, let's get those accounts cleaned out."

"I forgive you," Jen said quietly, ignoring Dan and digging deep for every scrap of love she'd ever had for her husband, and there was more than enough. So much more than enough. How could she have doubted him? Ted had made a mistake—a terrible one. But he'd never stopped thinking of his family, and she should have always known that. "Do you hear me, Ted? You need to know this. I love you. I *love* you, and I'll never stop. Tell me you understand."

"I don't deserve your forgiveness," he said hoarsely.

"You have it. You have me. Just focus on staying strong. We *will* get out of this."

"Jesus, what is this?" Dan demanded. "The fucking Hallmark channel?"

As Dan grabbed Jen's arm and marched her out of the bedroom, she realized there was one question Ted hadn't answered.

She still didn't know where he'd been all day yesterday.

★★★

The funds transfers went without a hitch. When the call was over, Dan took her back to the basement.

She rushed down the stairs. Livvy had been huddled on the couch under a quilt, but she jumped up as soon as the door opened. "Where've you *been?*" she demanded, and then they were hugging, holding on hard. Jen held Livvy, swaying gently and murmuring that it would be all right, until she finally relaxed a little.

They sat back down on the couch, and Livvy haltingly gave her an account of what had happened. Jen could tell that she had been crying, her hair straggly and knotted, her eyes red.

"I just thought if he went to the Sterns', at least we would know he was safe. He'll know how to get to their house, won't he?"

"Of course he will, sweetheart," Jen said with as much confidence as she could. They'd walked to the Sterns' dozens of times when the weather was good, but Teddy had never gone alone, and Jen wasn't sure he paid attention to the route. "You were so smart to think of that. And brave, too."

"But it's my fault Dad got shot. If I hadn't tried anything, maybe Ryan wouldn't have done it."

"Oh, honey, no, it is *not* your fault at all. You are not one bit responsible for what those…lunatics do."

"Is Dad hurt really bad? Ryan wouldn't let me see. He dragged me back down here right after and I didn't see him. Is he going to be okay?"

Livvy hadn't seen how badly her father was hit, and so Jen minimized it. "The bullet went through clean. And I don't think it hit anything important." Which might be true…but probably wasn't. "He's alert and talking. You did good, honey. You did so good, I'm proud of you."

"But, Mom…I feel like I made everything worse. Dad's hurt and Teddy might get lost and it's so cold out there."

"It's going to be fine, sweetie," Jen said with a confidence she didn't feel. "Teddy will find his way and Mrs. Stern will take care of him."

"Do you think there's any way he'd be able to tell her? About what happened?"

Jen hesitated. Sure, it was possible. The therapist said that Teddy was making great strides in his exercises at school. But these things didn't have a timetable. And in a situation like this, under stress, it seemed to her that Teddy was *less* likely to verbalize, not more.

"I don't know about that, honey, but we just need to focus on getting through tonight, and then tomorrow it will all be over."

"Why, what's going to happen tomorrow? Where did you even go?"

Jen gave her an abbreviated version of the bank trip, saying only that she had to wire funds that would be ready tomorrow. "It went smoothly," she lied. "We just have to go back and pick up the money, and then Dan and Ryan can leave."

She could feel Livvy relax in her arms and prayed she was right. The money would land in the account by tomorrow afternoon. They'd return to the bank and get the cashier's check before it closed. Of course, one little hitch would mean that they were up against the weekend, and then there was a good possibility that the money wouldn't be ready until Monday at the earliest and—

Stop, Jen told herself. She forced herself to take several slow breaths, the way she'd learned in yoga, imagining breathing in vital oxygen to fill her lungs and exhaling her worries.

Teddy was fine. She could believe that. She *would* believe that. Cricket would take care of him. If she came to the house, Jen would lie brilliantly and talk her into keeping Teddy for the night. She'd say Livvy was sick—she could even use that excuse for not inviting Cricket in. Tomorrow, when Jen didn't show up to pick Teddy up, she'd be worried enough to do something. But that was good. Once Dan and Ryan left with their money, Cricket could bang on the door, call the cops, do whatever she wanted.

The breathing helped. After a while, Livvy's eyes fluttered shut and she dozed in Jen's arms, and it was almost peaceful. Ten minutes passed, maybe more, and Jen even began to get a little sleepy herself when the door at the top of the stairs opened again.

Dan came down carrying a pot in one hand and a couple of bowls and spoons in the other. He set them on the coffee table as Livvy sat up groggily, rubbing her eyes.

"You better eat," Dan said, lifting the lid off the pot. He'd made macaroni and cheese and stirred in what looked like cut-up pepperoni. Jen felt a faint wave of nausea and struggled not to show it.

When neither Jen nor Livvy made a move toward the food, Dan spooned half the macaroni into each bowl, shoving them back across the coffee table. Jen picked up her spoon and took a bite, trying not to gag on the cooling, powdery noodles.

"Okay, I've made some decisions," Dan said. "We're going to go look for Teddy, me and you, while it's still light out. If he didn't make it to his friend's house, I want that damn kid back here where we can keep an eye on him."

A bit of pasta lodged in Jen's throat and she started to cough. The coughing turned to gagging for breath, and Dan cursed and looked around the basement.

"Where's the water? Come on, Livvy, where's the damn water?"

But Livvy was already up, grabbing a bottle from the top of the washing machine where Ted had left them and twisting off the cap. "Mom, drink," she said, shoving the bottle at her mother, and Jen lifted it up and took a drink. The water forced the food painfully down her throat, and she gasped for breath.

"Here's what we're going to do," Dan said, when she recovered. "We'll go out the back, search from the woods until we get to the edge of the neighborhood. If we run into anyone you know, you tell them you're giving me directions. If we don't find him, we assume he made it to his friend's place."

"You don't have to do this," Livvy protested. "Even if Teddy runs into someone, he can't tell anyone his name or address, and he can't write."

Dan pressed his lips together. "Maybe we should send you," he said to Livvy. "You and Ryan, you can go look while I stay here with your folks."

"No," Jen said quickly. "If someone has to go, I'll go with Ryan. Or you go and take Livvy. *Please.* I don't want her alone with Ryan."

Their eyes met and held, and the comprehension in his expression frightened Jen. He knew what she was asking—and he didn't disagree. He was worried about Ryan, too. Which meant that he didn't believe he could control his partner.

"Yeah, okay, that could work. I'll take her. You'll know where to look, right, Livvy? It's, what—" he peered at his watch, a cheap Timex "—nearly three now. Plenty of daylight."

"Mom," Livvy said, squeezing Jen's hand hard. "I don't want to."

"It's all right," Jen said gently. "You'll be safe with Dan. Nothing's going to happen while you're with him."

She cut him a look, trying to let him know that if he hurt Livvy in any way she'd make it her life's purpose to make him pay. "Right, Dan?"

"Sure. Right. Look, the sooner we go, the sooner we'll be back. I'll get your coat. Where is it?"

Jen told him where to look, and after he'd gone upstairs and locked the door behind him, she turned to Livvy and took both hands in hers. "Listen. I know it's hard, but I need you to be brave. You can do that, right?"

Livvy swallowed. "I'm not scared for me. I mean, I am, a little. But only of Ryan. I don't care about Dan. I just don't want to leave you here."

"I know, honey. I know. But you'll be okay."

"How's Daddy? Tell me the truth, Mom, is he really okay?"

"He's just fine," Jen said. "It looked so much worse than it is. It's not bleeding anymore."

Livvy nodded. Jen could tell how much she wanted to believe.

"Listen, honey…I know this is difficult." Jen bit her lip hard to keep from tearing up. "I know it's scary. But we're going to get through it together, do you hear me? We're going to do what we need to do, one step after another, and it'll be over. I promise. It'll be like when you had to get your wisdom teeth out. You remember how scared you were? Everything—getting up that day, and driving to Dr. Pearl's office, and waiting—it was just one step at a time, right?"

"I guess," Livvy said doubtfully. "I mean, you're sure about the money, right? All you have to do is get it tomorrow, and then this will be over?"

"Yes. Just like I said, one step after another. In a month, this will seem like…" She was going to say it would seem like it had never happened at all, but that was too far from the truth. "It will seem like it happened in another lifetime."

Livvy chewed her lip, an old habit that only showed itself when she was anxious. "Is Dan bringing his gun?"

"Yes, I think so, but he's not going to use it, not out in the neighborhood. You're just going to help him look for Teddy."

Livvy nodded, looking miserable. "Mom…what if all of this is my fault?"

"We talked about that, sweetie. You can't control those men. They're *criminals.* When Daddy got hurt, that was their fault. They made the decision to shoot, not you."

"I know but—I mean, what if it's my fault they're even here? That they came here in the first place?"

Jen drew back and looked at her daughter carefully. "How could that possibly be true, honey? How could you have done anything to make them target us?"

"I don't know," Livvy whispered, not looking at her. "Just…somehow."

"You need to stop thinking like that. You didn't do anything wrong. You're just…we're all just in the wrong place at the wrong time. But we're going to get through it."

Livvy nodded, her chin down. “Do you want me to try to escape?”

It was tempting. God, it was so tempting. If only Livvy could break away, too, then nothing else would matter. Jen would stay behind with Ted, and they would be together, and if the worst happened—if Dan and Ryan killed them both—their children would still be free, would be safe, and Jen could accept that trade.

But what she’d said, about Dan not using his gun—she knew that was naive. He was a con. He was dangerous, and if he felt threatened, if he lost control of the plan, there was no telling what he might do.

“No, sweetie, just go along,” she said. “Help him look, or at least pretend to help him look. Do what Dan says, and soon you’ll be back.”

“But if I see Teddy I am *not* going to tell Dan,” Livvy whispered fiercely. “I *won’t* help him. I hope Teddy’s so far away by now.”

“I know. Me, too,” Jen said.

She thought about how, just days ago, she’d had it all. Healthy children and a loving husband and a beautiful home and good friends. How could she not have known how lucky she was?

Livvy was innocent. Ted had been punished. Teddy had escaped. Only Jen couldn’t yet tell what part she played in this terrible story. Had she brought disaster to her family by not valuing what she had? Was she being punished for taking it all for granted?

Chapter Sixteen

Livvy walked along the neighborhood streets with Dan, dragging her feet. Every time she got too far behind he would turn around and tell her to hurry up, and wait while she caught up. He didn't know about the shortcut from the end of the street to the cul-de-sac the next street over, and Livvy wasn't about to tell him, because sometimes Livvy took Teddy that way when they were going to the park, and maybe he remembered. The people whose backyard they cut through had a little brown dog that they tied up every afternoon, rain or shine or snow, so it could do its business, and Teddy loved to stand just beyond the limit of its chain, talking to the dog while it strained at its collar and wagged its tail.

She hoped maybe the people who lived in that house saw Teddy outside with their dog and got worried about him and went outside to talk to him. Maybe they had him wrapped up in a blanket with hot chocolate right now, while they tried to figure out where he lived. She wasn't going to take a chance that Teddy would look out their glass doors and see her and Dan walking by. If Teddy saw her, she knew he'd come running, and that was the opposite of what needed to happen.

"There's a path that runs along the back of these houses," she said instead. "If we follow it, we can see into all the backyards."

Dan grunted his assent and followed her back to the deer path. It was little more than a faint trail in the summer, but in the winter the deer trampled the snow away until there was just a thin layer of dirty ice on the frozen earth below. Livvy chose it because no one ever walked on it; there were too many exposed roots and rocks. She didn't think Teddy even knew it was there.

Livvy tried to figure out how to talk to Dan while they walked. Ever since Ryan first touched her, putting his hand over her mouth when they forced their way through the front door, she had been sure this was Allie's vengeance. Allie hated her so much that she wouldn't think twice about putting her cousins up to this. Especially after what had happened at the party and the way Sean had been talking to her at the locker.

The blue-black cross tattoos on the insides of Ryan's arms—that was a gang thing, she was pretty sure. The way he'd pulled back her hair, caressed her skin with the gun, it was like he was taunting her. Showing her what happened to girls who went after Allie's boyfriend.

She could totally imagine how Allie talked them into it, too: *Give her a scare,* she could have said, *and then take whatever you want.* Because there was lots to take.

Looking back on it, Livvy couldn't believe how stupid she'd been. One Sunday last winter when her parents had taken Teddy to Elk River to see her great-aunt, she'd stayed home to study for finals and instead Sean came over—and she'd showed him everything. She had been trying to impress him, trying to find any way to keep him, because already he had begun moving away from her. She showed him the paintings her parents got on their honeymoon and her dad's collection, the sound system her dad had put in the living room. And it had been wrong, all wrong. Sean had gotten so quiet, Livvy finally figured out it made him uncomfortable, all the things they had. When his family was poor.

And Allie…she couldn't stand thinking about him telling Allie about it, making her hate Livvy all that much more. Hating her for what she had, when all Livvy had ever wanted was Sean. But once Allie knew, all she had to do was tell her cousins. They'd know who to call. But it got out of control. They weren't happy with just the stuff in the house; they made her mom go to the bank. Her poor mom, she was totally unprepared for this—she was just a nice suburban lady who had no idea what went on in the real world. Hell, her mom thought everyone should just be polite and the world would fix itself; she was always writing thank-you notes and cleaning the table when they went out to eat to make it easier for the busboys.

"You should leave my mom alone," Livvy blurted as her boots crunched through the frozen leaves, walking ahead of Dan.

"I'm not trying to hurt anyone," he said. She could tell he was really pissed to be outside, that he was stuck trying to fix Ryan's mistake. "I'm just getting the goddamn job done. You want to blame anyone, blame yourself for letting your brother go."

"*Ryan* let us upstairs," she said. "It was Ryan's fault, not mine."

Dan just grunted, and they walked without speaking for a while.

"Listen." Livvy decided she had to know. It wasn't like it would make anything worse. She stopped, and Dan was forced to stop, too, because the path was only wide enough for one person. "I just want to know something. You can just say yes or no, you don't have to tell me the whole thing. But did a girl from my school put you up to this? I mean, her cousins? Their last name is Morris. I think."

Dan raised his eyebrow. He swiped the snow off his hair, then wiped his hand on his pants. "What the hell are you talking about? What kind of crazy question is that?"

"I'm not going to tell," Livvy assured him. "I just want to know. For personal reasons."

"Christ," Dan said, more to himself than her. "Turn around and get moving."

They walked for a while without saying anything, and Livvy was convinced he wasn't going to answer her.

When he finally did, it wasn't an answer at all. They were walking along the edge of the ravine, where the black water flowed over the icy rocks down below, and you could look across at the electrical lines and dumpy houses on the other side in Hastings. They came to the bend where the path turned back toward the edge of the neighborhood, when Livvy tripped over a root and almost fell. She grabbed for a branch and managed to scramble back up, but Dan did nothing to help, just stood there watching her.

"You think you got it bad," he said, gazing gloomily over her shoulder, at the backyards of all the houses on Dogwood Lane, with their play structures and barbecue grills and outdoor furniture covered with snow. "You think you got something to complain about.

"Christ," he muttered again, and spat, the gobbet landing just a few inches from Livvy's boot.

Chapter Seventeen

Dan and Livvy had only been gone a few minutes when Ryan came down into the basement. Jen jumped up off the couch, glad for the coffee table that separated them.

"Your husband won't shut up and he smells like shit. If I'm going to be stuck here another day I don't want him keeping me up all night. We're going to bring him back down here."

"We can't move him now," Jen protested. The more they disturbed his arm, the worse it would be for the wound, not to mention painful for Ted.

On the other hand, she didn't want Ted alone with Ryan. So far he'd shown no trace of human emotion or compassion. He seemed to care nothing for anyone else, including Dan. Wasn't that the mark of a psychopath? Since shooting Ted, he hadn't shown any remorse. What would stop him from hurting Ted again, just because he felt like it?

"We *are* moving him," Ryan said, shoving the table against her legs, bumping her knees painfully. "He'll be fine. Now get your ass moving and help me."

Jen knew that arguing would get her nowhere, so she started up the stairs, with Ryan following close behind. When she opened the door to the bedroom, the smell hit her first, the metallic sweetish scent of blood mixing with Ted's sweat and the mustiness of the room. Ted grunted and his eyes fluttered open, but Jen couldn't tell if he saw her.

Ryan went around the bed and started working at the knots that secured his good hand to the headboard. "You got scissors or something up here?"

Ted coughed. "Wire snips in the box on the bathroom floor," he rasped. "In my toolbox."

Relief took the edge off Jen's nerves: Ted's mind was still clear. As Ryan headed into the bathroom, she thought that now would be a great time to get the gun from the bedside table, if they were those kind of people. She scanned the room for something she could use, something heavy or sharp or otherwise potentially deadly. But the familiar landscape of their bedroom held nothing useful: the polished ebony jewelry box, the wicker clothes hamper, the cashmere throw draped on the chair on her side of the bed. The leather tray…

The little slip of goldenrod was still there, undisturbed since she first noticed it. *Thx tons, Thursday 2pm Firehouse xoxoxo.* Jen looked from the note to the hamper, remembering the missing clothes, the gym bag in the closet. The fact that he still hadn't explained where he'd gone Wednesday, or last weekend when she'd gone to Murdoch with Tanya.

Betting on some game wouldn't have kept him out all night. And besides, he swore he was finished with gambling. So what was he doing last Saturday? And he had still never said where he went Wednesday, when he'd said he was getting the car fixed. Two times in one week that he hadn't accounted for, even after coming clean about the money. A faint tendril of doubt worked its way into Jen's mind, clouding her sense of purpose.

But no. Ted lay in a pool of his own blood, and his only thoughts had been for her and the kids. Even now he was struggling to smile for her, his eyes full of pain. "Are you all right?" he asked. "Livvy? How's she doing?"

She shook her head very faintly because Ryan had come back into the room.

"Your daughter's helping Uncle Danny look for your kid," Ryan said as he started cutting through the ropes. "You better hope they find him."

"It's okay," Jen said quickly. "She's got her coat. They're just looking around the neighborhood. There's nothing—"

Ted moaned as Ryan tore off the ropes more roughly than necessary, jostling his arm.

"This shirt's disgusting," Ryan said, lifting a corner of the hem with distaste. "Get him something else."

He leaned against the wall with his arms crossed and watched as Jen unbuttoned the filthy shirt and eased it off Ted's body, wincing when he cried out. She used the snips to cut through the sleeve, and again to remove his T-shirt, taking as much care as she could near the wound. The arm was swollen and purpled, the area around it dark and painful looking, the skin radiating heat.

"Please, let me put a bandage on him."

"Whatever floats your boat, long as you do it in the next three minutes." Ryan yawned and looked at his watch.

Jen wondered if he was enjoying Ted's pain. She got the first aid box from the closet and dug frantically through the bandages, the rolls of medical tape, the squares of gauze. None of them would be adequate. Finally she grabbed a length of ACE bandage and a tube of antiseptic.

"You've got about a minute and forty-five more seconds," Ryan drawled. "Then he goes, no matter what shape he's in."

Jen grasped Ted's arm above the wound and steeled herself against his sounds of pain, centering the bandage against the worst of it and wrapping the arm as fast as she could.

"Time's up. Put a shirt on him."

She grabbed his old fleece-lined chamois from the hook on the closet door and eased his good arm into the sleeve, but he had begun to shiver violently and she didn't dare try the other arm. Ryan reached under Ted's shoulders and lifted him to a sitting position, and Jen draped the shirt around his shoulders.

Ryan hoisted Ted from the bed, straining under the weight. He staggered a couple of steps, cursing. Ted was trying to stand, but the sheets were tangled around his legs and he couldn't keep his balance.

"Help me out here!" Ryan barked, and Jen took Ted's other side, and they eased him into the bedside chair.

"Holy shit, you're one heavy motherfucker," Ryan said, breathing heavily. "You managed to get up here without help. Can't you walk now?"

"I can try," Ted said, and took another step, but then he started to list to the side. Jen struggled to keep him upright. He grabbed the edge of the dresser to support himself.

Ryan noticed blood on his own shirt. "Aw, man…" He tore off the shirt, wiping his hands on it before throwing it into the corner of the room. Underneath, his chest was white and hairless. "Did I get it on my pants? Jen, do I have any on my pants?" He turned around, looking over his shoulder.

"You're fine," Jen said.

"Okay, look," he said. "Wrap up all those filthy sheets and stick them in the bathroom. Get a clean blanket or something so Ted here doesn't stink up the chair. Ted, you'll be fine in the chair for a few minutes. I'm going to change my shirt. But I'm keeping an eye on you," he added.

Sure enough, he backed into the closet and watched her while he grabbed one of Ted's clean shirts off a hanger.

"So we're…not moving him?" Jen asked.

"Not unless you can lift him yourself. Here, use this," he added, tossing her a cashmere throw that she kept in the closet.

"I thought—I thought you said—"

"You thought I said *what?* Are you questioning me, Jen? Is that what you're doing? Because last time I looked I was still the guy with the gun—" He pulled the gun out of his pants and pointed it first at her and then at Ted, and then back to her. "And you're supposed to be cleaning up your husband's mess."

"Hey," Ted said, trying to turn toward Ryan. "Don't you—"

"It's okay," Jen said quickly, putting her hand on Ted's shoulder. "Honey, relax."

She was afraid Ryan was close to losing his temper, and she had no idea what he'd do if he was angry enough. The plan was falling apart, and he seemed to be losing his focus, as well. She laid the throw across the chair and helped Ted sit down. Once she tucked the blanket around Ted's body, she started on the bed, glancing at Ryan out of the corner of her eye. He pulled the shirt on, a royal-blue polo shirt with a pink whale embroidered on the chest. It was too big for him, and it made him look skinnier than he was.

Jen tugged the comforter and sheets and mattress pad off

the bed. Under the linens, a stain at least two feet wide and twice as long was drying to brown at the edges, bright red in the center. She grabbed two pillows and set them on top of the stain, and folded the rest of the linens so none of the blood showed and put them in the bathroom, closing the door.

Ryan seemed to have calmed down. He wandered to Ted's side of the bed and picked up the remote from his bedside table, turning on the TV and then muting it. A group of men sat around in an industrial shop of some sort. Most of the men had beards and tattoos. After watching for a few minutes, Ryan laughed and turned it off. "That fucking *Overhaulin'*." He chuckled. "Man, I love that show."

Jen sat down warily on the edge of the mattress closest to the chair. She reached for Ted's good hand and gave it a squeeze. His skin was hot and moist.

"So, Jen." Ryan abruptly tossed the remote onto the mattress and sat at the foot of the bed a few feet away. She tensed, feeling the mattress shift beneath his weight. "How long you guys been married?"

"Nineteen years." Jen kept her voice even.

"Yeah, see, I don't get that. All that time, same person? I mean, I'm making assumptions." He laughed, and Ted stiffened.

"Watch it," he muttered, his voice sounding thick, like his mouth was stuffed with cotton.

Ryan laughed again. "Hey, hey, chill. I didn't mean nothing. I mean, what a man does outside the home, you get a little on the side, a little taste, that's your business, right? I mean who can blame you?"

"I don't know what you're talking about," Ted said. "And I'd appreciate you not talking that way in front of my wife."

"Calm down, I'm just talking man-to-man here. You keep yourself fit, take pride in yourself? Drive a nice car, throw around some cash? That gets the ladies' attention, am I right?" He chuckled, scratching at his chest near his underarm. He kept glancing between Jen and Ted, and she got the sense that he was digging, trying to find a way to stir them up. "Not bad at *all.* I mean, a guy like me, I'm just a regular guy, but I do okay, right? I got no expense account, got no four-hundred-dollar shoes. All's I got's what the good Lord gave me."

He put his hand on his crotch and gave it a squeeze. The gesture was so crude and so unexpected that Jen shrank away from him.

"Hey." Ted tried to stand but immediately fell back again, his legs seeming to crumple under his weight. The stale smell wafted from him.

"Ted, don't. It's all right. Just sit."

"Nice," Ryan said, grinning. "Nice. I like it. I like how you're there for him, Mrs. G. Standing by your man. Letting him know that, no matter what he did, you're there for him. Man, you don't see that a lot these days, right? Am I right? *Women*—they'll screw you first chance they get. But not you, Jen. Come here, come sit a little closer." He patted the mattress between them.

"I'm fine," Jen said, eyeing the expanse of quilted cotton.

Ryan leaned toward her. "I just want to sit next to you, have a little up close and personal."

"You leave my wife alone," Ted snarled, but his voice was slurred, his syllables running together. He slumped into the corner of the chair, his wounded arm resting on his lap, the fingers upturned, useless looking. The arm had swelled further. The fingers were puffed and pale, and the flesh darkened near the wound, an angry purple fading to gray.

"Oh, I don't know about that. Seems she's been spending a little too much time alone. Seems to me someone's been neglecting his duties. Am I right, Mrs. G? Are you getting what you need at home? You can tell me. I care, I do. I want to know."

He was speaking just to her now, his words lilting and hushed. She could feel his breath on the side of her face. "I don't know what you're talking about," she said.

"Oh, I think you do," Ryan said, chuckling softly. "Come here and talk to me about it."

Ted suddenly lurched forward off the chair with a strangled cry, his good hand crabbing against Ryan's chest, reaching for his throat. Any advantage he had in size and weight was lost the minute Ryan shoved him backward. Ted slid to the floor next to the bed, his head bouncing off the seat of the chair as he went down.

Ryan stood and kicked him hard in the ribs.

Ted's garbled cry was horrible, cut off by a second kick that left him gasping for breath. Then Ryan lifted his foot and Jen saw it coming, watched the arc of his shoe in the air—an oversize skate sneaker like the boys at Livvy's school wore. Jen pushed herself off the mattress, trying to prevent what was about to happen, but she was too slow, and Ryan smashed his foot down on Ted's wounded elbow, and then there *was* screaming, unearthly desperate sounds as Ryan put all his weight on that foot and twisted.

Jen grabbed Ryan's arm and pulled him off Ted, and he was lighter than she would have guessed. He went crashing into the dresser and fell back on his ass. She knelt down in front of Ted. His gasps turned to vomiting, and when he started to choke she grabbed the collar of his shirt and forced him to turn his head so it went on the floor. He heaved several times before taking several ragged breaths, and his groans turned to whimpers. She didn't look at his arm, couldn't bear to look at it, but even in the periphery of her vision she saw the bright red stain spreading on his shirt, fresh blood, the arm surely now injured beyond repair.

"That's disgusting," Ryan said behind her, and then she felt it on the small of her back, the cold hard contact of a gun. "Get away from him. You'll get puke all over you."

"I can't leave him like this," Jen protested. She put her hands on Ted's face and tried to make him focus on her, but his eyes were rolling up inside his head. "He needs help.... He needs a doctor—"

"He might as well have done that to himself," Ryan said calmly. He used the gun to trace slow curves on the skin of her back, sending shivers of revulsion through her body. "He left me no choice, coming after me like that."

"He was only trying to protect me!" Jen twisted, slowly, carefully, trying to draw her body away from the gun.

"Not much of a man," Ryan said. "Like I said. And now he's going to have to watch—"

Suddenly there was a jarring blast of music, heavy metal rendered tinny and static. Ryan cursed and dug in his pocket, held his phone to his ear. "Yeah?"

His scowl deepened as he listened. Jen could hear a voice, but not what the caller was saying.

"Don't you think I'd call you if he showed up?" Ryan said shortly. He paused and turned toward Jen. She wanted to look away but couldn't. Ryan was blocking her view of Ted, but at least his gun was hanging loose in his free hand, and not pointed at either one of them. "She's fine, but, Dan, funny you should mention, about Ted, he seems worse. I don't know, just *worse.* Blood and shit, I don't know, man." He paused again. Dan's voice was louder now, and Jen thought she caught the words *risk* and *fuckup.*

"Yeah?" Abruptly, Ryan turned away from her, jamming the phone harder against his ear. "Well, I'm not the only one deviating from the plan, am I? I mean, if we did it my way, none of this would have happened. We'd be done and on our way. Uh-huh…well, I guess that's a matter of opinion, since ain't either one of us—hey—hey—God*damn* it, you want to stop fucking interrupting me?"

And then he was staring at his phone, his eyebrows knitted together incredulously. The call was over, but Jen couldn't tell who had ended it. For a moment she thought Ryan was going to throw the phone at the wall. Instead he slid it with great care back into his pocket. When he turned to Jen, he was smiling.

"No sign of Teddy," he said calmly. "Jen, you're going to have to go back downstairs now."

"What about Ted?"

He closed his hand around her upper arm, tugging her away from her husband.

"Ted's fine. He's going to be fine. Let's get you settled, and then I'm going to hang out up here with him, okay? Nothing bad, I promise. You believe me, right? 'Cause I wouldn't lie to you, Jen. I'm not going to hurt him."

Jen said nothing as Ryan pulled her along. She took one last look at Ted before they left the room. His eyes had rolled up and his mouth was open, and he was taking rapid, rasping breaths. Ryan led her down the hall, pulling her roughly. He pushed her ahead of him down the stairs, all the way to the basement door. He slipped the key in the lock, and Jen knew that this was the moment. If she was going to fight him it had to be now, because once she was on the other side of the door she would be powerless to do anything but wait for the next terrible thing to happen.

Ryan put his hand on the small of her back and gave her a gentle shove. It was his hand—not the gun. The gun was gone. He wasn't going to shoot her, not right this second, anyway, but just as she was gathering up the courage to do something, anything, he closed the door the rest of the way, leaving her standing on the landing in the dark.

No, she wanted to say. *Wait, come back.* There had been a moment when she could have changed something. But the moment was gone, and she hadn't been brave enough or quick enough or strong enough to save anyone at all.

Chapter Eighteen

In the afternoon, the moms and little kids came out in force, taking advantage of the first bright sunshine all week. Teddy abandoned the little playhouse when a trio of older boys crowded into it. He took one last look around the parking lot for Livvy, and then he walked back around the edge of the playground where the picnic tables were.

Near the far end, someone had left a coat on a table. Teddy could tell it had been forgotten because there were no other belongings nearby, no diaper bag or picnic basket or bucket of toys. A mom would probably come looking for it tomorrow when she realized it was missing, but after staring at it for a long time Teddy decided she wouldn't mind if he borrowed it for now. It was red, with a fuzzy lining. Teddy was suspicious that it might belong to a girl, and he didn't want to wear a girl's coat, but he put it on, anyway, and it warmed him up fast. The coat was much too large; the sleeves extended over his hands and the hood left only a little of his face exposed when he zipped it all the way up.

On a table nearby was a torn brown bag. Through the flapping paper Teddy could see juice boxes and Doritos. No one was looking in his direction; all the moms were busy with their kids or talking to each other. Teddy walked up to the table and waited a little longer to be sure, but no one saw him, so he took two juice boxes and the big bag of Doritos and turned around and walked away, up the hill overlooking the park. He found a hiding spot behind some bushes and ate some chips and drank some juice.

Soon he was feeling better, but then two women came walking up the hill, one of them carrying a baby, and Teddy was worried that the food he had taken might have belonged to them. Maybe they were trying to find the person who took it, and he would be in trouble. He squeezed himself farther in between the bushes, the branches scratching his hands and face.

The women didn't see him. They went to the flat part of the hill, where the snow had all melted away, and helped the baby practice walking between them. He stumbled every few steps, making a face like trying to decide if he wanted to cry. Every time he fell down, the women cheered and clapped, and eventually he smiled and got up and tried again.

Teddy started to get antsy waiting in the bushes. He found a plastic soda cup that had blown into the bush and started making a worm house out of it. First he put a layer of dirt in the bottom. Next he picked little tufts of grass to make a soft bed, and searched for tiny rocks and small sticks that would be fun for the worm to dig under.

When the baby got tired and began to fuss, one of the women picked him up and they started coming back down the hill. Teddy wasn't able to wiggle out of sight, and they saw him. After conferring briefly, they walked over to the bushes.

"Well, hi there," the younger one said. Teddy decided

she must be the baby's mom, and that the other one was his grandma. The mom gave the baby to the grandma, and he started to cry, his face crumpling up and turning red. The mom crouched down in front of Teddy and smiled at him.

Teddy made himself keep looking at her so she wouldn't worry. He knew that when he didn't look at people when they were talking to them, they thought he wasn't listening to them.

"What have you got there?"

For a moment Teddy worried that maybe the cup belonged to her and that he was in trouble because he had filled it with dirt and grass and sticks, and then he remembered that grown-ups never thought that trash was good to play with. He held it up so she could see it wasn't really trash anymore, now that he had the worm house started.

"Wow! Well, isn't that—you're making something special, aren't you?"

Teddy nodded, glad that she understood. He knew it would be easier for people to understand him when he started using words, but he still wasn't quite ready. Sometimes, when he was working with Mrs. Tierney, Teddy felt like he was almost ready, but then he'd get busy with other things and the moment would pass. He had tried to explain it to his mom, that the words were all there, waiting.

"So, is your mom here?"

Teddy looked down at the cup in his hands. Some of the bits of grass had fallen out, lifted by the wind and blown gently back into the dirt. He wasn't sure what to do now. If the women started looking for his mom, a lot of people were probably going to come over and ask him questions and then get upset when he didn't speak. It had happened before, when Livvy was supposed to be watching him at the mall.

If the two women would just leave him alone, his mom would come as soon as her errands were done. She always did. If he could tell the women his mom's name they would probably go and get her, but he couldn't do that, so it would be better if they just went away.

"Beth," the older woman said in an irritated voice. She was jiggling the baby from side to side, which was making him cry more. "I think he's hungry, I can't get him settled."

"Just a sec," the mom said. "This is important."

Teddy looked down into the park, where there were fewer moms and kids now. It was almost dinnertime, the sun slipping down in the sky and his stomach rumbling with hunger. But there was still a group of moms over by where the benches were, next to the sand lot, chatting while the kids played on the jungle gym.

Teddy pointed to the mothers gathered below, moving his finger, trying to decide which one to choose.

"Oh, your mom's down there?" the woman asked, sounding relieved. "Does she know you're up here?"

Teddy nodded, exaggerating the motion to make sure she understood.

"It's kind of cold up here, isn't it?"

Teddy shook his head. He wasn't really cold anymore. The coat came down almost to his knees and made a sort of blanket to sit on, and he was able to pull his hands into the furry sleeves whenever they started to feel too cold.

"Okay, well…have fun up here. Go back to your mom if you get too cold, okay?"

The woman stood up and took her baby back and settled him onto her chest. He let out a loud burp, which made Teddy smile. She took the baby's hand and waved it at Teddy, and Teddy waved back as they went down the hill.

When they got to the playground, the mom turned around and looked back up at him, and then over to the women on the benches. She and the grandma stood there for a minute talking and then they went into the parking lot and put the baby in his seat in a big silver car, got in and drove away.

Teddy went back to his cup. Soon he'd have the house all nice and ready, and then he'd just have to find a worm.

Chapter Nineteen

"Where's Daddy?"

Livvy had to repeat the question twice. Jen was so relieved to have her daughter back unharmed that she wasn't able to do anything but hold her, warming Livvy's cold hands in her own.

"He's resting upstairs, honey," she said, hoping Livvy wouldn't see the lie in her face. She hoped that Ryan had at least helped Ted back up onto the bed. Maybe he'd even given him something for the pain, a few Tylenols or some of the Vicodin she was pretty sure was left over from when Livvy had had her wisdom teeth out.

"So you didn't see any sign of Teddy?" she asked, helping Livvy unzip her jacket.

"No, nothing. We went through the woods and along the ravine. We looked in all the cul-de-sacs and over by the gas station. He wasn't anywhere, Mom. He's got to be at the Sterns'. Is Daddy doing okay? Did you get to see him?"

"I did, actually," Jen said lightly. "I went up there with Ryan to help. Ryan wanted to, um…he wanted to wrap up Daddy's arm better. Why don't you come sit with me."

Livvy seemed skeptical, but she didn't voice her doubts. Maybe she didn't want to know the truth—maybe she couldn't bear to know.

"Mom, listen, I was thinking, while we were looking for Teddy." Livvy sat on the couch and ran her hand under the edge, coming up with the toy receiver. "We *have* to try to call Jake on the walkie-talkie. It's going to be dinnertime soon, and you know Jake will have his on, especially since he missed us last night."

Jen glanced at the window. The light was failing fast. Her tongue felt sluggish in her mouth, the sense of possibility making her faintly dizzy. "I'm sorry, sweetie, I just don't know how we would manage it," she said.

"Mom, come on! Please!" Livvy drew a frustrated breath, pushing the button on and off.

Jen calculated: Could it actually work? Their house was well within the units' one-mile range, but they only worked when both boys were by the windows above the trees, without a lot of buildings or branches in between.

And being denied the nightly call last night would probably only make Jake more hungry to talk to Ted. He adored his uncle, and Ted hammed it up for him— "Hey, Jakey my man, calling Jake the Snake 1—2—3—4, one foot on the floor, one hangin' out the door." So the odds were very good that Jake would have his unit turned on. But unless they got out of the basement, it would never work.

"There's just no way for us to get up on the second floor."

"We have to find a way," Livvy said. "I'll just say I want to see Daddy."

"Honey. Listen." Jen took her hand, lacing their fingers

together. "This is a great idea, and I think we should try to figure it out, but I just don't want you to get your hopes up. And I don't want you to worry, because everything is already all set up. The funds were wired today. Tomorrow Dan and I will go to the bank and get the money and then they'll leave and this will all be over."

"Mom!" Livvy exclaimed, pulling her hand back. "Daddy is *hurt* and Teddy is *gone,* and it's all my fault. We can't just wait around doing nothing. We have to get help."

Her voice dissolved into tears, and Jen hugged her close. "Baby, no, it's not your fault. You've got to stop thinking that way. Sweetie, come on, you've been so brave…."

As Jen tried to comfort her daughter, she wondered if Livvy had stumbled onto an idea that might really work. God willing, Teddy was safe at the Sterns', but at some point Cricket was going to come to the house to find out what was going on. And the longer Ted went without medical attention the worse it would be. She didn't know much about medicine but it seemed likely that there could be infection, blood loss, shock, things she didn't even know the name of. Frankly, if Ted got through this with anything left of his arm she would be grateful.

"Honey. All right." She gave in to the lure of hope. "I'll try to get upstairs."

"Tell them you have to see Daddy," Livvy said, wiping her eyes on her sleeve. "Tell him we need him back down here with us tonight. Maybe they'll let you go up there to help bring him down here."

"I don't think that's a good idea, since he's stable where he is." Jen couldn't let Livvy see Ted's arm, couldn't let her see how weak he was. "I don't think he should be moved."

"It doesn't matter…you just have to say it," Livvy said impatiently. "Say anything, whatever it takes to get up there. But it has to be at seven, Mom. Jake always tries right at *seven.* If we're too early or too late, it won't work."

"How are we going to figure out what time it is? I don't even have a watch down here, a phone, anything—"

"Mom!" Livvy's voice was increasingly hysterical. "You have to! Just think—come on, you always figure things out. You *always* do."

Hearing Livvy's desperation, Jen knew she would fix this because she *had* to fix it. She couldn't let Livvy down.

She looked around the room. The basement had accumulated more clutter than she'd realized. She scavenged the shelves, searching for something, anything that would help them.

"What are you looking for?" Livvy said, following in her wake.

"I don't know—something to tell us what time it is. I thought maybe I could find that souvenir wristwatch we got you in Disneyland."

"Mom, I was in seventh grade! That was four years ago!"

Jen kept looking. Maybe she'd find that silver-plated clock they'd received as a wedding gift, the one that Ted had insisted they display for years just in case his aunt came to visit. There had to be *something* among all this detritus from their past, the hundreds of possessions they simply had no room for, enough to furnish entire homes, blocks, villages.

In a box Jen found the Easter decorations she had lovingly

packed away last April, the hand-painted eggs from the little import store downtown. In a dusty unlabeled Rubbermaid tote were dozens of juice boxes and Clif Bars, the product of Ted's fleeting enthusiasm for disaster preparedness. There were boxes of outgrown toddler clothes, little overalls and turtlenecks Jen hadn't quite been ready to give away.

Jen worked her way around the room, getting splinters in her hands from the rough plywood shelves, but finding nothing that would help them. She was reaching behind stacks of plastic shoe boxes filled with the kids' school papers when her hand brushed against something soft—the silken nap of synthetic plush—and she knew immediately what it was and she gasped because she'd forgotten she'd kept him.

Licorice.

Her fingers tightened involuntarily on his soft paw and the room seemed to tilt. Her vision flickered and faded, and she gripped the post holding up the shelves. She tried to speak, but nothing came out of her mouth as she slowly slipped to the floor.

Chapter Twenty

Jen could feel the cold concrete through the fabric of her pants, but she couldn't seem to stand up. Her strength had left her, all but the hand that held on to Licorice.

Hold on to him and forget everything that happened tonight.

Tanya had said that. Long ago, the night she gave Jen the stuffed bear. But why? What had happened? Jen tried to remember, but it was like someone lowered a screen over the memory every time she got too close. She remembered that it was August and their mom was getting sicker. She spent all her time at home on the couch, and she was missing a lot of work. Jen and Tanya didn't talk about it. It was like they had worked out a deal without ever discussing it, that neither would acknowledge what was happening to their mother—and maybe then it would stop being true.

Tanya was staying away from home more and more, hanging out with her friends at the Soul Patch or going for drives with boys. That night she had gone to the carnival with some boy, and Jen pretended she didn't care. But the night dragged out long and lonely. Jen lay in the upper bunk listening to

Jackson Browne on her Walkman and trying to focus on the problem set she was working through from the math book.

Jen didn't blame her sister for wanting out for a few hours. She wanted out, too, but the sort of escape Tanya favored—the boys and the loud-revving cars and the smell of cigarettes on her clothes, the sticky lip gloss and front-porch manicures and shorts made even shorter by rolling the hems—none of that was within Jen's grasp. So she waited for her sister to come home on nights like this, and as she drifted off to sleep in the upper bunk, she'd listen to Tanya's whispered accounts of skinny-dipping in the lake and making out at Suicide Point and someone's older cousin buying them beer. And it would be enough, even with the sweltering heat and the clacking fan, the sweat on her pillow, to get her to sleep—just knowing that Tanya was there below her, anchoring them both, making it all okay.

Around eleven she heard a car pull up and tossed the math book to the floor and yanked off her headphones. It was here that the memories became hazy and unreliable. Sometimes she remembered watching for her sister through the window. Other times she thought she might have gone out on the porch. Sometimes she thought she remembered the boy, a lanky senior named Dwayne, who had a farmer tan and a car he'd saved up for by working at his father's scrap yard. Other times, she couldn't remember anyone bringing her sister home that night.

This time, the memories took her further. Treading softly, she passed through the living room—her mother had managed to get herself to bed, the afghan was folded on the couch and her bedroom door was closed—and let herself out the front door. She didn't want to wait through some long make-out session. Whoever the boy was, the sight of Tanya's little sister on the porch ought to be enough to cut short his ardor. And Tanya wouldn't mind, not too much. That was the good thing about her—she didn't stay mad at Jen for long, not these days.

Standing on the porch, worn-paint boards cool under her bare feet, she inhaled the overripe smell of river and exhaust that drifted up their street on summer nights. The porch light hadn't worked in ages, but the moon glimmered in and out of a bank of chalky clouds. A car. How could she have forgotten that car? It wasn't one she recognized, a long sedan like someone's dad would drive. It was parked carelessly, front tires sunk into the edge of the yard, and the driver had left the motor running.

Jen tried to see who it was. She squinted and took a few steps forward. She could see the oval of his face, glowing pale under the moon, but all the features had been erased. The car shimmered and shifted, changing from the dark sedan to their mother's car and back, refusing to stay still long enough for Jen to understand.

She took a few more steps forward toward the car, trying to peer around the faceless figure to see if her sister was in the passenger seat. The face shook slightly. It was laughing at her—somehow Jen knew it was laughing, even though she couldn't see its eyes or mouth. Why couldn't she remember who had come that night?

A sound behind her caught her attention, and she turned. Her body felt light and graceful; it seemed to move without her moving a muscle. The house loomed in front of her, dark and foreboding and empty, the way it looked later, after their mother had died and they had moved away and no one lived there at all, broken glass on the porch and the windows boarded up and graffiti on the front door.

When she turned back around, everything had changed. In the yard lay a listless mound that resembled a heap of rags more than a person—except for the sounds that emanated from it.

The car was still there and the engine revved, but no one was at the wheel. The tires spun on the wet grass and then found purchase, kicking up cinders and dirt as it backed off the lawn. For a moment it idled there and then it was gone, taillights disappearing down the street and around the corner.

Silence. The heap of rags on the lawn twitched.

Jen walked across the yard, treading softly like she and Tanya used to do when they were in grade school, playing Indian scout and making no noise. She slowed as she approached the thing on the ground. A few feet away, she saw that it was a man, lying facedown, limbs splayed. But that was *Sid's* coat, wasn't it? His scruff of thick black hair was like a wet hound's, his squared-off fingers scrabbling at the grass. He was making sounds like a man carrying a sofa up a flight of stairs, grunting and trying to sit up.

But suddenly Tanya was there in front of her, materializing out of nowhere to stand between Jen and the man. Under her arm was a big stuffed animal, a prize from the arcade at the fair. Around its neck, a bow of shiny satin reflected moonlight.

"I never remembered this part before," Jen said. She wasn't sure if she was speaking out loud as her mind flickered between the present and her memory. "Sid being here."

"Go on back inside, now," Tanya said, smiling. "It's awfully late for you to still be up."

"But it's Sid," Jen said, pointing at the thing on the ground.

"Don't you worry about that." Tanya held out the stuffed animal, a big-bellied stuffed bear with a smile stitched on its snout. In the moonlight it appeared to be the color of blood. Jen took it and hugged it against her chest, ducking her chin into the soft place between its head and its floppy front legs. It smelled like the cotton in an aspirin bottle.

"You know, he had it coming," Tanya said, her voice echoey and far away, like she was speaking from another room. "You go on inside, and I'll come get you in a few minutes when I need you."

But Jen didn't go inside; she sat down on the porch steps to watch, the bear in her lap.

Tanya took her keys out of her pocket. She had a little mini flashlight on her key chain, and she shone it down onto Sid. His shirt was slick with blood, the plaid disappearing into the dark of it. Tanya used the toe of her shoe to hook him under the arm and roll his body over. Sid groaned and his hands went to his gut as fresh blood leaked out.

"Someone from the roadhouse did this," Tanya said. "He got into a fight."

"He got into a fight," Jen echoed. Her mouth was pressed against the bear's soft fur and her words came out muffled.

"They brought him here and dumped him, so now *we* have to deal with the mess." She shook her head, clucking, a show of exasperation exactly like their mother's—at least, how she used to be, before she got to feeling so bad all the time.

Jen remembered the featureless face, the way it shook when it laughed. Confusion made her words come out slow, like they were getting caught behind her tongue. "But I don't think—"

"He got into a *fight,*" Tanya said, not mad, but insistent. "Say it, Jennie."

"He got into a fight?"

"Yes, that's right. Good."

Tanya reached down and picked up the old canvas drop cloth from the shed, wadded up and sticking to itself where paint had dried. It hadn't been there before, but Tanya didn't seem surprised. She spread it out across the backseat of their mother's car, which was idling in the road where the other car had been. How it got there, Jen had no idea, but Tanya didn't seem surprised by that, either.

"I guess since you're out here, you can help." Together they dragged Sid over to the car. They each took an arm. Jen tried not to touch him anywhere there was blood, which was hard to do because he had it on his hands and his shirt cuffs. He tried to talk a couple of times, but Jen couldn't understand anything he said. Dragging him was like dragging a dead person, the way his ankles bumped along in the grass.

"Time to go," Tanya said, breathing hard, after they'd maneuvered him into the backseat.

Tanya wasn't supposed to drive, because she didn't have her license and, anyway, Dwayne had only barely started teaching her, but Jen got in the passenger seat, anyway. It seemed like the minute she closed the door and got her seat belt on, they were at the roadhouse outside town past the paper mill. They could hear music from inside, drifting through the muggy summer night. Tanya parked next to a jacked-up pickup that blocked the view from the door. Jen helped Tanya pull Sid out of the backseat and drag his body along the ground, muttering and shivering. They laid him by the Dumpster, his arms flung out like a snow angel.

"That's it," Tanya said, wiping her hands on her shorts. "Don't worry, Jennie, our part's done now."

"Our part's done," Jen agreed.

Someone was tugging on her and wouldn't stop. She squinted, trying to make out who was standing next to her now. The memory went wavy, the roadhouse and the pickup truck and Sid lying on the ground, and then it all disappeared like a snuffed-out flame.

Livvy. Livvy needed something and Jen had to help. She made a mighty effort to focus, blinking to dispel the dark. Livvy's outline became clearer, shimmering above her, her long hair inches from Jen's face. She tried to look back and see Tanya, but she wasn't there. The house was gone; the car was gone. It was all gone. Her eyes adjusted to the light and she saw the shelves behind Livvy, felt Licorice's paw in her hand.

"What do you mean, our part's done?" Livvy said. She looked so scared that Jen forced herself to sit up. She let go of the bear and rolled onto her knees, waiting for the dizziness to pass.

"I just meant we need to get our part done." She rubbed her temple, trying to clear out the last of the confusion from her fall, or fainting spell, or whatever it had been.

"I know. I've figured it out, Mom. But are you okay? What happened?"

"I—I guess I just got a little dizzy because I haven't eaten," Jen said. "But I'm fine now."

"What is *that?*" Livvy pointed to the stuffed bear, which was bedraggled with age, its ribbon flattened and faded.

"It was mine when I was about your age. Aunt Tanya gave him to me."

"Oh." Livvy picked it up and set it back on the shelf. Jen flinched when she touched it; she didn't want her daughter near the musty old thing. She should have thrown it out. Why hadn't she thrown it out?

"Listen, Mom, maybe you should eat something now. And drink some water, okay? This'll take me a few minutes. I'm going to hook up the TV so we can find out what time it is. Then right before seven we'll figure out a way to get upstairs. We only need a minute or two on the walkie-talkie, right? Just long enough to tell Jake to have Aunt Tanya call the police."

"But how can you hook up the TV?" Jen said, trying to cut through the cloudiness in her brain. "There's no cable down here."

Livvy gave an exaggerated sigh. "Have just a little bit of faith in me? Okay? Just a *tiny* bit of faith? I'm not an idiot."

"I never said you were an idiot," Jen protested, but Livvy was already stalking off to the corner of the basement.

Jen dragged herself over to the couch. Her body felt sluggish and weak, her mind slow. She drank some water and forced herself to eat a handful of crackers while Livvy got tools from Ted's workbench and climbed up on the stepladder. She worked in silence as Jen ate a pear, and suddenly the silence was broken by the voice of Leroy Edwards, evening anchor on Channel 2.

"There," Livvy said, a note of pride in her voice. She tapped the channel controls on the clicker and brought up the cable guide. "Six forty-three, Mom, we don't have much time."

"Mute it, honey—we don't want them to hear. I can't believe you figured…" Jen stopped herself and tried again. "It's really impressive, that you knew how to do that, sweetie."

Livvy rolled her eyes. "It's *nothing.* Jeez. Two seconds. Now we need to figure out how we're going to get them to let us go upstairs."

"Livvy, I just don't want you to get your hopes up. Even if one of us can get upstairs, and somehow we get a moment alone, which in itself would be a miracle, what are the odds that Jake's going to be listening?"

"Really freaking good, Mom," Livvy said impatiently. "Jake never misses a night."

"But still, I don't want you up there alone. I should be the one to go. I'll just tell them I need to see Dad."

"Okay, if you want, but, Mom, you have to be really convincing. You have to make them understand that you need a moment in private with him somehow. You have to make them *believe* it."

"I know, honey, I'll do my best. I won't let you down, Liv."

"You only get one chance, Mom." Livvy hugged herself, her voice wavering. "Dad's hurt bad, isn't he? You aren't telling me because you think I can't take it."

"No, no, that's not true," Jen protested, and instantly regretted it. Livvy's trust wasn't something she could afford to squander now. She and her daughter had come into this nightmare already fractured, their bond weakened by the stresses of adolescent rebellion and Jen's own failures as a mother. But that didn't mean that Jen couldn't do better, even now, even here. "Wait, Livvy…it's true. Dad's hurt pretty bad. The bullet, it went in near his elbow."

She traced a gentle path on her own arm with her fingertip, showing where the thing had lodged.

"Did it go through?"

"Maybe…I don't know. But, honey, it wasn't just the bullet, he had some other damage, too. That part of his arm was…" *Crushed,* that was the word, stomped and mangled. Jen tried to think of some gentler alternative. "There was a lot of trauma around the elbow. I don't think he's losing much blood anymore but that arm is going to need a lot of attention. He certainly can't use it right now, and I don't know how much use he's going to get out of it for a while."

That was close to the truth, wasn't it? Livvy nodded, and Jen could tell from her expression that she'd read meaning between her words. "Why didn't you tell me before?"

"Oh, sweetheart, I just didn't want you to worry more than you had to."

"I'm not incompetent. Or fragile. It's not like I'd fall apart. I'm not the one who falls apart around here."

"I don't think you're either of those things," Jen said carefully, trying to not to upset Livvy further. "I think you are wonderfully competent in so many ways. And if I treat you like a child sometimes, honey—"

"Whatever," Livvy said and sat on the sofa, her body turned slightly away, not looking at her. Jen sank into the love seat. The seconds ticked by slowly, and Jen watched the digital numerals at the bottom of the screen, wishing she knew what to say to Livvy, how to reassure her.

Because what if these few minutes were their last?

"Okay," Livvy said when the guide at the bottom of the screen flickered 6:53 p.m. "It's time. You need to get Dan to take you upstairs. Remember. You've got to make them *be-lieve*."

"Got it." Jen stood up and took a deep breath. She'd pre-tend with everything she had.

Chapter Twenty-One

"I just remembered," Jen said. Standing on the second step from the top, she had to look up to see Dan's face. It had taken him a few moments to answer the door when she started pounding on it, and he didn't look happy. He stood in the doorway with his arms folded, smelling of fried food and cigarettes. "Ted's supposed to play basketball tonight. If he doesn't call, his friend is going to come by to pick him up."

"Yeah?" Dan looked dubious. "Why should I believe you?"

"His friend sends his son up to the door to get Ted," Jen said, coming up with the story on the fly. "He's fourteen. There's no way I'm letting another child walk in on this."

Dan stared at her for a long time, and Jen could feel herself starting to perspire. But she didn't look away.

"Let's say I let Ted make a call," he finally said. "How do I know he's not going to start yelling his head off the minute his friend picks up?"

"He wouldn't," Jen said. "Not if I explain." *Not if you've got that damn gun pointed at me.*

Dan cursed and smacked his hand on the doorjamb. "Goddamn it. You tell your husband that he can't fuck this up."

He led Jen up the stairs. She didn't dare to turn around and look at Livvy. Instead she touched the outline of the walkie-talkie in her pocket to reassure herself that it was there. In the kitchen, Dan grabbed Ted's phone off the counter. Passing by the office door, Jen glimpsed Ryan inside, using Ted's computer with his feet up on the desk.

In their bedroom, the smell was stronger, the dirt-and-metal odor now tinged with something sick and even more foul. Dan flipped the switch, and the room was bathed in the soft glow of the silk-shaded lamps on the nightstand.

Ted was back in the bed, a motionless form under a mound of blankets. Jen couldn't see his face. It took a second to register that the blankets were from Teddy's bed; Dan must have taken them to replace the soiled ones in the bathroom after he got Ted moved back to the bed. He hadn't bothered with restraints this time; the ropes Ryan had cut off were still in the corner of the room where he'd tossed them.

She moved closer, and Ted shifted and she saw his waxy, gray face. She tried to compose herself as he opened his eyes. "Hey, you," he said thickly, trying to lick his cracked lips.

Jen bent and kissed his forehead gently. His skin was hot and moist. She lifted the sheets to take a look at his arm and almost wished she hadn't. It was easily twice as large as it had been before, at least below the injury. The flesh was a purpled gray, swollen and shiny, his fingers spread wide and fat. Jen touched her fingertips gently to his forearm and was shocked at the burning heat. Ted winced and she took her fingers away.

"How are you feeling?" she asked, not wanting him to see how shaken she was.

"I'm okay. How's Livvy?"

"She's doing fine, sweetheart. Don't worry about her." She laid a hand on his forehead. The fever had taken over his whole body now; his skin was damp with perspiration.

Dan grabbed her roughly by the arm and pulled her back to the foot of the bed. He tossed Ted's phone onto his chest, where it landed in the tangle of bedcovers.

"Honey, you need to call Phillip and tell him not to pick you up for basketball today," Jen said. Ted looked at her in confusion, and Jen hoped Dan would think he was just slow from the pain, not because she was lying.

"We can't risk Luke coming up to the door," she said carefully. "You have to call and tell him you're sick."

"Make the call," Dan said. "But don't even think about trying anything funny." He put a hand on Jen's neck and pulled her back, away from the bed, until her back was pressed against him, and she felt the hard cold barrel of the gun on her forehead.

"Oh, God, don't hurt her," Ted mumbled. It took him two tries to pick up the phone, and then he tapped at it clumsily with one hand, using his thumb to find the number. It took a long time before Jen heard it, faintly, ringing on the other end. Three, four, five rings… When Phillip's message played she felt weak with relief.

"Hey, Phil, Ted here." His words sounded hollow and rough. There was a pause while he bit down his pain and gathered the energy to continue. "Listen, I'm not feeling well… don't think I'll make the game. So. I'll give you a call next week. Take care." He ended the call and let the phone drop back on his chest, exhausted.

"Not bad," Dan said, lowering the gun. Jen could still feel

the barrel's imprint on her skin. "You sounded like shit. I'd say it was convincing."

Ted's eyelashes fluttered, but there was no other response. She had to act now, before Dan forced her back down the stairs.

"Dan…can I just go to the bathroom?" she asked. "Just real quick, before we go back down?"

"What for? You've got one in the basement."

"It's…" Jen tried to think of something, anything, that would convince him. "I wanted to get the Tylenol out of the hall bath."

"How come? You got a headache?" Dan's voice was mocking. "Thinking of yourself when your husband's lying here like this?"

"No, I just…it's for Livvy. Please."

"Okay, whatever, let's go," Dan said. He put a hand on her waist and shoved her toward the door to the hall. "Move it."

Jen reached for Ted, but she was already too far from the bed to touch him. *I love you,* she mouthed, but Ted's eyelids were half-closed, and she couldn't tell if he saw her.

"I'll just be a second," Jen said, when she stood in front of the bathroom, her hand on the knob.

"Uh-uh, no way. I'll come with you."

"But—"

"Get the Tylenol, then you can do whatever else you need to do downstairs."

Jen saw her chance disintegrating. "Please," she said, her voice thick with despair. "*Please* just let me go by myself."

But Dan pressed past her with an exaggerated sigh. He went through the medicine cabinet, found the Tylenol and tossed it to her. The little bottle bounced off her wrist and fell to the floor. When Jen bent to pick it up, the blood rushed to her head, and she had to grip the sink to keep from falling.

"Keep it together," Dan snapped. "We can't afford another one down."

She slipped the bottle into her pocket, where it clacked against the walkie-talkie, but Dan didn't appear to notice. That was it, then—the plan wasn't going to work. She'd lost the chance to make the call, their only chance to get help.

As Jen followed Dan back into the hall, she felt weak from the magnitude of her failure. She lingered for a second in the doorway, and reached into her pocket and pressed the button on the walkie-talkie—just once, long enough to hear a single syllable of her nephew's voice. It sounded like "two"—as in "testing, one, two, three" or perhaps "too" as in "are you there, too?"

Dan glanced over his shoulder at her, and she cleared her throat. "What did you say?"

"Nothing."

Ryan appeared at the top of the stairs. Jen hadn't heard him come up. His hair was sticking up on one side, as though he'd been napping.

"We need to move him back to the basement," he said to Dan, ignoring Jen. "I'm not sleeping up here with that smell tonight. And he never shuts up."

"He's fine where he is."

"Okay, well, I'm not fine where he is. Let *them* deal with him."

"Ryan..."

"Come on. I'm asking you for one little fucking thing. This whole time we've done everything your way."

For a moment the two men stared at each other. Jen recognized Dan's beleaguered frustration; she had felt that way herself so many times when dealing with Livvy. But Livvy wasn't a psychopath. Livvy didn't hurt people to amuse herself. She prayed Dan would refuse Ryan, that he'd let Ted stay here instead of subjecting him to a move.

"Okay, fine," Dan finally said. "Get over there on the other side." He yanked off the sheets and blankets and pulled Ted's legs toward the edge of the bed. Ted moaned in agony.

Dan gave a heave and Ted was sitting up, swaying while Dan struggled to get an arm around his shoulders. Ryan took the other side, grunting with the effort of helping to lift him up. Once Ted was vertical, he took a small, tentative step.

"Don't pass out on us," Dan demanded.

"I'm fine," Ted muttered through gritted teeth.

They made their way down the hall, shuffling like zombies, Ted in between the two men, his legs buckling every few steps. Jen followed behind. She thought about trying to lag behind and call Jake, maybe ducking into Livvy's room. But she couldn't say what she needed to Jake in the amount of time she would have before they came for her, and she couldn't risk them finding the walkie-talkie she was hiding. Besides, if she tried anything, they'd let Ted fall to the floor while they dealt with her, and she didn't think he could take any more trauma.

The stairs took forever. Dan went first, and together they eased Ted down each step, their progress punctuated by his moaning from the pain. When they reached the first floor, all three men were sweating. Dan and Ryan dragged Ted down the hall past the kitchen, Ted barely even able to move his feet, and then Ryan supported all of Ted's weight while Dan fumbled with the lock. *Now,* Jen thought, now would be the time to go for it. Dan's gun was still jammed in his pants, near the front where his gut was fleshiest. She could make out the top of the grip, pressing into his stomach. She could get to it, she was pretty sure, though she had no idea if she could figure out how to shoot fast enough, and she'd have to aim to kill because anything short of that was just bound to make things worse.

Dan turned the key and the basement door swung open. Once again, she was too late—stalling, deliberating too long. Useless.

Dan grunted as he got in place to help Ted down the stairs. His face was red with exertion.

"Daddy!" Livvy shouted from the bottom of the stairs.

"Back off," Dan barked, reaching for his gun. Jen barely saw him move before he had it out and aimed at Livvy, but in the process he let go of Ted, who started to sway, unable to grab for the handrail with his damaged hand. Ryan tried to hold on, but his hands slipped on Ted's sweat-soaked shirt. If he fell, there was nothing to stop him but the flimsy rail, nothing below but the concrete floor. Jen lunged for his belt, straining to hold on to him, but she wasn't strong enough.

Ted wobbled and then crumpled. He fell down hard on the top landing, dragging Jen down with him. Livvy was running up the stairs, but then Dan seized her arm and forced her back down, twisting her wrist up and behind her back. When they were at the bottom he yanked up hard and she mewled with pain. "Do *not* come up those stairs again, do you hear me?" he snapped.

"Yes," Livvy whispered, then repeated it, louder, when Dan pulled at her wrist again.

Jen felt something hard jab the small of her back, and she twisted around to see Ryan nudging her with one of his shoes. "Get up," he snarled, and she pulled herself up.

"Come on, honey," she murmured to Ted. She looped her arm under his armpit and, leaning on the rail for support and praying it wouldn't give way under their combined weight, guided him down one faltering step at a time.

"Can I help my mom?" Livvy sniffled, her voice thick with tears as she rubbed at her wrist. Jen wondered if it was sprained. "Please?"

Dan shrugged, taking the rest of the stairs slowly. Livvy rushed to Ted's other side and pressed her face to his soiled shirt, careful not to touch his injured arm. "Oh, Daddy, what happened?"

And then, quickly, so quietly only Jen could hear, she muttered "Did you do it? Did you call Jake?"

Jen shook her head. "I couldn't," she whispered.

"Give it to me." Livvy's hand went around her father's waist, hugging him tight while her fingers sought out Jen's hand. She made hiccuping crying sounds that were so real Jen wouldn't have been entirely sure her daughter was acting except for the fact that when she didn't react quickly enough Livvy pinched the soft flesh of her stomach and hissed *"Now."*

Jen slid her hand into her pocket, fingers closing on the little walkie-talkie. Coming down the stairs behind Dan, Ryan said, "Aw, ain't that sweet."

Livvy pushed her hand into Jen's pocket and took the walkie-talkie. Jen could have stopped her; she could have held on tighter. But what did it matter, now? Ted was downstairs. There was no excuse to go back up, and no time, either. Livvy twisted as though she was helping her father, pulling his arm up and over her shoulder as she jammed the walkie-talkie into her jeans pocket with her other hand. It made an unmistakable outline in her tight skinny jeans, but Livvy managed to tug her sweater down over the pocket before she limped to the sofa with Ted and helped him sit down. Ted collapsed into the corner of the couch, his eyes fluttering closed as he puffed out a breath.

"What happened?" Livvy wailed, turning on Jen. "I thought you said it wasn't bad!"

"Honey, it isn't— I wasn't—"

"Mom, there's *bone* sticking out. What did they do to him?"

"Honey, I don't..."

Livvy clutched her stomach. "*God,* I think I'm going to be sick."

Jen tried to put her arm around her, but Livvy shook her off. "*Don't.* You're just making it worse."

"Your dad's going to be okay," Dan said gruffly. For the first time, he looked a little embarrassed. "This was all an accident. Things happen. He's just in shock, the body protecting itself. When we leave tomorrow, we'll get someone over here."

"Right," Jen snapped. "You'll make that 911 call on the way out of town, I bet. Top of your priority list."

Dan wheeled on her. "I didn't ask you to talk. You're lucky if we don't just leave you high and dry here."

"Please...can't you just take me up to the bathroom?" Livvy

pleaded. "I don't want to throw up down here, we'll all have to smell it. *Please.*" She added a convincing whimper and put her hands over her face.

"Too damn bad," Dan said, but Ryan was already at Livvy's side.

"I'll take you up," he said. "Last thing we need in this house is more stink, that's for sure."

Livvy cast her mother an inscrutable glance over her shoulder, and Jen's heart constricted: Livvy had done it; she had found a way upstairs. But she was going with Ryan, and Dan wasn't doing a thing to stop them.

"Livvy, *please*—"

But Livvy didn't even glance at her. As she walked up the stairs, Jen noticed her daughter's thin shoulders sloping up to her delicate collarbones and elegant neck; her long, glossy hair curving down her spine; her perfectly rounded behind tight against her jeans. Jen's mouth went dry, knowing what men saw when they looked at her daughter. She cringed as Ryan's hand slipped down Livvy's arm to her wrist. He slipped a thumb down into her palm and stroked suggestively.

Ted moaned, oblivious in his haze of pain.

Dan muttered to himself, and Jen knew he'd completely lost control of the situation.

And as she followed Ryan up the stairs, her daughter never even turned around.

Chapter Twenty-Two

Control what you can control. It was something Mr. Marvin, her drama teacher, always said. Livvy took a deep breath, held it in her lungs for a second and then let it out slowly, counting off in her mind the way she'd learned to do during warm-up exercises in his class.

It was hard to focus as she climbed up the stairs, trying to stay ahead of Ryan. She could still feel the place on her palm where he'd put his thumb. The skin where he'd touched her felt warm and clammy, and she wished she could claw it out. She knew what Ryan was thinking, and she saw how her mother looked at her with horror like Livvy didn't know what Ryan wanted to do, like Livvy was some innocent fragile thing.

But Livvy wasn't fragile and she knew things and she was going to use them. She could smell the liquor on Ryan's breath; he was drunk the way the boys got at parties, early in the night when they were showing off, splashing and joking and crushing cups in their fists. Later they got quieter, cagier, meaner. But at first they were like this, loud, confident.

But with Ryan it was scary because there wasn't anyone

else around for him to bounce all that energy off. There was just Dan, and Livvy was pretty sure there was something bad going on between the two of them. Dan didn't trust Ryan, and Ryan didn't like Dan. Livvy couldn't understand how it worked, who was the boss. When she had asked Dan about Allie's cousins it was like he really didn't know what she was talking about, but maybe they only brought Dan in because he had more experience. Like he was the professional and for Ryan it was more personal. Except, now it seemed like there was something personal between *them.*

As for her dad, she didn't even want to think about what had happened to him, couldn't stand to remember the way his arm looked. There was no way that shooting him was part of the original plan. She really believed they had meant to pull this off without anyone getting hurt. But now everything had changed. In the movies, the minute the plan started to fall apart, all the loyalties shifted and the bad guys turned on each other. Which made things more dangerous for everyone.

And Teddy—it had been hours since he'd run out the door, and no one had knocked on the door, no one had tried to bring him home. Teddy was super smart and everything, but no kid should be wandering around, getting lost, wondering why no one was coming to get him. The thing about her brother was that he wasn't like other little kids. She knew he wouldn't look for a grown-up. She could see him totally staying out all night and never even thinking of finding someone to ask, just wondering why his mom didn't come for him, and getting colder and colder.

Which was why this *had* to work.

At the top of the stairs Livvy dashed for the bathroom and

jammed the door shut, twisting the lock and leaning on it, her heart racing. Outside, Ryan's voice was way too close.

"Hey, don't you lock that door!" he called as he pounded the door.

Livvy turned on the bathroom fan and ran the water. "Just give me a minute, please!" she said, making her voice sound weak and helpless. She flipped up the lid on the toilet and made retching sounds while her thumb found the button on the walkie-talkie. She moaned and coughed, keeping up a steady stream of sound.

She pressed the button and put the thing to her ear and listened. When she heard the click of Jake answering—thank God, she wasn't too late—she flushed the toilet and talked fast and quiet.

"Jake, listen, it's me, Livvy," she hissed. "We're in trouble over here. You need to have your mom call the cops and tell them to come to our house. Do you understand?"

"What?" Jake's voice was tinny and distant. These cheap things were crap, just toys. "Livvy? Is that you? Where's Teddy?"

"Teddy's not here," Livvy said, pushing down her fear and speaking as slowly and clearly as she could. She flushed again, knowing this was her last try. Ryan would get suspicious if she didn't finish soon. "Tell your mom to call the police and have them come to our house. Say it back to me, Jake."

"You want my mom to call the police? Why?"

Livvy's hands clutched the little plastic unit so tight she thought it might break. "Bad men are in our house, Jake. We need help."

There was a silence, too long. Finally Jake clicked on again. "What?"

"They have *guns*. I have to go. Promise me you'll tell your mom."

"I promise, Livvy." He sounded scared now, and Livvy felt bad about that, but she needed him scared so he'd tell Aunt Tanya.

"Go," she said urgently. "Do it *now*. Love you, Jakey."

She stood and slipped the walkie-talkie back into her pocket. She washed her hands at the sink, scrubbing hard, and then brushed her teeth. Ryan started knocking, and she said, "Just a minute" while her mouth was full of toothpaste. That should help, that should make it authentic.

She wiped off her mouth and looked at herself in the mirror. She looked like someone else, as dirty and unkempt as a homeless person, fear and exhaustion giving her deep circles under her eyes. But that was all right. She'd rather be someone other than herself right now. She took a deep breath and opened the door.

Ryan was leaning against the wall, arms crossed, grinning at her.

"Done yakking?"

She cleared her throat. "Yes. Thank you."

"You brush your teeth?"

Livvy nodded, but she didn't like the way he was looking at her. She touched her pocket and was reassured by the feeling of the hard surface of the walkie-talkie under the fabric. Now what? If Jake told Aunt Tanya, if she called 911, it shouldn't be very long until someone arrived.

"Excuse me," she said, looking down at the floor as she tried to step past him, back toward the stairs.

He put out a hand, blocking the way. "Not so fast."

"I'm good now. I can go back in the basement with my mom and dad," Livvy said, then blushed because it made her sound like a little kid. Little and scared.

"What if I don't want you to go back down there yet?" Ryan said, taking a step closer to her. She could smell his breath, and it smelled like he had been eating Fritos with his beer. Now she really did feel nauseous, her stomach diving and rolling.

She forced a smile. "I just thought, because my mom and Dan have to go to the bank tomorrow? To get your money? I mean, I should probably get down there so everyone can get some rest."

She'd hoped the mention of the money would distract him, but Ryan just raised an eyebrow and kept smiling.

"I don't think rest is what you need, little girl."

And then he reached for her face, and Livvy made herself keep still. Somehow she knew it would be worse if she flinched, if she tried to duck out of the way, so she didn't move. His hand landed softly on her skin, his fingers cupping her chin, and they weren't rough and hard like she expected but warm and soft, like a girl's. His thumb went to her lips and rested there for a moment, and Livvy could feel the warmth of her breath reflecting off his hand back at her.

Then he started rubbing, gently stroking her mouth. Livvy didn't dare say anything because talking would make her open her lips. Instead, she pressed them together tightly. But he rubbed harder, turning his thumb on edge so his nail grazed against her skin, not quite hard enough to hurt. He moved closer, his face only a few inches away from hers.

"Suck it," he whispered, his voice all weird and harsh.

She shook her head, tears forming in her eyes, her heartbeat getting faster. She put her hand on his wrist and tried to push his hand away but he grabbed her behind the head with his other hand, his fingers splayed on her scalp, digging into her hair. They were locked in a silent struggle, and his thumb never stopped working, working, finally forcing its way past her lips, into her mouth, rubbing against her front teeth.

She clenched her teeth as tight as she could, but he squeezed hard. She whimpered deep in her throat, and he said, "Yeah, like that, suck it like that."

His thumb went in. He shoved hard, and it pushed against the back of her mouth, rubbing against her tongue, hot and salty and making her gag, and he was muttering things, awful things, his face bumping against hers, his tongue jamming inside her ear. She tried to pull away but he pushed harder, his mouth making wet noises in her ear and his thumb probing around in her mouth. Livvy couldn't breathe, she couldn't seem to get any breath in through her nose, and she tried to scream but it was impossible, with his thumb in her mouth. The tears had spilled over and the heel of his hand mashed against her cheek, spreading the tears and saliva around, and Livvy bit down.

At first it was just her molars clamping on his thumb but then she got a better grip with her front teeth and squeezed as hard as she could, imagining them slicing right through his skin, his callused knuckle, the bone and sinew and cartilage. She felt his blood fill her mouth, hot and metallic, and then he slammed her head into the wall so hard she let go, dizzying pain arcing out from her skull through her entire face.

"Fuck, girl, what the *fuck!*" he yelled, rearing back to take a swing at her, closed-fist, and she braced for it, had time to wonder how many bones in her face he would break, but it didn't happen, and after a couple of seconds she opened her eyes to see him still standing there squeezing his fist with his other hand.

"You're going to wish you didn't do that," he said softly, almost whispering.

The dizziness settled into a throbbing ache. Livvy spit blood on the floor and touched the spot with her fingers, feeling the lump rising on her scalp. Ryan held up his thumb, turning it this way and that. A smear of blood glistened wetly. That was *her* spit mixing with his blood, Livvy thought with disgust. She'd swallowed some of it. Her stomach rolled again, and she pressed her hands flat against it.

"What's going on up there?" Dan demanded, from the bottom of the steps.

"Nothing," Ryan snapped.

"You can't keep me up here," Livvy said.

"Oh, yeah?" Ryan wiped his thumb on his shirt, twisting his mouth back into the smile he'd had earlier.

"Didn't sound like nothing." Dan started up the stairs, his tread heavy like an old man's. He came around the landing, a concerned look on his face. Livvy felt such relief at the sight of him that she had to remind herself that he was also the enemy.

"What are you doing with her?"

"Nothing. She threw up, she washed up, that's it. She

yakked on her shirt so I'm taking her to change. Seriously, it's covered."

Dan was already shaking his head. "The girl goes back downstairs."

"No, she fucking doesn't."

Livvy could feel the tension between them, dangerous and out of control. Ryan's smile grew wider, and he grabbed her arm and yanked her close to him, and suddenly it occurred to her that maybe Dan *wasn't* the boss after all.

"I want to go," she said, swallowing hard. "I don't want to be up here."

"Yeah, you do," Ryan said, quietly, never taking his eyes off Dan.

"That's enough." Dan took two long steps and shoved Ryan, just hard enough to send him tripping backward. It was reassuring, how much bigger Dan was than Ryan, and Livvy wrenched her arm free and scrambled behind Dan, putting him between them.

"You might want to keep an eye on her," Ryan said lazily, but Dan had already grabbed her arm without even turning around. Livvy didn't mind, until he started squeezing, which hurt. He wasn't as gentle as she thought he would be. "Don't want to lose another one."

"I didn't lose the first one," Dan muttered. "That was you, boy."

"Oh, yeah, I forgot. I fucked up again, right? That's me, the family fuckup."

"No one said—"

"Only this time things are different. This time maybe I'm

not as dumb as you think. I got something you want to pay attention to."

"What are you talking about?" Dan seemed impatient.

"Can I go downstairs?" Livvy pleaded. "I won't try anything. You can just lock me back up."

"That's a great idea," Dan grunted, but he didn't move. "What the hell are you talking about, boy?"

Ryan held up his hands slowly, fingers spread wide. At first Livvy thought he was showing Dan the place where she'd bitten him, and then she figured it out:

No gloves.

"Where the hell are your gloves?" Dan demanded, reaching the same realization.

"Right here," Ryan said calmly. He jammed his hand into his back pocket and came up with a pair, pulling them on with a snap of latex.

"Why'd you take them off? Are you out of your mind?"

"Relax. I only had them off for a minute. Before you so rudely interrupted us. Some things a man has to do skin to skin."

The words made Livvy's stomach heave, and Dan's face only darkened with anger.

"We talked about this, Ryan. No taking chances. No taking *stupid* chances."

Ryan shook his head like he felt sorry for Dan. "Now there's that word again. *Stupid.* I feel like I've been called that a few times too often. But I got to say, I see it a little different. Maybe I'm not the one who's stupid, right?"

"What the *hell* are you talking about?"

"What if I told you..." Ryan let his gaze stray over to Livvy, giving her a wink like they were in this together, like they were sharing some private joke. "What if I told you I brought along some insurance? Some personal insurance, just to make sure everyone gets treated fair?"

A subtle change came over Dan, and suddenly he looked afraid. He didn't say anything, but his grip on Livvy's arm loosened. She wondered if she should try to pull her arm away and run, but Dan had surprised her before by how fast he could move, for an old guy.

"What sort of insurance?" he said slowly.

"Well. Tell you what. I'll give you one, for free. A show of faith. Come on down here."

Ryan sauntered down the hallway to Livvy's room and pushed the door open. Dan dragged her along, his grip like iron on her wrist.

She stood in the doorway to her room, but it didn't seem like hers now. The bed was unmade, just like she'd left it, covers puddled on the floor. The T-shirt she slept in—Calumet Hornets Lacrosse ALL THE WAY 2013, with the hornet outline in purple—lay inside out on the pillow. The dried flowers were still on her bulletin board from the last father-daughter dance before she quit Cadets in middle school. There was the box from Nordstrom, the suede boots her mom had bought her, even though she'd been such a brat lately. It seemed like that was months ago.

"Come on in," Ryan said, making an exaggerated bow. Livvy walked in ahead of Dan. Ryan shoved the door closed behind him, pressing his back against it to make the latch click. "Okay, you're getting warmer. Let her go, Dan, no need for that."

Dan stood in the middle of the room under the paper lantern light fixture hanging from the ceiling. Her mom had ordered it from PBteen as a surprise when Livvy showed it to her and said she liked it.

"Colder," Ryan said.

"This isn't some fucking game." Dan glared at Ryan, and if Livvy had been Ryan she would have been scared. But Ryan just laughed.

"So serious all the time. Okay, fine. See that basket up on the shelf? There, by the pig…look in there."

"I'm not gonna play, I'm telling you," Dan said, but they all looked at the basket. It was white with a checkered pink-and-white fabric liner. It was from before they redid her room, but Livvy kept it for barrettes and headbands. Next to it was a ceramic piggy bank she'd painted years ago with her Girl Scout troop at Art From the Heart. An ugly thing with splotched green-and-red glaze that ran together to make brown.

"For God's sake." Ryan rolled his eyes and went to the shelves and pulled down the basket. "Do I have to do everything myself?"

He hooked a finger inside and pulled out a white rag, dangling it in front of him for them to see.

Not a rag, though…Livvy saw the dark band of elastic and knew what it was: underwear. Men's underwear, the old-fashioned kind. They were wrinkled and dirty, with a racing-stripe stain that looked like it had been there through many washings, faded and gray.

Dan shot out a hand and snatched at the underwear. "What the hell?"

"They're yours."

"Yeah, I get it. What the fuck are they doing *here?*"

Ryan shrugged. "You ought to be more careful with your things. I found them under your bed last week. Didn't look like you'd been under there in a while. Dust bunnies and shit all over the place."

Dan glared at Ryan, and when he spoke again his voice was very quiet. "Why?"

"I think you know why."

No one said anything for a minute. Livvy was confused and scared, the sick feeling rising again in her stomach. She couldn't help looking under her own bed, wondering what she might find there, but all she saw was the corner of her sleeping bag sticking out, and a single pink flip-flop.

"It's not just those, man," Ryan finally said, now sounding bored. "There's shit all over this house. And every bit of it's got your fingerprints, your DNA, your everything. You'll never find it all, I promise you."

"You..." Dan lurched forward like he was going to grab hold of Ryan, but he stopped himself.

"Don't worry, I kept a list, and I know where every last thing is. You won't find 'em but I guarantee you, the cops will."

The pieces came together loosely in Livvy's mind. The cops, Dan's underwear, with his DNA...Ryan was setting him up. The gloves they wore wouldn't matter if they found other things, clues that led to Dan's identity. Ryan had double-crossed him. Which meant he and Dan were now enemies, didn't it? But why? They didn't even have the money yet.

She moved closer to Dan, and walked through a cold current of air. Only then did she notice that someone had opened her window several inches. Outside, a few flecks of ice floated down from the sky.

"Here's how it works," Ryan continued. "This whole time you been talking about trust and shit, you think I didn't know you were setting me up?"

"I wouldn't set you up," Dan said. His face was pale from disbelief.

"Yeah." Ryan chuckled. "Just like you'd never set up my *dad,* right? Blood's thicker than water, ain't that right? Dad told me once you were the only person in the world he could count on. He was your *brother,* man."

"Your dad and me… He never blamed me. I loved him. We had an arrangement."

"An *arrangement?*" Ryan said it mockingly. "He went to jail. That don't sound like much of a deal for him. Now he's dead I guess it doesn't matter. Anyway, tomorrow, you get back from the bank, you give me my money, I go on my little treasure hunt and I take all that shit back. Place'll be clean as a whistle by the time we leave. Oh, and I'll take the BMW. You go your way, and I'll take my own chances."

"You're…you're not coming with me?"

Ryan laughed again. "No, I'm not coming with you. You think I want to dick around on some beach with a bunch of old wetbacks for the rest of my life?"

"Ryan…"

"Look, man, it's time for you to go. Me and Livvy, we need a little privacy."

"You can't—"

"I can do whatever I want. *Think.* I got you here. I'm in charge now. I got your dick in a vise. Get it?"

Dan's face went ashen and Livvy prayed hard that he wasn't going to leave her here, but after a minute he turned without a word and let himself out the door. He closed it carefully, and she heard the soft click of the latch, and then his steps as he walked away.

And it was just her and Ryan.

"Get the light," he said softly. "It's too bright in here."

Chapter Twenty-Three

Jen held the bottle up to Ted's mouth, letting the water dribble in. "I got it," he said, taking the bottle from her. He drank deeply, his eyes closed, and then sighed, exhaling slowly. The water had helped; he'd managed most of the bottle already. The fever seemed to recede a little and he had been able to sit up on his own.

"Are you all right?" Jen asked softly, her hand on his leg, not sure how to touch him without hurting him. How long had it been since she'd touched him at all? Of course, he wasn't all right. Their son was missing, their daughter was upstairs with two criminals, and Ted had lost what seemed like gallons of blood. The fear and suspicion she'd felt earlier had ebbed as they struggled down the stairs, leaving in its wake an unexpected tenderness. He needed her, and that need brought echoes of other times, earlier times in their marriage when they'd relied on each other, when they'd been each other's everything. But God, what was she supposed to say to him now? What was she supposed to do?

Jen heard someone upstairs, moving around. She tried to track the location and guess what they were doing. Probably taking all their valuables, now that the plan was falling apart. If they were smart, they'd take her jewelry. It was worth almost as much as the money market, between the diamond studs and the tennis bracelet and the anniversary rings. The silver, the electronics, the art—with two car trunks they'd be able to take all of it.

Abruptly Ted grunted and sat up straighter, pushing off the back of the couch with his good elbow. He set the empty water bottle on the coffee table, his hand steady. "I'm feeling a little better. I was thinking, can you get one of those extra sheets? Let's see if we can make some sort of sling, or something. I feel like if we could just get my arm stable against my side here, I could move better."

"You can't move," Jen protested. "We can't risk making anything worse. We need to wait for a doctor to—"

"How can things get any worse?" Ted said, and it was the calm in his voice, the lack of panic, that got her moving. Yes. They should *do* something, anything. Taking care of Ted was better than just sitting here and watching him suffer. If they kept trying, then they weren't giving up, even as it seemed like there was nothing they could do to reverse the course of events.

She went to the big cardboard box she'd opened earlier and sorted through pilled fleece blankets and mismatched pillowcases until she found an old twin sheet, pink with yellow daisies scattered across the fabric, part of a set Livvy had outgrown years ago. She tore the sheet into four long strips, and brought them to Ted.

"I figure it'll be most stable if I bend my elbow so my hand's up on my chest," Ted said. He was definitely more alert, even if his arm didn't look any better. "Then we secure it there and it's out of the way."

"Won't it start bleeding again if you bend it?"

Ted shrugged. "I think it's mostly quit bleeding for now, and if not, the sling'll help keep it under control."

Jen knew he was guessing, hoping, but she had no better ideas. "Where should I…" she said uncertainly.

"I think what'll work best is if you move it into place. Like this." He showed her with his good arm, splaying his fingers over his heart. His hand came away bloodied.

Jen touched his injured hand tentatively, and found it swollen and still much too warm.

"Honey, you're going to have to do it," Ted said apologetically. "Be brave, okay? No matter what."

As he closed his eyes and clenched his jaw, his words echoed in Jen's mind: *be brave, be brave.*

Jen nodded and picked up the strips of pink cotton. She worked them carefully behind his back, so that when she got his arm positioned right she could tie it tightly into place. The ends dangled behind him like colorful streamers.

When she was ready, Jen gritted her teeth and put one hand on Ted's shoulder and laced her fingers through his and lifted the hand, the hand that no longer felt like her husband's, and kept moving it while he moaned, the sound coming from him unlike a man at all, a raw howl like an animal's. He began to tremble violently as she forced the hand up and against his chest. His elbow stood out inches from his side and Jen pushed her other hand at it, feeling the wet of blood and the sickening softness of the torn flesh and the sharp edge of bone as she pushed it hard against his body.

"Hold there." She grabbed the strips of cloth and wrapped them tightly around his torso. She tied the first tightly, the knot at his knuckles. He panted while she worked, short sobbing breaths, his entire body shaking. She took more care with the second strip of fabric, laying it above the first, stretching it as wide as she could across his shoulder so that it would brace as tightly as possible. The last two strips crisscrossed to stabilize the makeshift splint.

When she was finished, Ted leaned back against the sofa, exhausted, his face drawn and chalky. Jen examined her handiwork: a bouquet of knots blooming on a spreading red stain, a bow on a gruesome package.

Without warning, they heard the sounds of the door opening at the top of the stairs, and Jen leaped off the couch, running to see.

"Livvy?"

"No."

It was Dan, stepping heavily. When he got to the bottom of the stairs they faced each other, neither speaking. Jen searched his face and saw the fear written there.

"What?"

He merely shook his head, then walked past her to the little arrangement of furniture in the center of the room. The overhead bulb cast the room in a sickly pool of yellow light, and accentuated the shadows of his face, the deep circles under his eyes. His shoulders were slumped like an old man's.

"What?" Jen repeated, grabbing Dan's arm, digging her fingers into the cotton of her husband's shirt.

Dan looked slowly from Ted to her, his eyes haunted and dark. "There's a problem."

"There's a problem? There's a *problem?*" Jen felt the stirrings of hysterical laughter in her throat, the horror too big, tipping her past sanity, past what she could bear. "What do you mean? Where's Livvy? What have you done with her?"

Dan started to say something and stopped. He glanced up to the ceiling, and Jen knew it had to be worse than she'd let herself imagine.

"She's with Ryan, isn't she," Jen gasped.

"Okay, look," Dan said. "Ryan is...Ryan is a little unpredictable. He's become a danger, a liability. He's threatening to upset our whole plan here, and I—"

"He is with my *daughter,*" Jen said, her voice rising. She grabbed him by both arms and shook hard, and he tried to push her hands away, but she was stronger. "You go up there and you *stop* him, you—"

There was a commotion as Ted lurched off the sofa. He crashed into the coffee table, knocking over the water bottle, putting out his good hand to stop himself from falling. Grunting from the effort of gaining his balance, he took a staggering step toward them. A second step and he was standing upright, his good hand in a fist.

"Where is my daughter?"

Dan swallowed, his eyes skittering over Ted, the blood and the bandages, his useless arm like a folded wing. "She's in her room. Ryan is with her."

"You left that little fucker alone with my daughter?" Ted roared, and he came at Dan, picking up his feet with sheer determination and planting them hard.

Dan held up his hands in supplication. "We're gonna figure this out, buddy. We just have to—"

But Ted had closed his hand around Dan's throat, shoving into him with all his weight, sending him staggering backward. Jen screamed as Dan reached for the gun in his waistband.

"Stop, just *stop,*" she cried, putting her hands on each man's shoulder and trying to pry them apart.

But Ted wouldn't stop, he brought up his foot and slammed it with all his weight onto Dan's instep, and Jen felt the impact through the concrete floor and heard a snap. Then Dan was screaming, too, and Ted was yelling something, some muddled curse as he used his body weight to slam Dan against the support pillar near the stairs, the two of them locked in an embrace of flailing limbs. Ted was the bigger man, taller by a couple inches and honed by all that squash, all those early-morning runs along Glenn Road, but Jen knew it was the thought of their daughter that propelled him as he managed to get his knuckles into the hollow of Dan's throat. He shoved hard, his face a contorted mask of rage and determination, grinding against Dan's windpipe, and later Jen would realize that all she had to do was go for the gun, just two more steps and she would have had it, she could have taken it from Dan as easily as she took the remote from Teddy when his television hour was over.

But she didn't. She stood rooted as her husband used the last of his strength to destroy the man who had attacked her family. Dan wrenched the gun from his pants and nearly dropped it. It teetered in his palm, and then he managed to get his grip and take a shot—

The sound echoed through the basement, a sound more like a popped balloon than an explosion. Her husband jerked and then slid, slowly, down to his knees. For a moment he swayed there, his hand scrabbling over Dan's pant leg. He clutched his throat, trembling violently, and then Ted slipped the rest of the way down onto the floor. After that, the only part of him that moved was his eyes, rolling and searching until they found Jen and settled on her in apology.

Chapter Twenty-Four

Ted was looking at his wife, and he tried to hold on, but almost immediately her face went blurry at the center and all he could see was her hair, swirling around her shoulders and glinting gold and red in the light that shone on her from above. That hair of hers. He'd once loved to hold it in his hands, heavy and silky. He wouldn't have traded her hair for anything, not for gold, not for money. It was like that story, so long ago, he read it in high school, where the wife sells her hair to buy her husband a watch chain and he sells the watch to buy her a barrette. That story had touched him even then, before he'd ever met his wife, but he'd secretly hoped that he would meet a woman like her someday, beautiful and smart, a woman who loved him and smiled at him every time she saw him and held him deep in the night when he was afraid he didn't really know who he was or what he was supposed to be doing.

He'd tried to win her back. He'd tried to win, for her, to show her he still had it, that reckless luck that brought her to him in the first place. He could see now he'd gone about it all wrong. He should have listened to her, should have been beating down the bushes on the job front instead of messing around at the track, in the bars, playing the odds on the games. Once he started winning that made it so much worse. He was up a few thousand at Thanksgiving, thinking about buying her something knockout for Christmas. That string of Tahitian pearls the size of nickels they'd seen downtown—clasping those around her neck would sure as hell have said what he couldn't seem to say himself these days.

And then…the same old story, an idiot who believed in his own luck. He got further and further behind. Stolen hours in the long afternoons, hands sweaty on a beer he didn't drink, watching games that didn't go his way. They just never went his way. Until the worst, the unthinkable happened, and he had only a few days to make it right.

He sold his most prized possession, the one beautiful thing his father had left him. He wouldn't miss it; he wouldn't *allow* himself to miss it. It was the punishment he deserved, to know the coin collection would never belong to Teddy, that they'd never pore over the rows of beautiful mint issues together the way he had with his own dad. And that was his fault.

And even that hadn't gone right. Five days, the dealer wanted, to collect bids before making an offer for the lot. And the bookie only gave him three. Which left a gap that Ted had to make up. Which led him right to the money market account. Only for a few days. He planned to replace the funds the minute he got the check from the dealer. There would have been some explaining to do but he would have figured out what to tell Jen.

Except now he'd never get the chance.

She was fading, the image of her dancing into the darkness

deep in his mind. Nothing hurt, not anymore, but he had the curious feeling that his limbs were being dipped into very cold water, and he was bobbing along on its surface. He tried to move his fingers, but nothing happened. He tried his toes—same thing. There was a sound—someone was talking—but it was like Charlie Brown's teacher in the Christmas special. *Mwah, mwah, mwah.*

Ah, no matter.

What had he been so worried about, a minute ago? He needed to stop something, some bad thing from happening, and for a moment that concerned him, and he wrinkled his brow to think better, or at least he thought he did. Jen was closer now, shimmering in and out of the darkness, her sparkling and shining hair close enough to touch. He made a mighty effort to smile at her, to let her know it was all right. His beautiful Jen. God, how he loved her. He should have tried harder to make her understand that. The thing with Sarah—it had all been stupid vanity. He probably could have had her anytime. She was like that; she had always had a thing for him. She'd even told him straight out a few years ago when they were all out after work, back when she was engaged to that douche bag, but he hadn't taken the bait. He wasn't all that interested, when it came down to it. A harmless flirtation, a few emails, those notes she put in the mail—it made him feel…well, not better, really, but like a man. A man who could still get a woman.

Just not the woman he wanted.

Another face swam into view, next to his wife's, its features flickering and fading. It all came rushing back, killing the sweet buzz that had started to blur his mind. Dan and the terrible things he'd brought into his house. But it wasn't all Dan's fault. Because *he* was the one who had let the devil in. He was the one who had been stupid, who had been vain, who had given Dan the keys to his kingdom and the invitation to come and take it all away from him.

Chapter Twenty-Five

It had happened last weekend, when Jen and Tanya went up to Murdoch. It had seemed like such a good idea: Jen and Tanya could get some closure with their dad's passing while handling the few practical details, and Ted could get the messy part of the demolition done without interfering with the household. Not to mention, he could use a day or two to figure out how he was going to break it to Jen about the money he'd lost.

After Jen left with Teddy, Ted finished his coffee and got to work. He stripped away the tile above the tub, working at the old mortar with a hammer and a cold chisel. The hard work felt good at first. Ted was damn well finished with gambling, but there was something left of the restless energy, and he needed the physical labor to keep himself distracted.

But it wasn't an easy job, not by a long shot. By the time he'd cleared enough of the tile to take the tub out, he was sweating and filthy. And then the tub turned out to be a bear. The wise guy at the plumbing supply store told him the old stainless steel would be brittle and a few good swings of a sledgehammer would break it up. He and his coworkers probably had a good laugh about it in the back room. Ted felt the impact of the first few blows up and down his spine, the sledgehammer heavy in his hands. But the bathtub wouldn't give, barely a chip in the porcelain. Ted stared at the damn thing, breathing hard. That fucker wasn't going to break, at least not with him doing the swinging.

They sure didn't make tubs like that anymore: had to be more than three hundred pounds of porcelain over steel, seventy years old easy and not a scratch on the thing until he took the hammer to it. Ted would never admit it, but Jen might have been right. Leaving it in place and remodeling around it was sounding pretty good right now. Except for the fact that he'd removed the locknuts, the hardware, everything—it was all sitting at the bottom of the Dumpster—and cut a good six inches of plasterboard out all the way around. And he'd spent fifteen hundred bucks on a shiny new Kohler tub that was sitting in his garage.

Ted set the sledgehammer down on the toilet lid, wiping the sweat off his forehead with the bandanna he'd pulled through his belt loop. How had it come to this? He'd taken a wrong turn somewhere, between his youth in Thief River Falls, where his old man taught him to rebuild an engine and finish an attic, to the job at a global management consulting firm where he ran the metals team until the day they gave his job to a young guy fresh out of Stanford.

Ted wasn't who he used to be. But the problem was that he seemed to have lost track of who he was supposed to become. He'd been following the same path for so long he'd stopped noticing that his will had become weak: he dropped a hundred fifty bucks on his daughter's jeans and folded like wet cardboard when she asked for money to go out on a night when she was supposed to be grounded. He cried in a stall in the men's room the day he was let go. And he'd forgotten how to take care of his family.

The ache that had been nagging at Ted's lower back all week twinged, a reminder that he wasn't up to the task. There was no way he could do this on his own, not if he was going to finish before Jen and the kids returned tomorrow night. Maybe he could hire one of the Mexicans who always hung around the Home Depot parking lot looking for pickup work. Give him a couple of twenties, and have the job done by the end of the day.

The more Ted thought about it, the more it seemed like the sensible thing to do. He hunted down his wallet, sunglasses and car keys, feeling better now that he had a plan. He'd get the rough work done this weekend, then next week he could take his time with the rest. Maybe he'd even bring Teddy up to help him, or at least watch. Put a hammer in the boy's hand and let him feel like he was part of it. Ted wanted his son to grow up as he had, knowing his old man could fix things, could build things with his hands. That his old man took care of things. Sure, Teddy was only four, but that's how old Ted was the first time he'd learned to turn the crank on his father's vise, to glue a broken chair leg.

The Home Depot lot was jammed with weekend warriors, which was both an annoyance and a relief. When he came on weekdays, Ted always felt self-conscious in the checkout line with a handful of housewives while it seemed like all the other men in the place were lined up at the contractor desk. On a Saturday it was just guys like him, clutching lists written by their wives and loading up the backs of their Range Rovers and Pilots.

Ted found a parking spot in the crowded lot and headed toward the entrance. Near the hot dog truck stood two or three men, their collars turned up and no hats despite the cold. Their hands were jammed in their pockets, and they stared at the ground, not talking. There would have been more of them earlier; these were the leftover guys, those who arrived last or maybe already finished a job and came back to make a few more bucks.

Ted walked toward them slowly, threading between the shopping carts and cars pulling in and out of spaces. He'd done this before—he'd hired a couple of these guys last summer when he tackled the old retaining wall out back—and it wasn't hard, but there was always that weird moment, practicing what you were going to say in your mind. *English okay? Want to make a few dollars?*

Ted walked up with his smile fixed in place, already nodding.

"Hey, how are you all doing? I'm looking for a little help with a project at home. Just an hour or two, nothing big."

A couple of them exchanged an appraising look. Maybe they didn't want to go out just for an hour. Maybe he shouldn't have said that. He'd *pay* for more, that wasn't the issue—it was a dick move to give them just the ten an hour, he always slapped on an extra bill—but that wasn't something you said up front.

"It's this old tub I need to get down the stairs," he continued, getting the words out around that stiff smile. "And a little scrap hauling maybe."

"You doing a bathroom?"

From the opposite side of the hot dog truck came a voice without an accent—Ted hadn't seen him there, standing a few feet away from the other men. A red-cheeked white guy with a knit cap and a couple day's beard, chewing on a toothpick. He wore a faded red sweatshirt hood over a beat-up leather jacket.

"Yeah. You interested?"

"I got some plumbing experience. And a little time." The guy shrugged, modestly.

Already the Mexicans had stepped back under the overhang; they weren't about to argue.

The guy had been polite, kicking the mud from his boots before he got into Ted's car, whistling softly when they pulled out of the parking lot. His name was Evan. He hailed from down by Mankato. He'd been over at the Hormel plant until a month ago—"Let us all go the Monday after Thanksgiving, you believe that? I mean, who's gonna hire before the new year, right?" That hit Ted in the gut, and he almost added his own story, that he was laid off after the firm posted their best quarter in four years, forced to walk out with the crap he'd accumulated in his desk piled in a box from the mail room, unable to meet the eyes of the people gathered to say their awkward goodbyes. But that moment passed, and for the rest of the drive back to the house, they talked about whether the Wild would ever have a shot at the play-offs. When Ted led Evan upstairs to the master suite, he was embarrassed, more than he would have been with one of the Mexicans, frankly, which wasn't something he liked admitting even to himself. He saw the way Evan looked at the rug, the gleaming floors, the upholstered headboard, the way his lips pressed together as he walked faster.

"So here it is," Ted said heartily when they got to the bathroom, laying a hand on the tub. "The beast itself."

It had taken them nearly an hour to get the thing down the stairs, and they'd knocked a chunk out of the plaster and put a deep gouge into the floor—Jen was going to have a fit—not to mention the strain on Ted's back, which was raging by the time they finally set the tub on the frozen winter-dead grass near the curb. But Evan had borne the worst of it: his middle fingers on the left hand had gotten mashed between the tub and the newel post somehow and were already swollen and an angry red. Ted offered Evan ice, an ACE wrap, Advil—but Evan waved it all away, rubbing the hand on his shirt and wincing.

"At least a beer, man," Ted found himself saying.

He hadn't really meant to. He'd hoped to make some headway on the floor today. He'd bought a new tile saw, a table-mount DeWalt, and he was looking forward to trying it out. And there was Jen, of course. He had promised her she'd be able to use her new bathroom by Valentine's Day, and he wouldn't mind seeing her face light up when she got home tomorrow, when he showed her what he'd accomplished with a few uninterrupted days to work.

But Jesus, those smashed fingers. Ted's hand hovered over the vegetable drawer in the fridge, where he kept the good beer, but he reached for the Sierra Nevadas lined up along the back of the bottom shelf instead, popping the tops off and grabbing a can of smokehouse almonds.

Evan stood hesitantly in the doorway to the living room, surveying the pale green sofa, the cashmere throw folded neatly over the arm.

"Maybe we should sit in the kitchen," he said. "I'd hate to leave a mess for your wife."

And so the kitchen it was. There were only four Sierras left, and those went down pretty quick. They traded stories about growing up in rural Minnesota. Evan recounting fishing trips and summers spent baling hay and detasseling corn. Ted reciprocating with a few self-deprecating anecdotes from college, the juvenile stunts the guys from his fraternity had pulled. He even shared the embarrassing nickname he'd been given in business school, Tonto to his best friend's Lone Ranger, since he was the quieter one, the one who always ended up being the wing man.

By then it was getting dark outside and the talk grew more serious. Evan was divorced, but saw his middle-school-age daughter whenever he could. She had an orthopedic issue that required some sort of shoe insert that cost four hundred bucks a pop. "Not that I'm looking for sympathy," Evan added, staring down at his chapped and swollen hands. "She's a blessing."

And then Ted, who hadn't really eaten anything since a couple of toaster waffles and a folded mound of deli ham with his coffee, found himself talking about Teddy in more detail than he could remember talking to anyone but Jen. It was easier, somehow, to tell a stranger, someone who'd never met his son or wife. How sometimes he worried that Teddy would never catch up. How you could never be sure if all the therapists and teachers knew what they were doing. How you always wondered if you were doing enough yourself.

Evan listened with interest and the right amount of sympathy—no pity, maybe it was because he'd been through something with his own kid. Ted tossed some tacquitos and pizza rolls in the oven, grabbed a couple of the Feldschlösschens by their long frosty necks and set them down on the kitchen table with enough force to make the empty nut can skitter.

"See what you think," he'd said, to cover his embarrassment. "The Swiss can make a few things besides chocolate."

The beer honestly didn't taste a whole lot different from the Sierra at that point. Evan lifted his bottle and knocked it against Ted's after his first sip. Ted belched and wiped his mouth with his sleeve, and they laughed like thirteen-year-olds.

"Still, it's cool, you guys got a nice setup here," Evan said quietly. "Great place for the kids to grow up, with the cul-de-sac and all."

"Yeah…yeah, it is," he said, matching Evan's tone, a moment of solemnity, something they were sharing. "We've been blessed."

For a moment neither man said anything, Evan nodding slowly and Ted sipping at his beer. It was good—something he hadn't known he'd missed so much, the company of another man. One—and he knew this was part of it—who was in the same boat as him, who'd lost something, not just a job but a part of his identity, of who he really was. A guy who understood what it was like.

"S'cuse me a minute," Ted said, and when he stood he realized he was drunker than he'd thought. He walked carefully to the bathroom, trailing a hand on the wall to steady himself, and while he urinated he closed his eyes and focused on the sensation, the pleasant emptying, the splashing into the porcelain bowl. A *man,* he was still a man, and maybe he just needed a day like today to bring it back to him, working with his hands and sharing the fruits of his good life with someone who accepted him for what he was, hiding nothing, being himself.

Back in the kitchen, Evan was standing in front of the fridge, looking at the photos and invitations pinned up there. "Wow, is this your *wife?* Beautiful lady," Evan said. Ted was there in the photo with Jen, their arms around each other's waists, last August at the lake with his brother's family. Jen was wearing a pale sundress that brought out the gold in her brown eyes, and he remembered how she'd smelled that day, sunscreen and warm skin and perfume, and how after the picture had been taken Ted had chased her up the hill from the dock and into their room with its pine ceilings and fluttering curtains and they'd made love and napped all afternoon.

And then he'd been laid off the next week. "I'm a lucky man," Ted said automatically, but that got him thinking about the task ahead of him, confessing to Jen, telling her he'd gambled away their rainy-day fund. And the worst part would be that she wouldn't blow up. She'd keep her anger to herself, and probably just redouble her efforts to get him to focus on the job search, ask him if he'd followed up on every lead when he hadn't had a nibble in months. She'd wonder out loud if he should update his LinkedIn account or get his hair cut, never telling him straight out but *wondering.*

Nagging, not to put too fine a point on it. "Though she keeps me on a pretty short leash," Ted said, covering his instant regret with a fake little laugh. But he couldn't seem to stop, now that he'd started. "Kind of nice to get a day or two to myself, if you really want to know."

Evan shrugged. "But a woman like that—that's worth a little trouble, I imagine. She on you with the honey-do list, that kind of thing?"

"No, no, not that," Ted said.

And then he proceeded to tell Evan the rest. How tight Jen could be with a nickel, how she'd blow a fortune getting her hair done and then throw a fit when he bought a single roll of paper towels instead of the multipack, because the per-roll price was higher. How she insisted on keeping a crazy amount of money in a money market, close to a hundred grand, so they'd have liquid assets that could be easily tapped in the event of some catastrophe even she couldn't name.

Ted realized when he finished that he might have been insensitive, given the fact that Evan was forced to hire out as day labor to make ends meet, and by way of apology he swerved into a wandering account of when Jen had harangued him for days about misplacing the remote to her car before she found it in the bottom of a purse she wasn't using.

But that just made it worse. He'd cast his wife as a shrew, the kind of wife men sought refuge from in exactly the sorts of places he'd been spending too much time himself. He could imagine him and Evan having this same conversation in the bar where he met his bookie, where the big-screen TV was the only fixture that had been changed in the past thirty years. Tired men, cheap drinks, the bar sticky and dirty, the floor worse. And the bitterness thick in the air.

Ted felt like he'd sold Jen out. He'd quit the gambling and supposedly he was rededicating himself to his family, and yet here he was criticizing his wife in front of a stranger.

"Thing is, she's had a lot to deal with," he said, the words coming out a little slurred. "My wife. Her dad just died, and she and her sister had to go up and see to his affairs. He was a son of a bitch, too."

"Yeah?"

"Left the family when the girls were just kids. Went to live in a two-bit little town up north—you heard of Murdoch? After that he just messed around, didn't work steady, never sent a dime to their mom. My wife grew up with nothing, lived over in Hastings—you know where the dollar store is now—back behind there used to be a dead-end road with a few shacks on it. Whole block got condemned ten, twelve years ago. Probably could have bulldozed the whole block with a rider mower."

"That's a tough break, man, kids growing up that way," Evan said sorrowfully.

"Don't I know it. Jen lived in her aunt's basement for years, put herself through school working two jobs." He shook his head morosely. "Now she and her sister are up there making sure her dad gets a decent burial. And the whole time he was alive their dad didn't give a shit about them."

"You hate to hear a story like that."

"I'll say." Ted lifted his bottle in a toast. "Good woman. I don't deserve her."

After that, the mood seemed flattened, and they finished their beers in silence. The countertop was littered with bottles and frozen food boxes and crumpled paper towels when they made their unsteady way to collect their jackets. Ted drove Evan to the nearly deserted Home Depot parking lot, where his old Sentra looked especially pathetic parked near the far edge. They said an awkward goodbye, promising to stay in touch. Ted pulled out of the parking lot without looking back, driving slowly to make sure he didn't attract the attention of the Calumet cops, given that he probably couldn't pass a sobriety test.

When he got home, he turned off the lights downstairs, leaving the mess for the morning, and crawled into bed in his clothes, sighing deeply and throwing his arm over the place where Jen usually slept.

Right before he drifted off, he realized two disturbing things: he had completely forgotten to pay Evan—and he'd never gotten his last name.

Remembering that day now, Ted felt like crying, the pleasant sparkly blur wrecked and drained, because it was too late now, wasn't it? Evan—Dan—whoever he was, he'd won. He'd come to take everything Ted had, and Ted had failed to stop him, and now Jen was going to have to take care of this mess without him. Because what was he going to do from here, without fingers, without toes, with his body floating away in the water that was going getting colder by the second?

Chapter Twenty-Six

Teddy searched for a long time in the dirt, but he didn't find any worms. All he found were some roly-polies and a dead-looking beetle with long green wings folded up on its back. When Teddy reached for the beetle, it surprised him by jumping, but he caught it and put it in the worm house with the roly-polies. Teddy thought maybe the beetle would eat a roly-poly, but it only shivered its wings once and then went still again.

When darkness began to fall, Teddy began to get a little scared. He had been waiting a very long time, and now it seemed clear that Livvy had forgotten to tell their mom to come get him. He walked down the hill, holding the worm house carefully, but he couldn't help shaking the cup, and the dirt jostled into his careful arrangement of sticks and grass. Teddy worried that getting shaken wasn't good for his beetle, so he set the cup down on the picnic table. Someone would find it tomorrow and be very excited to see the good job he'd done with it.

He was still wearing the coat he had borrowed, but there wasn't anyone left at the park so he knew it was all right if he kept wearing it. His mom could drive it back to the park tomorrow, after he got home and warmed up.

Teddy figured he might as well walk back home. He didn't want to see the men, but surely by now they were gone. And if they weren't, at least his mom would be home, and she would be glad to see him. Teddy had been walking for a while along the road that led away from the park, when he realized that it didn't look familiar. There was a gas station on the corner that he thought he recognized, so he walked to it and stood on the corner, looking into the brightly lit shop, the racks full of snacks. The cashier was reading a magazine, looking bored. His mom sometimes bought him slushies here. The memory made him even more homesick, and he started walking again.

But in the dark it was hard to tell if he was on the right road. His stomach hurt from being hungry, and the cold reached in under the cuffs of his borrowed coat and made his fingers hurt. Cars went by, but none of them slowed down. Maybe they didn't notice him standing there; his mom was always telling him to be careful because the cars couldn't see him.

When he saw the Walgreens he knew where he was, on the edge of downtown, which was not the same direction as home. He didn't know how to get home from here. He crossed the street at the corner where the light was green and walked to a restaurant he had been to with his family before. His stomach rumbled when he thought about the people inside eating dinner. He couldn't go into the restaurant because he didn't have any money, but he watched the people through the window. There was a family sitting in a booth, the two kids drawing on their place mats with crayons. The free crayons and puzzle place mats were Teddy's favorite thing about this restaurant, and he wished his family would come so he could go inside.

Two girls came out of the Starbucks next door. Teddy recognized one of them; it was Livvy's friend Kate. Both girls had long hair and puffy jackets, and they were talking and laughing, but they stopped when they saw him.

"Teddy, is that you?" Kate said. She was on the soccer team with Livvy, and sometimes she came over before games and she and Livvy braided each other's hair with ribbons to match their team colors. Kate was bossy, and Teddy didn't like her very much.

"This is Livvy's little brother, Teddy. He doesn't talk," Kate said to the other girl in her bossy voice.

"Never?" the girl asked. She looked at him curiously. "Hi."

"He won't answer you. Teddy, is Livvy here somewhere? Is she in there?" She pointed in the restaurant window. "You can just nod or shake your head."

Teddy shook his head no.

"Hey, are you crying?" Kate said, but Teddy was embarrassed, and he shook his head no again, wiping away his tears with the back of his hand.

"Well, where's Livvy? Are your mom and dad here?"

If he said they weren't here, then Kate would probably take him to a grown-up. Teddy didn't want to go with Kate, but he really wanted to go home.

"You're here by yourself?"

Teddy nodded. The other girl had her phone out and she was texting, not looking at them.

"Seriously? You're not here with anyone? You didn't walk here by yourself, did you?"

"Hey," the other girl said. "Davis got our tickets. He says meet by the front. They're waiting."

"Okay, but Teddy's lost. Are you lost?"

Teddy shook his head, because he wasn't lost, he was downtown.

"We need to *go,*" the girl with the green jacket said.

Kate flicked her hair over her shoulder impatiently. "You sure you're not lost?"

Teddy wasn't sure what to do, because he didn't want Kate to leave him alone. He didn't want to go with her, either. Maybe she could call Livvy for him and tell her to come. He pointed to the other girl's phone.

"You want Lauren's phone? He wants to use your phone, Lauren," Kate said. She laughed, even though it wasn't funny.

The girl named Lauren kept texting. "Yeah, well, I'm using it. Seriously. Kate. Come *on*."

Kate got out her own phone. Its cover was pink. "I'm going to text Livvy, okay, Teddy? You stay right here. Promise me you're going to stay right here. I have to go, but I'm going to text her and tell her to come get you. You're not going to go anywhere, right?"

Teddy shook his head. The other girl was already walking away, and Kate started texting while she walked fast to catch up. "See you soon," she said, but she was looking at her phone and not at him.

Chapter Twenty-Seven

"That's better," Ryan said, his voice going rough after Livvy turned the lights off.

She stood near the door, hand on the wall switch, shivering. She couldn't believe Dan just *left* that way, left her here with him *alone.* Ryan was in charge, but how could that be? Ryan was just some nothing with a bad haircut, a guy she and her friends would never give a second look to, someone who you could tell right away wasn't from Calumet and wasn't from anywhere you needed to care about. If he knew Allie's cousins, he had to be like some low-level guy, the one they gave the worst jobs to. She'd seen Allie's cousins, they picked her up at school sometimes, leaning up against their SUV while they waited; their arms were thick with muscle and they wore shiny track pants and designer polo shirts and their expressions were unreadable. They were nothing like Ryan.

But after everything that had happened, it didn't even matter anymore why Dan and Ryan were here. Whatever this had started out being, it had turned into something else, something much worse. If there had ever been a chance for them to get away fast and clean, that chance was long gone. Livvy understood what Ryan had done, leaving clues all over the house that the cops could use to identify Dan, but so what? They'd never catch him. If things went smoothly tomorrow, Dan and Ryan were leaving with their money and their cars and they weren't ever coming back. Dan was going to Mexico, and Ryan was going on his own, and if he was smart they'd never find him, either. In six hours he could be over the border in Canada, and he'd have enough money to become somebody new.

But that was the *best*-case scenario. He wasn't gone yet, and the longer he was here, things just kept getting worse.

There was a muffled sound like wood breaking coming from downstairs, and Livvy and Ryan both jumped from the surprise of it.

"Was that a gun?" Livvy demanded. "That was a gunshot, wasn't it?"

"Naw," Ryan drawled. "Probably someone knocked something over or slammed a door."

"No it wasn't." Livvy's voice went high with panic. "It was a *gun*. I know it."

Ryan went over to the door. He put a hand on the knob and looked at her for a moment before he opened it. He leaned out into the hall as if testing the air, but after a second he closed the door again. Then he twisted the lock.

"If it was anything, Dan will take care of it," he said. "Now get on over here."

Livvy stood frozen in place, trying to make sense of what he'd said. If Dan had shot her mom or dad, there would be screaming or yelling, right? It was probably another warning, like when her dad tried to force open the door. But her dad was so messed up from his arm, half-unconscious or in shock, there was no way he would have tried anything. And her mom—would her mom have taken a risk like that? Especially when Livvy had come up here to call Jake on the walkie-talkie. It didn't make sense.

"I said, get over here." Ryan had gotten up on the bed, *her* bed with the deep purple comforter and the pillows her mom fluffed and put back in place every day while she was at school. Ryan patted the sides of the quilt. He wanted her to get on the bed with him. Livvy felt sick and exposed, like he could see under her clothes.

"I want to stay here," she whispered.

"Well, I don't want you to." Ryan smiled, showing his teeth. The top ones were straight and white, but when he smiled like that, she could see that the bottom ones were crooked and one of them was gray.

While she was staring at his mouth, Ryan's tongue came out, slowly, like a snake slithering out of a hole in the ground, and ran slowly around his lips. "Mmm, hmm," he said. "I think you should get that sweet little ass of yours over here."

Livvy whimpered and hugged herself, shifting from one foot to another. Ryan's tongue was long and pink and had a pointy end, and his mouth glistened wet.

"I'll scream," she said.

Ryan laughed. "Yeah? Okay, I'll scream, too. You think that's gonna change anything? With these fancy windows your rich daddy put in? You don't even have neighbors back there—there's nobody to hear you. But if it makes you feel better, go ahead."

Livvy bit her lip and stared at the floor. It was true—the

only people who would hear were her parents and Dan. And her parents couldn't do anything about it, and Dan wouldn't, and it would just make things worse.

"I ain't playing, Livvy," Ryan said. A sharp tap made her look up: he had the gun held casually in one hand and was tapping it against her nightstand. "You can make this hard or you can make this easy. Hell, you might even like it."

Livvy shuffled toward the bed, her feet dragging. She stopped a couple of feet away, and Ryan sat up and swung his legs over the edge of the bed. He grabbed the front of her shirt and pulled her closer, making her stumble, until her thighs were touching his knees.

"Unbutton your shirt," he said.

Livvy breathed through her mouth, short breaths that didn't fill her lungs enough. She put her fingers on the top button, wiggled it a little. It was round and smooth, like a bead that had fallen off a broken necklace. Her mom bought her this shirt in the Denver airport last Thanksgiving when they'd gone to see her uncle Gar and his family. She got stuck babysitting her little cousins and Teddy, and she'd taken advantage of the fact that her mom felt bad about it and convinced her to buy her this shirt and a new set of earbuds that she ended up leaving on the plane.

"Damn, girl," Ryan said, and he reached up and pushed her fingers out of the way, grabbed where the button was and yanked. Her neck snapped backward, but two of the buttons flew off the shirt. Livvy unbuttoned the last few herself. Ryan used the gun to push the shirt slowly open, sliding the end of the gun up over her breasts and hooking the collar to ease it off her shoulders one side at a time. The shirt got stuck at the wrists, but Livvy was afraid of being shot by accident and she wriggled the cuffs over her hands until the shirt fell to the floor.

She was wearing her pink bra. She'd put it on so long ago, Thursday morning—was that only yesterday?—along with the matching pink panties with the white trim. Was he going to make her strip to her panties?

"Show me." He was breathing hard, staring at her breasts. "Take your hands away."

She had her hands tightly crossed over herself and it was like she had to pry them off, like she was working against herself. Livvy didn't like people looking at her; she never had. She shied away in the locker room before gym class, or when they were getting ready for a game, because she didn't want anyone to see her. Some of the girls decorated their bras, they pinned on lucky ribbons and wrote with puffy fabric paint, and they chased each other around the locker room with bottles of Gatorade, calling each other by their team nicknames, and it was all in *good fun,* Livvy knew that, but she still hated it and she still changed as fast as she could, head down and a blush creeping across her face. At home she stared at herself, holding up the round mirror so she could see her back, the bumps of her spine, the birthmark, all the ugly details that didn't add up to something she could stand to see. And Sean… after Sean it had been worse, because he had gotten so close, he made her almost believe it was all right, that she was pretty enough for him.

"Let me see," Ryan said, his voice sounding half hungry and half angry, and then his hands were on her, on her breasts, under them, lifting and squeezing. She looked down and saw his thumbs making dents in the soft flesh, his thumbnails dirty and too long. He was fumbling at her bra clasp, but this clasp was tricky, you had to bend it a certain way and it snapped apart, and he was doing it wrong, getting frustrated.

"Get this fucking thing *off*," he demanded just as her hands went to the clasp. As she opened it, he added, "Or I'll rip it off you."

Livvy squeezed her eyes shut, not wanting to see any more, not wanting to see her breasts naked and exposed.

"Your pants," he said. Abruptly he released her, and she staggered back a step. Her eyes opened, and she saw his hand go to his own zipper, tugging his shirt over his head, getting frustrated when the collar got stuck against his chin. He ripped it off and worked at his jeans, jamming them down over his narrow hips. He wore plaid that looked too small for him, that hugged against his white, hairless stomach. He looked younger than some of the boys in her class did, at the pool, but Livvy knew it was all an illusion, that he had done things and seen things and knew things that none of those boys did.

Because Ryan was *not* a boy; no matter what he looked like, he was a man. He was a dangerous man and he was going to do dangerous things to her and it would be nothing like it had been with Sean.

Ryan yanked at his boxer shorts and Livvy looked away; she didn't want to see. She was backing toward the door, her hands scrabbling behind her for the desk, trying to remember what was on it, anything she could throw or hurt him with but all her seeking hands found was the chair. You couldn't hurt anybody with a flat little chair cushion, that was for sure, and Ryan was making some weird sound in his throat and his hand reached inside his pants.

"You want a taste?" he asked, grinning. "You'll like it. Got some sugar for you right here. Come get on your knees, girl, I'll show you what to do."

Livvy's hands were behind her now, the back of her thighs pressed against the chair, her fingers skittering over pens, her chem book, the case that held the glasses she was supposed to wear for reading but never did. The case was hard plastic, and she thought about throwing it, but it was next to nothing; you couldn't kill a bug with it.

Her fingertip nudged something cold and hard. The mug her friend Paige got her when Seether played Mill City, shiny black with the letters like they were made out of bones. Livvy kept her pens and pencils in it. She slipped her fingers into the handle and threw it as hard as she could, and it cracked against Ryan's face.

The doorbell rang.

Ryan yelled *fuck* and stumbled sideways, his hands going to his forehead where the mug hit him. Livvy grabbed the doorknob and twisted the lock. Sometimes the door stuck, but not this time. It flew open and bounced against her dresser. She crashed into the edge of the door, hitting her ribs and knocking the breath from herself. If she'd opened the door with a little less force, she would have been out and down the hall and at the front door before anyone else could get there. But instead she had to grab the door frame to keep from falling down. She was halfway through the door and into the hall when Ryan grabbed her arm. He yanked it so hard she went down, skull bouncing off the door, hip hitting the edge.

"You bitch, you filthy fucking cunt," he screamed while he yanked up his pants.

The doorbell rang again, and there was the sound of running, heavy steps on bare wood. Livvy could see Dan standing halfway up the stairs, his mouth open and panting.

Ryan had her by the hair; he was pulling her up with it. Livvy stumbled to her feet, covering her bare breasts. Ryan pushed her into the hall, not letting go.

"Dave!" Dan said, in the very same tone her dad used on her when he was really angry. But who was Dave?

"I'm getting this door," Dan growled. "Get that girl dressed and stay upstairs. I'm coming up after. You put one hand on her and I swear I'll break your fucking neck."

And to Livvy's amazement, Ryan let go of her hair. Whatever was between them, whoever Dan was to Ryan, he was still a little afraid of him. The way he'd been in her room earlier, the underwear, the sneer on his face when he was threatening Dan, that's who he was now, she could see that. Pure mean and pure bad and smarter than he looked.

Dan yelled at Ryan and hesitated just long enough to give Livvy one second. One second to run.

She took the stairs full speed, bracing herself with her hand on the banister, bare feet slapping on the wood. She came at Dan with her arms grabbing, pulling at him. She was naked on top but she didn't care.

The ringing had turned to knocking, the brass ring against the door hollow and thunking. "Jen?" It was a thin voice—Aunt Tanya. Jake sent his mom. She hadn't called the cops; she'd come by herself instead.

Dan lifted his hand, and for a second she thought he was

going to smack her across the face but he just pushed it flat over her mouth. “Do not say one fucking word,” he muttered, quiet and furious. He started dragging her, one hand on her mouth and one on the back of her neck, down the hall toward the basement door. Livvy struggled against him, her feet slipping on the slick wood surface and her fingers clawing at his hand over her mouth, but he was much stronger than she would have thought, hands like iron for an old guy. He kept talking as they went, voice low and angry. “You stay down here and keep quiet. So fucking quiet, I don’t want to hear a word, not a sound. You hear me? Or I’ll give you right back to Ryan and tell him to do whatever he wants with you, you understand?”

Livvy was crying, snot dripping down onto Dan’s rough knuckled hand. She tried to nod but she couldn’t, not with the grip he had on her. “If you mess this up,” he continued, “I will come down the stairs and I will *hurt* your mother and then I will give you to Ryan. I have had just about enough of this, and I won’t have it. I won’t *have* it. I will wash my hands of you, every damn one of you.”

They had arrived at the door, and Dan took his hand off her face to turn the key. Even with only one hand Dan managed to keep her still and quiet, his fingers and thumb pinching into the back of her neck like it was nothing more than a rag, squeezing the tendons so she gasped. As he opened the door he gave an extra squeeze, and Livvy’s vision went gray and flickering, the air cut off to her brain, little choking sounds coming out of her.

He pushed her through the door. Hands grabbed her, and her mother’s frantic voice shouted “Livvy, Livvy” and then the door shut and the key twisted. Her mother wrapped her arms around her and Livvy hugged back hard, crying and gulping for air.

"Are you all right?" her mother asked when she caught her breath, and Livvy was trying to say yes, that he hadn't hurt her, he hadn't done anything to her. She had gotten away before anything really bad could happen. Even though she would never forget the memory of his hands on her skin.

"I hit him with my mug," she finally managed to choke out, but her mother just kept asking if she was okay. Finally she grabbed her mother's hands and squeezed them hard.

"I'm *okay,*" she said, catching her breath. "How's Dad?"

But her mother just held her tighter, sobbing into her hair.

Chapter Twenty-Eight

Jen finally managed to catch her breath. "Were the police at the door?"

"No, Mom. It's Aunt Tanya—"

"Tanya's here?" Jen should have known the plan would never work, that whatever Jake told Tanya, she would come here to check it out for herself. And now Tanya was stuck with them, sucked into this nightmare, and it was her fault for letting Livvy try something so desperate and doomed to failure.

She had to keep her daughter from going down the stairs, because Ted was down there, and Ted was dead. He had died in her arms. There was no way Jen was going to let her baby girl see that, her girl who had already been through so much. Ryan sickened her, and if Jen was given the smallest opportunity, she would kill him for what he'd done.

It was all too much: her husband was dead, her baby was missing, her sister was about to walk into a nightmare and she had failed to protect her daughter. From the start, Dan had promised an orderly resolution, a simple transaction from which they'd all walk away. Instead, Jen's world was shattered, and all that was left was for her to die, too.

Through her agony, she heard her sister's voice, muffled by the door.

"Jennie! Oh, my God, Jennie, what is going on?"

Dan said something Jen couldn't make out, and then Tanya cried out, her screams high and unintelligible.

All Jen could do was to pull her daughter close and try to cover her ears. In the next second, someone opened the door and pushed Tanya through. She fell into the wall, as the door slammed shut. Jen grabbed for Tanya to prevent her from falling down the stairs.

"It's okay. I'm okay," Tanya said but Jen couldn't speak, and somehow the roles all shifted. Tanya gathered her and Livvy into her arms, and there was a shadow of a memory, another time when Tanya had held her like this. Another time when Jen was sobbing so hard that she couldn't speak, couldn't breathe, and Tanya had saved her. No, that wasn't exactly right. Tanya had...she had helped her, or found her, or—the past was getting all tangled up together with the present.

"We're going down the stairs now," Tanya said firmly. She supported Jen on one side and Livvy took the other. They went down the stairs in a tight scrum, the three of them clutching each other, Tanya making sure they didn't fall, that everything would be all right.

"Don't let Livvy see," Jen whispered and Livvy twisted her body, trying so hard to look, but Tanya was stronger. She'd always been strong, a wiry alley cat. She'd only lasted one year on the cheerleading squad before she was kicked out for what happened after Homecoming, but during that year she'd done all the most dangerous stunts, held up girls heavier than she was, supporting their weight on her hard, knotted shoulders.

At the bottom of the stairs, Tanya took off her coat and helped Livvy into it, zipping it up over her bare torso. She didn't ask where Livvy's shirt was. Between the two of them, she and Jen got her over to the couch, shielding her from a view of Ted. But Jen had seen his body lying on the floor, curled like a letter *c*, his hand still clutching his wound. And she knew that Tanya had seen him, too.

"Mom—" Livvy gasped for air. Jen rubbed her back and exchanged a look with Tanya. Her sister's face was pale as paper, her eyes wide and questioning. "What happened to Dad? Tell me. Please, I have to know."

"Oh, honey..."

"He's dead, isn't he? Dan killed him. Dan did it, didn't he?"

Jen hesitated, wishing she could keep the truth from her, that she could send her daughter back forty-eight hours into the fairy tale of Before, into the dumb luck good fortune of the life they never appreciated enough. She would happily give up her own life, if she could make things right for Livvy.

But that wasn't possible. And now, her job was to let go of everything they couldn't ever have again, and seize hard on what was left. What was left was her children and now her sister, a ragged and desperate cohort. Jen wanted to sink to the floor and fade away, but instead she had to be like Tanya: strong and fearless.

She swallowed, her throat raw. "Livvy...yes. Dan shot Daddy when he was trying to get help."

Livvy made a sound that broke Jen's heart: a wretched exhalation of grief and loss that sounded much too old to come from her baby girl.

"Daddy was brave and he was strong and he was going to

get help, just like you went to get help. I am so proud of you both. I won't ever be able to tell you that enough, honey. You and Daddy did everything you could because you're fighters and you are strong and you are better than—so much better than these monsters. And that's why we're going to..."

She faltered, because what were they going to do, exactly? What reserves did they have left, what weapons to fight against the evil upstairs? She'd thought Dan could be reasoned with, but he'd proved to be just as reckless and dangerous as Ryan. They'd used all their wild cards, and all they had managed to do was ensnare Tanya, too, and now she was trapped in the same bloody, deadly web.

If only Jen could just lie down next to Ted and die with him. It was too hard—it had all been too hard, not just the invasion but the days leading up to it, the family that seemed to splinter a little more every day despite all her efforts to keep them together, the love that had escaped her marriage like smoke carried away on the wind, the sweetness of the babies she'd held in her arms. The past that never seemed to leave her but never came into focus, a shroud that prevented the joy from getting close enough to take hold of. The losses—her mother, her father, even her sister, all slipping away from her when she had tried to hold them tight. Wouldn't it be best to just let it end, to go where the dead go?

But she couldn't, and the reason was Livvy, holding on to her so tightly that she could feel the outline of every one of her daughter's fingers against her back. And Teddy, out there somewhere. She would give everything for her children. She would find the strength; she would find the courage.

"We're going to get out of this," Tanya said, finishing the sentence that Jen had started.

"I'm sorry," Livvy wailed. "It's my fault. I thought Jakey would tell you to call the police, I never thought that you would—"

"He did, honey. He did exactly what you asked him to," Tanya said. "You both did perfect. It was me…it was my fault. I didn't believe him. I thought he was just making things up, trying to get out of homework. But I've been calling you guys, I called your mom's cell yesterday, and I kept getting voice mail on the house phone, and, well, I just thought… So I left Jake next door with Mrs. Bassett and then I came over here."

Jen put her hand over her sister's and squeezed. Their eyes met and Tanya nodded faintly, letting her know it was okay. She was taking care of Jen even now, even after all these years.

Somewhere along the line, Jen had lost faith in Tanya. But Tanya had never wavered in her faith in Jen.

"I'm here now," Tanya said, squeezing Jen's hand back. "I'm here, and that makes three of us, three brave strong women. Now tell me what the hell's going on, and we'll figure out what to do."

Jen told the story quickly, leaving out the details she didn't want Livvy to hear. Tanya winced when Jen told her about Teddy, her eyes darting to the window wells, inky dark now.

"And you think he's at your friend's house?" she asked softly. "If he got away when you were at the bank—I mean, honey, that's more than twelve hours. Wouldn't she have come over here by now to see what was going on?"

"She's probably called a bunch of times."

Jen told Tanya about the bank account, the money she kept sitting there in a vain attempt to feel safe, a notion that now struck her as so ridiculous that it was no wonder Ted had teased her about it all those years.

"But I don't understand what happened to the money," Tanya said when she got to the part about the bank visit. "It was just gone?"

Jen nodded. "It had to do with the construction," she lied, aware of Livvy watching her. "He had to cover the cabinetry and...all those expenses."

Jen could tell that Tanya knew she was lying, but she played along for Livvy's sake. "Yeah, that makes sense. And then you got the transfer lined up, so tomorrow..."

"I don't know. I mean, I guess...in theory we could still do it like we said we would. Me and Dan could go back to the bank. We could get the money."

Which would mean leaving Livvy here with Ryan. And Tanya, yes, but all Ryan had to do was take her daughter upstairs again and do whatever he wanted. He would be angry now, frustrated, vengeful, brimming with whatever poisoned brand of bile he carried.

He and Dan were unpredictable. Really, what were the odds that they could pull off a trip to the bank tomorrow? Even if Dan let Jen fix herself up, even if she could disguise her emotions with makeup and clean clothes and pull off a convincing performance...it would never work. There was a wildness in Dan's eyes, a grim realization that everything was fucked up. *Fucked up* on a cataclysmic scale, and what did guys like that do in situations like this? You only had to turn the TV on, any of those action movies Ted liked, to understand that when the chips were down the bad guys cut their losses, they left their dead, they got the hell out of Dodge.

"If I were them, I would be figuring out what I could take with me," Tanya said. "I'd be looking around the house and taking everything that was worth anything that could fit in the cars. And I'd be doing it fast."

"Because the longer you're gone..."

"Yeah, for all they know I have a husband at home, people wondering where I went. Maybe I told my husband I wouldn't be gone long, and now he's worried about me. Or maybe I really did call the cops."

"So maybe they'll just go," Livvy said hopefully.

"Honey." Jen gently stroked her daughter's hair. "Maybe you're right—maybe they'll decide that this has gone far enough and they have to look out for their own best interests, and they'll leave. But we have to be ready for the possibility that they won't. That they..."

"That they come down here and kill us," Livvy said flatly.

"Oh, sweetie, no," Jen protested, both her and Tanya pressing closer, protecting her the only way they could. "Not that."

"But it's true, Mom. Dan's DNA is all over the house, but Ryan knows where it all is, and if they clean it up, they can still get out without leaving any proof it was them. But if they let us live we can ID them."

"Baby, no..." But Jen knew it was true.

"Like Aunt Tanya said, they have to be worried about someone knowing she's here. They've already killed Dad—" Livvy's voice caught as she said it, but she swallowed hard and continued, her words running together fast. "And Ryan's, like, *crazy* so you have to figure they aren't going to think twice about killing anyone else."

"So we have to be smarter than them now," Tanya said grimly. "And stronger. It's all or nothing time."

"All or nothing," Jen repeated, the words tasting like metal.

They had no reason to hold back now. And whatever shred of decency she'd thought she'd detected in Dan—the evidence that he was human, that he still operated from some moral code deep inside—she didn't trust it now.

"Well, what are we going to do, then?" Tanya said, standing. "We aren't just going to sit here and let them come to us, Jennie. There is no fucking *way* we are going to do that."

She paced in front of the sofa. She reached in her pocket and pulled something out, something narrow that glinted in the dim bulb, something…familiar. It had a round loop at one end, a metal key ring, and she stuck her finger through it and twirled it around her finger nervously as she paced.

"What…" Jen said, but the more she stared at the thing the fuzzier it got, the twirling arc of it making her dizzy, making her vision swim.

"Oh, honey, you know what this is," Tanya said, stopping in front of her. "Come on. Sid's knife? I've carried it with me ever since that summer."

Jen stared, trying to fight through the swirling haze of memory and forgetting, of the past reaching out for her. It pixelated and scattered, grains of sand swept by the wind, leaving only what Tanya held in her hand. Near one end, something winked in the burnished metal, a coin of red, before Tanya jammed the thing back into her pocket.

"Mom!" Livvy hissed, grabbing her wrist so hard that it

hurt, yanking her back. "I hear them. They're walking around again."

"We have to be ready," Tanya said grimly.

"But how?"

"Well, we're not just going to sit here and wait for them to come get us." Tanya grabbed Jen's hand and pulled her up.

Livvy stood, too, the quilt falling from her shoulders to the floor. She put her hands through her mother's and aunt's arms, linking them all together.

"I think I know what to do."

Chapter Twenty-Nine

After Kate and her friend left, Teddy waited for Livvy, but she never came. Eventually the family he'd seen through the window came out of the restaurant, and one of the boys waved at him. Teddy followed them for a while, keeping his distance, but at the corner they crossed the street when the light was yellow, and by the time he got there it was red.

He walked in the other direction, where the girls had gone, hoping he could find them. But the streets were almost empty. An elderly couple got into a car and drove away. Teddy decided that if someone asked him if he was lost, he would say yes now. He would nod his head and if they still didn't understand, he would try to use his words.

But no one else came along. Teddy walked down the empty street, passing all of the shops that were closed for the night. When he got to the corner, there was a store whose entrance was shielded from the wind and cold. For a long time Teddy stood in the entrance, hoping someone would come along. Finally he got tired and sat down, pulling the coat's hem over his knees and shrugging his hands inside the sleeves to keep warm. But the tiled floor was too cold even with the coat, and Teddy started to cry. The mucus from his nose froze and became crunchy and painful. He wondered if Livvy and Mom and Dad were all looking for him now, unable to find him, and the thought made him cry harder.

After a while he stopped crying and rubbed his nose on the sleeve of the coat. He tried the door to the store, but it was locked. He looked in the windows. Inside, a few lights were on, illuminating window displays. One mannequin wore a dress and black boots and a jacket and a purple scarf. The scarf looked like it would be really fuzzy. Her plastic wrists held several bracelets. In the other window was an orange purse with a big tag sticking out of the top. There were other things, too, shoes and socks and jewelry. Things his mom might like.

If his mom was here, she would rub his fingers and his toes between her warm hands and they would tingle as they warmed up. She would make cocoa on the stove and let him put in the marshmallows, as many as he wanted. She would wrap him up in the soft green blanket and say "Where did your arms go, Teddy? Oh, no!"

Teddy lay down inside the coat. He pulled the hood more tightly around his face and closed his eyes. A little while later he put his fingers in his mouth. He had promised Mom he wouldn't do that anymore, but he was very sad right now, and sucking on his fingers made him feel a little better. Inside the hood, his face was warm. He had drifted off to sleep when he heard people yelling.

Teddy sat up and saw three teenage boys across the street, sitting by the bushes at the end of a parking lot. One boy was on a skateboard, rolling it slowly back and forth, and the others were sitting on the curb. One of them had leaned a bike against a light pole, a trick bike with a low seat and thick tires. Teddy decided he wanted a bike like that when he got old enough.

The boys were smoking, which Teddy knew was one of the worst things you could do. Also, none of them were wearing helmets. Teddy wondered if their parents knew that they were riding around without helmets.

A police car pulled up across the street with its signal casting a strobe of blue light. The boys leaped up and scattered. One of them jumped on the bike and pedaled away, and the other two ran, leaving the skateboard behind. They made it around the side of the building, dodging trash cans, and disappeared.

Two policemen got out of the car, not hurrying. One of them picked up the skateboard and said something to the other policeman and they laughed. Teddy stood up uncertainly. His mom had always told him he could go to a policeman for help anytime he was lost or scared. She said he didn't need to be afraid of them, and that he could tell a policeman anything. She had shown him how to talk to a policeman. Teddy pretended to be a police officer, and Mom pretended that she was lost and afraid, and she practiced saying her name and their address. She said he could practice, too, and they had switched and then Mom got to pretend to be a police officer. She was good at it. Teddy thought she would be a really good policeman.

Teddy walked slowly toward the policemen, his heart pounding. He was a little bit afraid of crossing the street, even though there were no cars. He looked both ways, left, right, left again. He started across the street, and one of the policemen noticed him.

"Hey," the policeman said, looking surprised. "Hey, what have we got here?"

When Teddy got close, both officers bent down so they could look at his face. The light on top of their car was still lashing the street with its light, making Teddy blink.

"Hey, where'd you come from? One of those guys your brother?" The policeman pointed in the direction where the boys had run. But Teddy didn't have a brother, and even if he did, his mom would never let him come out here at night.

"You out here by yourself?"

"Where are your parents? Are you lost?"

The officers took turns asking questions, and Teddy pushed his lips together and tried not to start crying again. He hoped they would let him get in their car. He wondered if they had the heat on. The sleeves of the borrowed coat dragged along the ground and, too late, Teddy wondered if they would think he had stolen it.

"Did someone bring you here?" The policeman was talking slower now. He was starting to look worried. "Hey, listen, son, what's your name?"

Teddy opened his mouth and made the shape of his name. There were two clicks with his tongue, for the 't' and 'd' sounds. He had practiced it many times before with Mrs. Tierney.

"I can't hear you, little guy. Can you tell me your name?" The other policeman seemed nice. His nose was pink, and he had ears that stuck out from his head, and he was smiling encouragingly.

Teddy shook his head. He didn't think he could say his name right now.

But he was so cold, and maybe, definitely, those guys that came to the house were gone by now, and Teddy just wanted to be home with his family. Teddy pushed out his breath the way Mrs. Tierney showed him to do when he was feeling scared.

"Do."

Teddy was surprised. Mrs. Tierney said the words were in there when he was ready to use them. At home, with his family, he never thought about where the words came from. But with other people, they stayed stuck inside.

He tried it again. "Do."

"Do?" the first cop said, like it was a question.

Teddy pushed out his breath again and then he said, "Do you know my mom?"

Chapter Thirty

Inches away, Tanya's eyes shone in the faint light that seeped behind the stairs. Tanya had the gift of stillness. She'd always been able to keep her body motionless. Jen was restless, a fidgeter, and her thighs and ankles were cramping from crouching so long under the stairs.

She couldn't see Livvy's face. Through the spaces between the steps she could make out only the curve of her bare shoulder, the quilt that had slipped off her as she dozed in the chair, revealing the swell of her breasts under the thin tank top that Jen had found in the giveaway box.

Of course, Livvy wasn't really asleep, and the quilt hadn't slipped down by accident. Livvy had arranged it very carefully after dragging the chair over near the wall so that someone coming down the stairs couldn't avoid seeing her lying there. She'd moved the lamp, too, so that she'd be bathed in light, almost spotlighted once they turned off the overhead bulb.

Jen worried that the plan was too contrived, too obvious, but she'd been outnumbered. After listening to Livvy's idea, Tanya agreed that it was their best shot, and when Jen questioned whether the plan had any chance of working, she said

"Come on, Jennie, they're *men.* They're driven by what's in their pants."

Because men, to her sister, were all alike, unable to ignore their animal natures. When Jen suggested that while Ryan would be distracted by the sight of her half-clothed daughter, Dan might have other things on his mind, Tanya only snorted.

Jen and Tanya crouched side by side under the stairs and didn't speak. As the minutes ticked by, Jen decided that it would be better if it was Dan who came down to kill them, and not Ryan. For one thing, he was slower and clumsier, more likely to hesitate when she and Tanya made their move. And she couldn't help thinking he was more likely to feel guilty and uncomfortable at the sight of her daughter stretched out seductively.

At last, when Jen's knees were numb and her ankles quaked from the uncomfortable position she was holding, they heard a sound at the top of the stairs, the key being turned in the lock, the squeak as the door opened on its hinges.

Tanya reached for Jen's hand and gave it a squeeze, a final encouragement, a promise to stay by her side. They heard footfalls on the stairs, slow and heavy, and Jen knew it had to be Dan.

"Jen?" he called. His voice was heavy, freighted with inevitability and exhaustion. "Aw, Livvy," he muttered as he descended, and Jen knew that she'd been right, that it wasn't lust that stirred in him when he looked at her daughter, but the weight of what he had to do.

But she also had a job to do. As his foot landed on the step in front of her face, she reached through the space between the stairs and grabbed his ankle, her hand closing around the smooth twill cuffs of her husband's trousers. She yanked with all her might, and he stumbled, cursing as he scrambled to keep his footing, but Jen held on. Tanya made a sound like a rabid dog tearing the throat out of a rabbit and jammed their father's knife into the back of Dan's ankle, and Jen felt the tendon snap like a fistful of rubber bands, and he screamed and fell down the stairs.

Livvy had burst out of her pretend slumber the minute Dan stumbled, diving to the floor and rolling out of the way. As he went down, he shot the chair where she'd been lying a second earlier. A second bullet struck the wall, chipping the cinder block.

Jen still had his pants cuff in her fist, and she held on for dear life, even as he kicked at her with his good leg, smashing her knuckles. His hips were on the bottom step, his torso on the floor, his arms flailing. He kept screaming as Tanya seized his ruined ankle and kept slashing at it. Jen let go and scrambled around the stairs in time to see her daughter kick Dan's face, landing a square blow to his jaw. It made a cracking sound, like snapping kindling for a fire. He kept yelling until Livvy kicked him a second time and then the sounds he made were more like wailing. Blood bubbled between his lips, and Jen figured he'd bitten his tongue. She hoped he'd bitten it clear through.

"Quick, get his gun," Tanya yelled. Dan grabbed Livvy's leg, and she lost her balance and went down hard barely two feet away. He managed to jerk his leg free from Tanya and rolled onto his stomach, and Jen watched in horror as he struggled up onto his elbow, never letting go of his gun.

The door at the top of the stairs banged against the wall, and Ryan clattered down the stairs. He managed two shots before he reached the bottom, but they went wide since he was trying to avoid hitting Dan. He stomped hard on Tanya's wrist, which still jutted through the stairs, and she screamed as Dan barked something and fired.

Tanya's body bucked and lurched, her head banging on the stairs above her, and then she slumped down to the floor, as formless as a bag of rice.

Livvy screamed, and Jen crawled the last few feet to her daughter, covering her with her body. Dan tried to get to his feet, and collapsed in pain, his gun falling to the floor and sliding out of reach, his useless foot twisted grotesquely. Ryan bounded over him and crouched inches away from Jen.

Up close, she could see a faint sprinkling of red along his hairline, the shadow of the acne that must have plagued him as an adolescent. She squeezed her eyes shut, waiting for the shot.

"Look at me!" Ryan shouted. Jen could smell his breath, hot and sour in her face. Livvy struggled to get out from under her, writhing and trying to push her off. But Jen would protect her daughter until her heart stopped beating. Her body would stop a bullet before it could reach Livvy, and if that was the cost of a few more seconds of her daughter's precious life, she'd pay.

"I said, *look!*" Ryan grabbed her neck, his thumb crushing her windpipe, shaking her. She opened her eyes and stared at him, taking in the foamy spittle at the corner of his mouth, the bottom teeth that crowded and pushed against each other. He had a faint scar under his chin.

"Do you have any *idea* how fucked up this is? Huh?" More shaking. "This is all on you. Not me, *you!*" He waved the gun around the basement. "You got enough shit down here for a whole other house. You want to know what's in my mom's living room? A La-Z-Boy she pisses in when she's drunk and a TV that weighs like five hundred pounds. How's that fair?"

Underneath her, Livvy went still for a second, and Jen thought she'd hurt her somehow, crushed the breath from her, but then she felt her daughter's hands at the back of her own head. She gave a mighty shove and Jen's neck snapped forward and her forehead smashed into Ryan's face, so hard she saw stars. The gun went off, and Ryan cursed and let go of her throat. Jen's vision had gone blurry, but she dived for the floor, trying to find Livvy's hand to drag her down with her.

Jen called her daughter's name and blinked until her vision cleared. Ryan had his hand over his wrecked nose and blood was pouring through his fingers. He was on his knees, his free hand frantically scrabbling around on the floor. Livvy dived, fast and sleek like when she was on the soccer field, and came up with his gun in her hand.

"Mom—" she yelled, but Jen was already there. She grabbed the gun from her daughter and watched Ryan spin on his knees, realization dawning in his eyes as his hand fell away from his nose. Jen curled her finger around the trigger, and was surprised by how easy it was, the way they made these things so that a nice lady from the suburbs who'd never fired so much as a Super Soaker would know exactly what to do. She squeezed, and the blast rocked back through her shoulder.

Half of Ryan's face disappeared.

A grunt behind her made Jen turn just in time to see Dan up on his hands and knees, crawling painfully toward his own gun, dragging his bloody leg. He had almost reached it when Livvy kicked it, and the gun went skittering across the concrete floor, spinning in a lazy circle as it slid, bouncing off the base of the shelves. Livvy stomped Dan's hand and then jumped out of the way.

"Don't you move," Jen screamed. "Dan, don't you do it."

He was crying out in pain, holding his smashed hand close to his body. It was already swollen, the skin angry purple, and Jen hoped her daughter had broken every bone.

"Livvy, back up," she said, needing her daughter outside the field of bodies. Tanya was sprawled next to the stairs, with one foot flung awkwardly over the other, an arm across her face. Ryan had fallen on his side, mercifully hiding the gore where his face had been. Dan was sinking slowly onto his stomach, whimpering and clutching his hand.

It was clear that Dan was beaten. Jen looked down at the gun in her hand. She turned it over so that she was looking at her fingers wrapped around the grip, her manicure still perfect except for a small chip in the polish of her ring finger.

She pointed the gun at Dan, aiming at his chest.

Dan had brought evil into her home. He'd shot her husband and her sister, and Jen would never have another chance to find her way back to them. Because of him, she had lost the two people who had loved her more than anyone else in the world.

Shooting Ryan hadn't exactly been a challenge, given that he was only a foot away, although she couldn't even remember aiming. But she'd done it. She had killed him. A shudder passed through Jen's body, a loosening of her bones. She'd taken a life, a life that had once meant something to someone.

The young man she'd killed—whatever his real name was—he deserved to die, after what he'd done to her family:

shooting her husband, allowing her son to escape, forcing her daughter to endure two days of terror.

But Jen didn't deserve to have to kill him. She didn't deserve to have to be a killer. She would carry that with her always, and the thought enraged her.

"You—" she said, her voice shaking, pointing the gun at Dan. "You came into *my* home. You don't *belong* here."

Dan winced. His gaze traveled to Ryan, and his face twitched in grief.

"Why did you choose us? Why did you choose my family?"

He didn't respond, too weak with exhaustion. Jen's finger ached to pull the trigger, and she contemplated killing a second man. This time it wouldn't be self-defense, as it had been with Ryan, but pure revenge. The tremor traveled from her finger up her arm, into her whole body, a shudder of longing. She wanted to kill him, badly. Hungered for it. Instead she edged carefully toward her daughter, giving him a wide berth.

"Livvy," she said, handing her the gun. "Stand here, right here, and if he so much as moves, shoot him."

Livvy took the gun from her and slid her hand around the grip. She didn't look frightened now.

Jen went to Tanya, crouching down next to her on the floor. Maybe she wasn't all the way gone, maybe there was life in her yet…Jen put her fingers to her sister's wrist, prodding gently, hoping against hope.

"Mom," Livvy said. "That was the doorbell. I heard it."

Jen glanced up sharply. Was that possible? Or was Livvy imagining things? It was the wee hours of the morning, the time when the neighborhood lay absolutely still under the blanket of night. Who would be out at a time like this? Could someone have heard the screaming, the gunshots? An insomniac out walking a dog, a teenager returning from a party?

But what if Dan or Ryan had called someone? Some lowlife friend of theirs who had come to help them carry away the loot from the botched assault on the Glasses' lives?

"Look through the peephole," Jen said. "If you don't know the person, if it's not a neighbor, don't let them in. Do you hear me? Do *not* let them in. Come right back down here."

"Okay," Livvy said. "But what about you?"

"Get me the other gun," Jen said, and her daughter went over to the shelves and picked up Dan's gun like it was car keys she'd accidentally dropped, like it was nothing. Livvy had to be in shock, Jen thought—the horror of the night would find her later.

She took the gun from her daughter and, watching her climb the stairs and disappear through the door at the top, she felt that same protective rage again, that surge of bloodlust. She was still crouched down next to Tanya, and Dan looked like he was about to pass out from the pain, barely able to sit up.

"Do you believe in..." she started as she reached for Tanya's hand. She meant to say "Hell," because if it existed, he would surely have earned his place there. But as she tried to say the word, her fingers found the thing that Tanya was still holding in her hand, the cold, ridged steel of the knife. Jen gently took it from her sister's fingers and examined it up close, the dot of red that wasn't a dot at all. How could she have forgotten? The image swam into view and fixed itself there, expanding until it took up all of her mind, the memory of it sudden and sharp like yesterday, and the gun fell to the floor as she closed her hands around the knife and remembered.

Chapter Thirty-One

September, 1983

Sid had been in the backyard since late afternoon, drinking beer and eating pistachios. He cracked them between his teeth and spit the shells toward the fence.

"He might leave soon," Jen said softly to her sister. She'd been hanging around Tanya all evening, unable to resist the draw of her sister's suddenly mysterious mood. Tanya smelled like the Amaris that she'd stolen from a boy and nail polish remover and cigarettes.

Tanya rubbed the cotton ball lazily over her toes, taking off the polish she'd put on only last week. "He's not going anywhere."

Lately Tanya's voice had sounded all wrong. Kind of… lifeless. And it wasn't just that: she didn't talk to Jen unless she had to, walking to school alone sometimes and pretending to be asleep when Jen whispered to her after they'd turned the lights out in their room. Jen tried to tell herself it was because her sister was in high school now, that next year when she started ninth grade, things would go back to normal. But

Tanya seemed to have veered off in some direction Jen couldn't follow, not because she couldn't learn to dress or talk or put on makeup the same, learn to like the same music and actors and mannerisms—Jen knew she could do all of that if Tanya just gave her a chance—but because Tanya had receded from her. And that both mystified and wounded Jen almost unbearably.

Sid was throwing his knife lazily at the stump he'd lugged down from the woods past the creek and set up on a pair of cinderblocks. He'd spray-painted a crude orange bull's-eye, the outer circle dripping down into the bark—a much more effective target than the cans he'd tried setting on the fence. He hit the circle about half the time. Whenever the knife lodged near the center, he'd laugh and take a long pull on his beer, belching and pounding his chest afterward. When he missed, he cursed and stomped around trying to find his knife in the mangy sod.

He swore he got the knife in Vietnam, but he was vague about how. It had a red bird embossed on the handle, an eagle or some other bird of prey, its beak wide like it was screaming. Sid said the knife was rare because it folded, said it was worth a lot of money. Once he said he'd killed the man who taught him to throw. Other times he said he taught himself. If he spent all the time he spent throwing the damn thing working instead, their mother said, he could have built her a whole new house by now. Or at least caught up on his child support.

Soon it would be dark, but Jen had an uneasy feeling her sister was right: Sid wasn't leaving anytime soon. He had been hanging around later and later, despite the fact that their mother had made a few threats to call the cops. In the end, she always gave up and just hunkered down on the sofa with her afghan pulled up to her chin, the TV droning on and illuminating the flat planes of her face with flickering blue. Sid had wormed his way further into their lives as the weeks went by, getting food from the kitchen when he was hungry, watching TV from the sagging love seat, going through their mother's mail. He was always gone by morning, but sometimes Jen would hear him walking in the hall outside their bedroom door as she drifted off to sleep.

"Go get the knife, Tanny-Bear," Sid called in his voice like coarse sandpaper. "Landed in the squash patch."

"Get it your own goddamn self," Tanya muttered, tossing the used cotton ball onto the porch and twisting the lid back on the nail polish remover.

"I'll do it," Jen volunteered, jumping to her feet, losing her place in her history textbook.

"No."

Jen glanced up, surprised by the vehemence in her sister's voice, but Tanya was already striding across the yard. Her mother had planted squash, along with a row of pole beans and lettuce, early last spring before she got sick. The beans and lettuce were long gone to seed, but no one had done a thing about the squash, and the vines trailed out of the bed, rolling their pale underripe fruit into the yard. Jen watched her sister push the moldering leaves and vines around with her foot, then bend to pick up the knife. Sid watched, too, drinking steadily from his beer, crushing the can in his fist as Tanya handed him the knife. He dropped the can to the ground, and Jen knew it would still be there in the morning, along with the plastic ring that held the six-pack together.

"I'm going to bed," Tanya said disgustedly as she stalked

past Jen, who hesitated only for a moment before she gathered up her sister's nail polish and remover and used cotton balls and went after her. By the time she'd brushed her teeth and changed into her pajamas—neither of which Tanya bothered with, stripping off her jeans and socks and shoes and leaving them in a heap by the dresser—her sister had her Walkman earphones on and was flipping through a magazine, nestled into the bottom bunk under the blankets that she never straightened. She didn't say a word as Jen climbed the ladder to the top bunk, and when she turned off her light a little while later, Jen did the same, even though she wasn't really tired yet.

Maybe that was why she heard it, later. Usually Jen slept like the dead, but this night—because she was restless, because she wasn't tired enough to fall all the way asleep—she heard everything. The click and whoosh that was the turning of the knob, the door dragging over the carpet. The rustle of her sister, below her, sitting up in bed.

"Tanny-bear." It was Sid's voice, a harsh whisper.

"Go away."

"Aw, don't be like that. Your mama won't give me nothin'." The stink of him wafted up, his drunkenness mixed with his sweat, metallic and sour.

"I'll scream—"

Tanya's words were cut off abruptly, except for a choked mewling. Jen's heart seized. She knew how strong Sid's deceptively lean body was. She'd seen him rip a fender off his car with his bare hands after he drove into a mailbox. She'd seen him snap one of her mother's kitchen chairs into pieces one night when she wouldn't fix him something to eat.

"Be a good girl, or I'll fetch your sister," Sid whispered. In response, Tanya squeaked, and a moment later there was a muffled cough as she tried to get air.

"Not here," Tanya whispered, and there was a quiet shuffling as she got out of bed and followed Sid out of the room.

Jen lay still for a second after she was sure they were gone. She rolled over and stared at the outline of the door in the darkness. She didn't want to know what was happening, but it was too late—she couldn't keep from knowing anymore. The way Sid watched Tanya when she reached for the plates in the cabinet, or bent to pet the neighbor's cat. Jen had seen her father put his hand on her sister's waist, his scarred and knobbed hands dirty from a shift at the garage, splayed over the pearly cotton of her tank top, and slide his palm down to the place where the hem of her shorts curved around the swell of her rear. *Don't wear those shorts around him,* Jen had wanted to beg, but that would make it real, this numbing and nauseating fear. And she couldn't let it be real, because what then? What could she possibly do about this evil that had worked its way so stealthily and relentlessly into their house? Their mother was powerless to stop it; the neighbors indifferent; Sid inveigling, twisting and sly, stealing and watching and waiting and wanting until his black-hearted desires burst from the very seams of him?

She heard the back door rattle; the screen door always did that no matter how hard you tried to close it quietly, and she couldn't let Tanya go out there alone with him. Jen tiptoed slowly through the house, heart pounding so hard she was sure it would wake their mother, and when she got to the back door she paused, her hand shaking on the handle. If Sid saw her… She looked around for something, anything, to arm herself with, but all she saw was a mason jar holding a few asters from the garden and the dinner dishes drying on a towel spread out on the counter. She couldn't see them through the screen, but the yard was dark, the only light seeping sickly from the house two doors down, where Mr. Birckenhoffer installed a light up on a pole over the shed after someone broke in and stole some of his tools.

But Jen could hear them. She could hear Tanya, anyway, quiet sobbing punctuated by the clank of metal on glass, probably the little patio table where her mom kept a pot of geraniums, every summer but this one, when she was too sick. Now there was just a pot with last year's dead roots.

"That's right," Sid snarled, barely keeping his voice down, then a deep groaning.

Jen squeezed her teeth together and pulled the screen door open, putting her free hand flat against the juncture of screen and frame to quell the rattle, and there was no sound as she stepped outside, bare feet silent on the rough concrete.

The light from down the street didn't reach the corners of the yard, the dark recesses and shrubby edges, but it managed to reach the side of the house just fine, casting a sickly pall over the rake leaned up against the siding, her mother's old gardening clogs that she hadn't touched all year…and her sister, backed up against the corner of the house, on her knees. Sid had his hand wrapped in her hair.

No. *No.* Jen made it in three steps, feet pounding sharp earth, and there were Sid's pants around his ankles and there was the table where he'd tossed his wallet, his keys, his…

The red bird seemed to wink at her as she closed her hand

on the handle of the knife. It was hard and cold and it fit her hand just right—it flicked open as easily as it had a thousand times for her father, and it slid into his side so smoothly, like slitting the Easter ham for cloves. She pulled her arm back and brought it down twice more before Tanya pulled her away, saying *Jennie no* but Jen couldn't stop. She had to keep going until she was *sure,* and how could she be sure unless he was dead? She struggled to break free of Tanya's grip so she could finish him off, and he watched her with fear in his eyes, clutching his stomach and huffing out wet bubbled breaths.

Tanya kept her arms wrapped around Jen but she still had that knife tight, so tight in her hand, slashing the air trying to reach Sid. If she could just get Tanya to let go of her, she would keep cutting him until he was nothing but pieces of flesh and a pile of bones, a gutted mess on the ground like a hunted deer.

Tanya twisted Jen around and the knife fell to the ground. Tanya picked it up and snapped it closed against her thigh and put it in her pocket, faster than Jen could move. She kept her hand on Jen's wrist—she was strong like Sid—and she didn't let go. Sid was on his knees, a spreading stain leaching from his shirt down his pants and onto the pavement. He started to lean, slowly tipping, putting one hand flat against the side of the house at the last minute to catch himself, then slipping down.

Jen whimpered, finally going limp in Tanya's arms. Their faces were inches apart. Tanya hadn't taken her makeup off before she went to bed, and her eyes were ringed with mascara. "Don't look at him, Jennie. We'll fix this," she said fiercely. "We'll make it so this never happened."

Jen could feel her legs starting to give out under her, aftershocks of adrenaline rendering her boneless. But Tanya gripped her tighter.

"Did I kill him?" she asked, words caught in the air between them. "Is he dead?"

"We'll look in a minute," Tanya said, but she didn't let go. "But it's going to be okay. You were just watching out for me, right, Jennie? You were just taking care of me. There's nothing wrong with that. You didn't do anything wrong."

Jen nodded, not sure at all if it was true. The feel of the knife going in, the twist as she yanked it back—she hadn't hesitated; each thrust had made the next one easier. The first to stop him, all the other times to obliterate him, to make it so Sid had never come back, so he'd never touched her sister.

"It never happened," Tanya said, pulling her close the way their mother used to, gathering Jen in her arms and nestling her face in the crook of her shoulder. "Do you hear me?"

Jen heard, and she wanted to believe it, wanted to so badly. But she couldn't.

Not at first, anyway. But later, when Tanya led her gently into the house and sat her on the sofa and washed her hands tenderly with a rag dampened under the faucet; when she wrapped Jen in their mother's afghan; it was starting to seem like it might be true. Because how else could Tanya be talking to her, softly and steadily?

"I need you to take these," she said, opening her palm to show Jen two of the little white pills her mother got from a friend who was a nurse, the ones she took on nights when the pain was especially bad. "They'll help you go to sleep."

"I'm not sleepy," Jen murmured, but she took the pills,

anyway, swallowing them down with a sip of water from the glass Tanya gave her.

"Now close your eyes, honey," Tanya said. She took a clean cloth and dabbed Jen's face tenderly with cool water. "I've got to go do something, but before you know it I'll be back."

"Don't go," Jen said drowsily. "Don't leave me alone."

"It won't be long, I promise. I'm going to take Mom's car. Don't worry. Dwayne's been teaching me to drive, I'll be fine."

"Mom'll be mad…"

"Mom won't know. We won't tell, okay?"

"Okay."

"You won't worry, will you?" Tanya asked anxiously. "Because I'm going to be right back, and everything's going to be okay."

"It never happened," Jen said drowsily.

"That's right, honey. It never did."

And she was gone.

When Jen woke the next morning, she was still lying on the couch, covered with the afghan and the blanket from her bed. Tanya was sitting in a kitchen chair pulled up next to the sofa. When Jen opened her eyes, Tanya was watching her, chewing on her hair with her knees pulled up to her chin.

"You're awake!" she exclaimed, and then tried to smile. There were dark circles under her eyes and her hair was lank.

Jen was groggy, trying to remember how she had come to be sleeping on the couch. It was something about Tanya. Tanya needing help, Tanya crying…no, was she the one who had been crying?

"I've got some bad news," Tanya said, grabbing Jen's hand

and holding it tight. "Listen, um, Sid got in a fight last night. At the roadhouse."

"Sid got in a fight?" Jen tried to collect her thoughts. The pieces seemed to slide away from each other and back together. Sid throwing his knife at the stump. Sid standing by the table where her mother's flowers—

"And he's hurt pretty bad. They didn't catch the guy who did it, but he had a knife. Sid got stabbed a bunch of times. They took him to the hospital. I just called over there. They admitted him."

"Sid's in the hospital?" Jen tried to sit up, and a wave of dizziness nearly took her down again. "I don't feel good, Tan."

"It's okay. Do you want me to get you some juice?"

"No, I…" Jen tried to think. Something wasn't fitting… something wasn't right. "Who did it?"

"They don't know, honey," Tanya said patiently. She stroked Jen's hair off her face, looking sad. "But I don't think he'll be coming over much anymore. And that's all for the better. We don't need him around. Me and you, we can take care of Mom ourselves, right?"

"Sure," Jen said, but that wasn't true, because they both knew Mom wasn't getting any better. Tanya was lying, but Jen knew it was only to make things easier, and she slid down onto the couch.

"I love you, Jennie," Tanya said as Jen floated back to sleep.

Chapter Thirty-Two

The gun lay on the floor between them, and Dan crawled toward it, grunting and garbling, his leg spasming and dragging through a smear of blood. Jen couldn't look away from the knife, the red eagle emblazoned on the steel. Her fingers curled around the handle, and she remembered how it'd felt that night, cold and heavy and inevitable in her hand. How could she have forgotten?

Why had Tanya kept it, all these years? She'd taken care of everything that night, somehow getting Sid's unconscious body into his car, driving to the roadhouse and walking all the way home. She'd created a version of the story that would keep Jen safe, and then made her repeat it, over and over, until Jen believed it herself. To make sure, she'd given her the medicine that made their mom so confused, the pills that sometimes made her forget what happened in the hours before she took them. Before night gave way to dawn Tanya had cleaned up the mess in the backyard, and the next morning there was nothing left, no evidence that anything bad had happened at all except for a twisting uneasiness where the memory should have been.

For the rest of that year, Jen had trouble eating and sleeping. Sometimes she had bad dreams that left her sweating and trapped in her knotted sheets, dreams that were lost upon waking, their details drowned in a wash of dread. But other things happened, things that took her mind off the nightmares: before long their mother was in the hospital and the school counselor had her in her office with a pamphlet on the stages of grieving.

How could she have forgotten, though? All those years when she felt like she was trying to outrun something, to stay a few steps ahead of the snapping jaws of the past, she'd thought it was just the desperate losing battle of her mother's cancer, the poverty that hounded them, the future that stayed maddeningly out of her reach. She'd run so hard, leaving everything behind—even Tanya. She saw that now—she'd sacrificed Tanya in her attempt to escape the shadow of what she'd done.

No wonder it had never worked, not really. Because Jen had been fighting the wrong enemy. It wasn't the wretched house she grew up in, the hand-me-down clothes, the sagging splintered porch where Tanya smoked and brooded. It wasn't even their mother's slow and painful death. It was Sid; it had always been Sid.

Jen's hand tightened on the knife's grip, fury flooding her veins like poison. She should have killed him. For years, she had been trying to run away from him and the evil he had brought into their family, the unspeakable things he had done, the sound of his black-hearted laughter as he threw his knife and threw it and threw it. The glimmer of her sister's pretty hair in the moonlight, trailing from her father's fist.

Jen's fingers were white from the effort of gripping the knife so hard. She'd been tasked with meting out hard justice once before. And now it was time again. *You were just taking care of your own,* Tanya had said all those years ago.

Jen watched Dan crawl across the basement floor, his fingers brushing against the gun, nudging it farther from his reach. He made an almost-inhuman sound, his lips stretching away from his teeth and his face drained of color. He drew one last gasping breath and flung himself forward, his face on the concrete floor, leg twisted beneath him, and propelled himself just close enough to grab the gun. She watched him pick it up, tears and mucus slick on his face, and use both hands to try to settle it in his trembling grip. Their eyes met, and everything she thought she'd seen in him at first—just a nice guy, he could have been anyone—evaporated as he pointed the gun at her face.

Jen brought the blade down.

Epilogue

On a warm spring day a few months later, Jen took Teddy to the cemetery.

"Hi, Daddy," Teddy said, kneeling on the flat slab of marble and putting his hands flat on either side of the deeply engraved letters.

"T, H, E, O, D, O, R, E. Just like you," Jen said, sitting down beside him in the grass. It was warm for May, warm enough that she'd brought an impromptu picnic when she picked Teddy up from school, banana and Nutella sandwiches with the crusts cut off and bottles of Orangina. The grass tickled her calves as she arranged her skirt over her legs. Sitting cross-legged in a skirt might not be ladylike, but there was no one else nearby to see.

"I'm going to give Daddy his present now."

"That's a good idea, sweetie."

Teddy had already given Jen her own present: a drawing he'd made at school that featured a creature that looked like it might be a dog but was actually a dolphin, according to Teddy. They were doing an under-the-sea unit at school, and as he unfolded the picture he'd made for Ted, smoothing the construction paper flat on the marble, she expected a crayon rendering of a fish or a shark. Instead she was surprised to see a half dozen figures on the page, one of them twice as tall as the others, looming over them. They were drawn in a variety of colors. It was only because the tall one—with arms that stretched clear across the page and five long fingers on each oversize hand—was green that Jen suspected it was meant to be her. Teddy took the subject of people's favorite colors seriously. His own favorite color was red, but none of the figures was red: there were two brown horizontal ones and two black vertical ones and one that Jen almost missed, because it was drawn in silver crayon, blending into the white page.

"Who's that?" Jen asked, tapping the silver figure.

"That's Livvy!" Teddy laughed, as though he couldn't believe she didn't already know.

"But Livvy's favorite color is orange."

"Yes, but this is her *hair.* With the lights."

Ah, yes—now that Jen looked more carefully, the figure did appear to be mostly hair. Livvy's recent highlights—her first, paid for out of her babysitting money—were a subject of endless fascination for Teddy, who liked to hold the bleached strands in his hands and stroke the pink tips. Livvy didn't mind. She had seemingly endless reserves of patience when it came to her little brother.

"And is this me?" Jen asked, pointing to the tall figure, which appeared to be holding a candle over the rest of the scene.

"Yes, that's when you killed the bad guys."

Jen winced. She had hoped to shield her son from the truth of what had happened that night, and she still wasn't sure who had told him. Of course, it was in all the papers. The kids at school heard their parents talking. He could have found out half a dozen ways.

"And see?" Teddy went on, moving his finger over the paper. "Here are the police guys. Here is your gun."

He pointed to each of the black figures, and then the object she was holding above the scene. Jen's heart skittered. The family therapist had cautioned her to allow Teddy to talk about what had happened whenever he liked, and not to interfere with his narrative, and Jen was fine with that, at least in theory, especially because his teachers all said he was doing great. Also, because once he started talking, he didn't ever stop again, a worry that had lingered at the back of her mind for a while, despite the reassurances from the speech-language pathologist. But she wished that he wasn't quite so fascinated with the deaths of the strangers who'd come to their house, and especially her role in them.

The hardest thing for Teddy to grasp seemed to be that Dan and Ryan had tried to hurt his family. Teddy had always been a trusting boy, and he couldn't understand why anyone would want to harm someone else.

The second hardest thing for Teddy was the move. They never went back to the house after that night, and Jen had to remind herself that for Teddy, it had never become a place of horror. After his sleepover in the basement the first night, he'd escaped the worst of it. When he didn't show up at the Sterns', Cricket called a couple times and then just assumed something had come up. Teddy spent most of the day in the park, as far as they could tell, though there was a rambling description of a house with worms in the floor, and when evening came he walked the wrong way and ended up in the downtown parking lot where the police found him. His memories of the day were of an adventure that he eventually tired of. So he couldn't understand why he never got to go back to his old room, and it was only when the movers unpacked his things in his new room in the house Jen rented near the old library—a sweet cottage, with a porch that ran along the front and an old-fashioned laundry chute, in walking distance to both their schools—that he quit demanding to go back.

Jen had returned to her old neighborhood only once, when the house went up for sale in early spring. Tanya had overseen the packing and the move, after spending only one night in the hospital and a week recuperating at home. Jen had paid for a nurse, which earned her an earful. The bullet had missed Tanya's organs and it was only because she'd hit her head on the stairs that she'd been knocked unconscious.

Jen drove over to Calumet on the Tuesday that the broker tour was scheduled. She wore sunglasses and parked two doors down, in the Camry she'd bought to replace her Audi. No one saw her. She watched people go in and out of her front door, wiping their feet on a mat she didn't recognize, admiring the brass fixtures and stone urns she'd once been so proud of. All the evidence of what had happened there was long gone, and the sooner the house was owned by some new family, the sooner she could let it go.

One by one she was releasing the pieces of what had happened. A week afterward, a man called from Redman Rare Coins to say he had a check for Ted's father's collection of eighteenth-century American coins, which explained how Ted had planned to cover his gambling losses.

Sarah Elizabeth Baker came to the memorial service on the arm of a man she said she'd been dating for six months. When she stammered her way through a few rushed and tearful sentences, Jen saw her for what she was, perhaps for the first time: a smart and slightly awkward young woman who'd had a crush on her husband, nothing more.

The media turned up more than she ever wanted to know about Richard Yost and his nephew Dave Husted, but she was surprisingly unmoved by the details. Yost had disguised himself as ordinary, an everyman. In truth he was even less, an empty vessel that took on the shape of whatever con he was working. And Dave—it seemed to her that all one needed to know was that there had been a dangerous fire burning in him, hidden behind those handsome features, and Jen felt no remorse from having extinguished it.

Jen picked up her purse and dug through the contents for her cigarettes, tucked into the pocket meant for a cell phone. Smoking was something she'd taken up during the waning end of February, an old habit that had taken a little of the jagged edge off during those days of police interviews and insurance adjusters and lawyers and school counselors. She was going to quit again—soon—but for now, just even touching the crinkling cellophane of the pack could calm her down, bring her back into the moment. And if that's what it took to be there for her children, then the surgeon general could just fuck off.

Jen flashed a quick grin. It happened, sometimes, a thought that would pop into her head that she would swear came straight from Tanya. She was still on careful footing with her sister, who had refused all her pleas to go to the family counselor. But at least they were spending time together.

Jake rode his bike over sometimes, and Tanya would pop by with a bucket of chicken, or Jen would take a casserole and a bottle of wine over to her apartment. Jen was thinking of inviting a few friends to Easter dinner, and Tanya had already said she'd help cook.

They might never be close again the way they had once been, all those years ago when they shared a cramped bedroom in a cursed house. But Tanya had risked her life to save her, just as she'd risked everything to save Jen once before. And Jen had once fought for her, as well. That story had been buried for three decades, and it would stay buried now. Jen would never tell it to a living soul.

For so much of her life, she had forgotten who she was. She had wasted so much energy trying to control everything around her, when the one thing she was meant to do had been in her grasp all along: she took care of her own.

Teddy had found a dandelion growing a few inches from his father's stone, and he was trying to uproot it without breaking the stem. At home, Jen paid him a nickel for every dandelion he dug out of the yard with the roots intact.

A yellow jacket swerved close and hovered near the sweet expanse of Teddy's neck where his blond hair curled, just as his father's always had. Without thinking, Jen shot out her hand and closed her fist around the insect. She could feel its wings beating frantically against her fingers as she carried it a few paces away. She released the yellow jacket behind a tall white marble monument, and it flew up into the sky.

Jen had let it live, and she wished it a good life—warm sunshine, blue skies and sweet nectar. But if it had harmed her son she would have crushed it.

Woe to anyone who ever threatened what was hers again.

Jen took in a breath and let it out slowly, allowing the fire that roared within her to return to a smolder. Teddy had managed to get the dandelion free and was now expanding the hole.

"Mom!" he said. "I saw a worm down there. A *big* one. Want to help?"

"Sure," Jen said, and together they dug, dirt under their nails, the sun on their faces and their dead at rest below.

* * * * *

Acknowledgments

This book was conceived over a lunch with two of the most dedicated publishing folks I know: my agent, Barbara Poelle, and my editor, Erika Imranyi. Little did they know that the fairly straightforward back-of-the-napkin outline I took home in my purse would take us on such an interesting journey. I would like to thank them for both high expectations and the grit to see the process through: this one is also for you two.

Thank you, also, to the Harlequin team for making me feel welcome at every step of the way. From warehouse to conference room to rooftop, you set the bar high, and I'm honored to be a part of the endeavor.

HOUSE OF GLASS

SOPHIE LITTLEFIELD

Reader's Guide

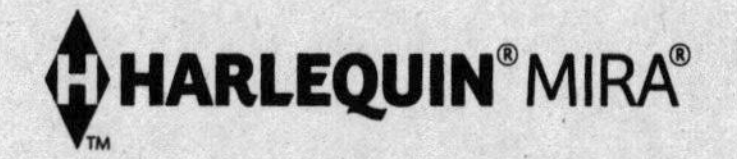

1. The Glasses' marriage is somewhat fragile at the beginning of the book. Are the issues genuine, or a product of Jen's imagination? Is she justified in doubting Ted?

2. Livvy is also at odds with her parents at the outset of the book. Is this normal teen behavior, or is there something more concerning at work? How does it affect her development as the story progresses?

3. Teddy has a condition in which he doesn't speak. Ted and Jen handle this very differently. Who is right? How does this condition affect the family and the Glasses' marriage? How does Teddy's decision to speak near the end of the book fit into the story?

4. Jen and her sister, Tanya, grew up under difficult circumstances. How did these dictate the choices each made in adulthood?

5. Sid's death brought up a variety of emotions for the sisters, especially given their estrangement. Are there lessons here on the consequences of grown children attempting to distance themselves from painful childhood memories?

6. Several red herrings cast suspicion on a variety of characters, including Sid, Livvy's boyfriend and even the family gardener. Given the circumstances, did Jen's speculation make sense, or was it merely the product of her hysteria?

7. Livvy endures a horrific encounter with Ryan. Where does she get the strength to endure and fight back?

8. Tanya's arrival marks a turning point in the course of events, but also results in her grave injury. Is she the true heroine of the story? Are there limits to what she would do for her sister and her family?

9. Ted's final moments are spent reliving the choices he made that led to the invasion. Does he ultimately bear the largest share of the blame, even posthumously? When, if ever, did he behave heroically?

10. As a mother, what are some of the challenges that Jen faces during the events of the novel, and how does she rise to confront them? How do you feel about her actions? Would you respond similarly or differently, and how?

House of Glass is an emotionally charged, ripped-from-the-headlines thriller about a family put to the ultimate test. What was your inspiration for this story?

A number of years ago, a home invasion took place in Connecticut. A family of four was imprisoned, abused, and all but the husband killed. Details of the case, and the subsequent trial and conviction of the killers, held the country in thrall and dominated the news for weeks.

I was unable to watch or read accounts of the case. Though I often write about violent characters and dark impulses, I have a low tolerance for real evil and suffering, and often take the coward's path, burying my head in the sand until the story is supplanted by fresher news.

But several aspects of the case were impossible for me to forget. One in particular: the mother was taken from the home by one of the killers and driven to a bank where she was forced to withdraw money. She believed that when she handed over the money, her family would be freed. She knew her husband had been beaten and her children were vulnerable and defenseless.

I can't imagine a more desperate moment for a mother. I decided to retell the story with a different outcome, giving her a bit of luck, a few unexpected allies and strength she didn't realize she possessed, from a source she had forgotten.

Like *House of Glass*, your previous novel, *Garden of Stones*, also featured a mother in a harrowing situation, forced to make a difficult decision in order to save her family. Is this a recurring theme in all your novels? What is the message you're trying to send about motherhood?

When my agent, Barbara Poelle, pointed out this recurrent theme, I was surprised. I hadn't noticed that it was such a consistent thread. Soon, though, I came to see that it is the element that binds my work in all my disparate genres.

It's probably no accident that all my published novels were written in 2007 or later. In that year, my children were twelve and fourteen, no longer children but not yet adults, and I had experienced some of the challenges of raising adolescents and glimpsed the long shadow of the challenges to come. A mother of an infant is fiercely protective; a mother of a teen—a person with some autonomy—must face the terrifying fact that she can't protect against all the danger in the world. I think my stories were an effort to direct all this helpless maternal protectiveness and fear.

Now that my children are nineteen and twenty-one, they have experienced and survived any number of hurts, and I have been forced to admit that I am no longer the axis around which their lives turn. This, too, is an aching change for a mother. But there is recompense: the older they get, the more frequent the glimpses of their own strength and capability.

In House of Glass*, both children are instrumental in helping the family survive. I didn't realize it at the time, but I think this reflects my own shift to seeing my children as powerful on their own.*

Is there a message there? Other than "Parenthood is not for the weak," I'm not sure. Maybe it would be more apt to see my work as a sort of therapy journal....

What was your toughest challenge, your greatest pleasure and your biggest surprise as you were writing *House of Glass*?

I was going through a divorce while writing this book, and as a result, my poor fictional couple was saddled with all kinds of angst that wasn't the least bit germane to the story. There was a memorable three-way phone call in which my agent and editor gently broke it to me that I had to go back to the drawing board and, in essence, reimagine these characters while remembering that they are not me. I don't think I will ever really learn this lesson—all my characters are me in some sense, from the most heinous criminal to the bratty kid down the street—but this experience did teach me to create a little distance in a very crowded creative realm.

My greatest pleasure was probably joking around with my sister about "her" character. Early in the first draft, Jen's sister, Tanya, was a feckless sort who brought about her own ignominious end—and also drank too much and had really trashy taste. I loved calling Kristen up and saying "You'll never believe what you did today." I figured it was only fair, since the early version of Jen was uptight, snobbish and dismissive. As the book progressed, I was able to report to Kristen that "her" character got stronger and wiser while Jen had to learn a few hard lessons. I'm very lucky that Kristen is a forgiving sort.

As for my biggest surprise—I suppose it would be the effortlessness of writing Ted, the husband. As someone who spends a fair amount of time bashing middle-aged white guys for any number of sins and irritations, I was surprised to find that I not only understood his motivation, his emotions and shame and longing, but that I had great compassion for him.

Can you describe your writing process? Do you outline first or dive right in? Do you write scenes consecutively or jump around? Do you have a schedule or a routine? A lucky charm?

I am still searching for my best process, and I'm getting the feeling that search will last a lifetime! True to my restless nature, I try lots of different things. I've written with detailed outlines and none at all; in chronological order and jumping around.

I do keep a detailed guide for every book and series. This includes a table of characters with their most salient characteristics, a timeline and a list of significant places. As for schedule...I adore the fact that this job lets me set my own hours. I work throughout the day—from first sip of coffee through the glass of wine that marks the end of most evenings—but I take breaks whenever I feel like it: to do chores, go to the gym or hiking, have lunch with friends, hang out with my daughter after school.

I have a variety of talismans in my office. There are three little plastic penguins, a mini Etch A Sketch on which my son wrote I Love You when he was eight or ten, a tiara given to me by a writing friend and the card that came with the flowers my brother sent to mark the publication of my first novel.

What can you tell us about your next novel?

In January of 2013, I visited a "man camp" in an oil boomtown in western North Dakota and was moved to write a story set against that backdrop. All of my assumptions were challenged: from what a rig would look like, to what an oilman—or woman—would be like, to how it would feel when my little prop plane touched down on a toy-sized runway on a zero-degree winter night. The story itself came to me in one blinding flash: two twenty-year-old boys go missing from their oil rig jobs, and their mothers must join forces to find them.